A NOT SO DEAD MAN'S JOURNEY

BOOK 1 OF THE BRICKBORN SERIES

C.J. JORDAN

For the countless family members, friends, and kind people who helped make this book a reality. A special thank you to Josh and Maya for quite simply everything.

MAP OF NISUROTH

CONTENTS

Chapter 1: A Proverbial Click

The path wound in front of him, cobbled from stones long since set. A beautiful blue sky above him was swallowed by a vast green ceiling of trees that weren't fond of sharing the sunlight. All Alden could think of was the black book behind the door and how it would elude him no longer. *Today is the day, I won't spend another hour staring through some magic veil. The spell will work and we'll catch him. I won't let this madman make any more corpses for us to bury.*

Plants he'd chopped down only a few days before seemed to have mysteriously returned. *Perhaps the foliage doesn't want the book to be found, it's incredible that they grow back in such a short time. Three months of clearing ferns and the stones still vanish into the undergrowth. How they ever managed to build a city here I'll never know.*

As wild as it was now, the path was nothing compared to three months ago when his family first moved to Mullentide. When he'd started coming to the ruins, seeing the cobblestones was a miracle only brought about by vigorous cutting.

I suppose I shouldn't be so rude to all the greenery. Without it there would be no point in coming here. Every relic, book, and artifact would've been stolen away centuries ago. Put harsh terrain and merciless monsters together and it's no wonder that the only copy left in the world has stayed put here all this time.

Alden bobbed and weaved under dangling branches as some small amount of sunlight trickled down through the leaves. Vines brushed his short brown hair as a fresh breeze began to blow past. Long, lime green grass rubbed against his sword and dagger as the sunny weather matched his mood.

One last trip to the library for the final trip to the tower, besides I know what Amara will say if I don't. 'Daddy I've already read all three of those ones you brought back last week', little conch-head's only ten and she's already better than me. Wonder if I could find a spell to pick up her clothes. Alden smiled at such an unlikely miracle.

His feet turned a corner closer to the ruins as he gazed upon an ancient glade. The soft green gateway led into the dark foreboding buildings of stone, overgrown with the ages. *Four hundred years old and it's still more advanced than most towns in Heanerath. Still there's a certain beauty in it now, an echo of what was. It'd be a lovely place to sit and think if not for the bloodthirsty insects.*

Giant trees seemed to steal away his sunny day as they wove themselves into a canopy over the city's highest structures, shrouding the dilapidated dwellings from the whole world. Willful weeds sprung from the nearly seamless stonework. Wooden crates and carts lined the thoroughfare, but only a few remained as the rest had rotten away. The Telendum enchantment had coated all of them at one time, but only those applied by very skilled mages had enough magic to endure this long.

As always, the first building on the right was a bakery who's bread no longer rose and its magical stove was now stuffed with vines. *Imagine it, using an eternal fire for baking. The supreme skill required of a master mage to create a portal from an elemental plane and they used it to make cookies.* Many little Ascendant boys and girls would've fetched lunch for their families here around noon. Their little skeletal hands paying for pieces of bread would've been a strange sight in most of the world, but certainly not here.

Alden didn't want to linger in the streets as he felt eyes begin to observe him. Heavy stones fell to the ground shattering the dead city's silence. *Still far off, perhaps it just saw a squirrel.*

Click. Click. Click.

Alden's heartbeat began to rise as he stopped moving to listen, but the moment he ceased stepping, so did the clicking.

What a clever bug, it's no wonder that everyone who comes here ends up dead. Best not linger, but I doubt it'll make much difference. Damn my luck. Quickening his pace, he pressed on towards the library.

Alden approached the library's dark wooden doors. Venturing through the soaring entrance revealed a grand collection. Fields of rotting books and creeping jungle vines that soared three stories above him. The walls were covered in faded red tapestries while the floors were smooth and dark as obsidian.

The building was beautiful, but the years had decayed much of the collection. Unfortunately, many of the preserving Telendum enchantments on the books had begun to fade away long ago. Only the spells added by the most skilled librarians had lasted this long and the masters rarely worked on anything trivial, a fortunate fact for a treasure hunter. Even spells from four hundred years ago were valuable trade secrets that only existed in the lost places of the world like this. Row by row, Alden had been slowly exploring the entire library, but today would have to be his last visit. His practiced eyes scanned each shelf for anything that might be useful. Previous visits had uncovered a variety of magical insights such as farming spells, enchantments, and even ways to pick very stubborn magical locks.

Finally, Alden's eyes stopped on just what he was looking for, an old elemental spell book. *Oh yes, she'll love this one. These variations of lightning magic are quite beautiful. She may be young, but Amara's a better magess than most at the Arcanum. Still, I'll need a story for Leonara to go along with it. I know, she can create a fire with it, that's practical.*

Well that's one book for a happy daughter and one left to catch a madman. Alden made his way out of the library just as a jarring clunk echoed through the stone city. Dust rose from an alley across the street. A shadow darted between the buildings as Alden began walking as fast as his legs would carry him.

Click. Click. click.

There it is again, I've fought far worse and yet my heart feels like it's in my throat. Can't it even do me the courtesy of just getting it over with? It's been over a month since the last one and they still give me the creeps. Might as well press on until this bug changes its mind.

Looming above him like a singular dark spear was the city's guild tower. Smooth dark walls and numerous glowing windows separated it from the lifeless city around it. A gaping wound peering into the interior had become Alden's entrance. *Even after four hundred* years it's majesty was still undeniable. A rising spire of endless blue dots in a sea of perpetual night. A fitting resting place indeed.

The chamber he entered into contained a large desk for pointing visitors where to go as well as the elevators leading higher into the spire. Surprisingly each one was intact and working when Alden had first arrived two months ago. *Shouldn't have been a surprise honestly, if a book can last four centuries then surely their only transportation would too.*

The ceiling stretched forty feet high and the magical chandelier's bright orange glow was as beautiful as a setting sun, illuminating tapestries and the silence of four-hundred summers gone by. *A mage channeled a bit of Lumendo all those years ago, I wonder if they'd believe it would still be delighting people after all this time.*

Alden had spent weeks combing the building, but only the final room occupied his mind today. His feet left the cluttered rubble of the lobby as he stepped onto the elevator.

Click, click, click.

Each echo came from the other side of the entrance wall. Dust descended to the ground with every step. Alden groaned at his bad luck. *I wonder how much longer he'll wait to make his move? Surely I've given him enough opportunities for a worthwhile ambush.*

Alden chose the only floor still withholding its secrets and pressed the corresponding button on the console. Pushing back against his finger the spell's blue interface shimmered above its stone dais. Springing to life, it's Autendum enchantment drove the elevator up the tower through the seamless stone tube.

I do love these older versions, without the Telendum shell the wind just flows right over you. Almost makes me forget I'm in the middle of a jungle except it stops and then my shirt is still as sticky as syrup.

He flew up the tower's spine and after going up twenty floors the stone elevator he was riding on stopped. Stepping off of it, Alden entered an antechamber he was far too familiar with. Several shelves of arcane books and ornate wooden tables filled the room, but his gaze did not deviate from the center. Covering the doorway in front of him like a sheet of sapphire was the lock that had denied him until today.

Beyond its ethereal blue glow was the guild leader's office and the only copy of the book he needed that was still known to exist.

Can a dead man's story truly save the living from a madman? For all our sakes I sure hope so.

The door was no new discovery, Alden had found it over a month ago, but like a drunk coming home at first light, he never could find the handle. For weeks he'd tried every spell imaginable to open the door, but nothing had worked until his recent discovery. Entombed under a pile of rotting scraps he'd found a book on removing barriers in the library.

To think that moving all the way to the southern half of Heanerath and digging through this ancient world has come down to one particularly powerful librarian. An ancient book to fight a modern enemy. I just hope Cassara is right about this, but I guess we'll know soon enough.

Standing before the door, Alden prepared to move his hand like the book described. *Right it's a twelve-point seal so I've gotta channel just the right amount for each particular hand configuration. It's almost like my fingers are like the teeth on a metal key. A simple metaphor for a complex spell, but thinking about it isn't gonna make this any easier.*

"Reserendum," he said.

Plunging each pattern into the veil one after the other, ripples danced across the magic sheet with every touch. Like picking any other lock, Alden waited for his proverbial click and luckily he got a real one. *That did it! Months of work and that was all I needed.* The blue glow faded with an elegant humming noise as Alden finally walked through the doorway. Inside the room was a sturdy wooden desk and shelves cluttered with magical objects he'd only ever heard of. Most interesting of all was the monolithic black tome sitting in front of him.

The moment of truth and my hands are shaking. Today we turn the tide and start saving people instead of burying them. Alden opened the book to discover it was exactly what they needed. It detailed the anatomy of some ancient ritual, cosmic theories of where the magical forces came from, and a discussion on its profound transformative power. In particular, the book seemed to wonder if souls were linked and if the power of the ritual could affect others.

Finally, this is the roadmap we've been waiting for. Wait, what are these parts in between? This isn't just theory, it's a record of experiments, brutal ones. Who could even think to replicate this? Little wonder most copies were burned after the war.

Alden packed the book away before turning to head back to the elevator. The sun was setting and a good stew seemed like a perfect ending to a profitable day. However, he was not the only hungry one in the spire today.

Click. Click. Click.

The familiar sound of scythe-like claws was coming from just below the overgrown window. Alden was a seasoned explorer, but this creature was quite good at cutting through matters and men alike. Only one beast could make such sounds and inspire a heart to hurry in these ruins, a Crawpike. Its plated head pierced the window's blue veil as it clambered into the room.

As in any profession, there are rewards and there are risks. The rewards lay in his rucksack, but the risk stared at him with six cold black eyes. The creature looked like a scorpion the size of a cow balanced upon two large, spear-like claws and a prehensile tail. Slime began salivating from the creature as it eyed Alden up and down. It wiggled its tail a bit like a dog, except most hounds aren't wagging a venomous sac which can melt an arm.

Dammit, I don't suppose he'd want to play fetch with me.

A terrible screeching bellow erupted from the insect shattering Alden's playful thoughts. His mind raced to figure out his way home to the stew instead of becoming this thing's supper. The Crawpike grew quiet and readied itself; the journey home had begun. Alden knew he had to act and decided to make the first move. *Fire ought to work, no animal can think straight while it's burning.*

"Flammorta!" he shouted.

Magic channeled through his palm as a burst of flames erupted onto the Crawpike. Screaming in pain the creature's face was lit ablaze. Cooking in its own shell, the insect rushed forward swinging wildly. A claw bigger than his leg flew within inches of his face as

Alden dodged just in time. The wooden desk in the room's center wasn't so lucky and shattered as it collided with the wall. Splinters rebounded onto his feet as Alden backed up to gain distance.

He tossed that desk like it was an apple! Still better the antique than me.

Alden swiftly drew his sword in time to parry the next swipe. Steel clashed against hard chitin as he blocked each strike. The creature began ruthlessly pounding away with its claws as he was forced to retreat. Its tail shot toward him, venom pouring from the stinger. Alden dodged right into a bookcase as pages rained down upon him. The spot he'd just been standing on had been reduced to a glowing green hole in the floor as he gazed back at his enemy.

It just soupified the floor. At what point is venom deadly enough because this is clearly past that.

Alden exhaled hard from the effort, but knew his opponent would afford him no respite. Brushing off rotten paper, he saw the Crawpike turn to him, its six eyes fixated. The bulbous tail swung back and forth, ready for its next strike. Alden began to raise his left hand for another spell, but was too slow. The creature leapt forward at lightning speed. Alden's chest was struck by its massive head, ramming him into the bookcase behind him. His breath was struck from his body as the insect pinned him to the wall.

Sharp and slimy teeth began to chew into his leather chest piece. Death inched ever closer through his armor as the knight dropped his weapon. *My sword's too long for this. If I start swinging it will only bounce off those hard plates. Gotta think of something quick or my chest cavity is going to spill out like a pot pie.* Alden's desperate hand reached for the belt and wrapped around the leather strips of a dagger hilt.

Swift as a songbird the small steel blade flew from its sheath into the Crawpike's neck. Its metal buried deep puncturing the creature's flesh with a satisfyingly wet sound. Screaming in agony, the beast began stumbling back to the window. Flailing erratically, its claws cracked the stone floor with every pained step as viscous green blood poured onto the floor.

Too bad, only one of us gets to have dinner tonight and it won't be you.

Alden braced himself against the raging storm he was about to unleash. Raising his hand, he shouted "Ventos," summoning a gust of wind from his hand which could pummel an oak. Losing its footing the Crawpike was blasted towards the window. Blood flecked onto the barrier as the creature tried to hook itself onto the window sill. It flailed like a drowning rat unable to find a foothold. With nothing to grab it began plummeting towards the street. Screeching all the way down, its cry was cut short by the sound of chitin shattering on the cobblestones below. Alden staggered to his feet as silence returned to the city.

Plopping down on the ground he uncorked his flask of Nisuri Sweetwater and drank deeply. *No more clicking for you bug. It's what you deserve, you ruined my leather coat. At least I got the book, it's not the worst trade I've ever made. It's a shame we're leaving, but if anyone else wants to enter this death trap then no Crawpike will attack them. That smell will be covering the whole city by dark with these winds.*

Either way, Alden really wanted that stew waiting for him back home. Picking himself up and retrieving his sword from the floor, he headed for the elevator. *Might be able to keep that little conch-head listening to story-time tonight.* A smile broke over his face as he set off for home.

Once he'd reached the lobby Alden saw the giant insect cracked open like a clam upon the street outside. Pausing for a moment, he lingered at the lobby as it would likely be his last chance to see it. Alden began his journey home, leaving behind the crumbling past and rejoining the far more pleasant present. A fading orange sky colored the air as flickering rays of light passed through the thick canopy.

Thinning trees let in more light as an approaching sunset painted the jungle. Alden couldn't help smiling at the crimson symphony of colors illuminating him. Rainforest turned to fields as the lights of the village dotted the darkness. The sapphire-like Otaton ocean lapped against the shore on his right. On his left the panoply of crops in the brackish farming terraces shimmered in the fading sunlight. *Even after dark the oxen constructs are still plowing? Must be nice to never run out of stamina with all that magic 'Nara poured into them. Hopefully the local guild mages will be able to maintain them after we head back.*

Mullentide and all its charm lay before him. Perched above the salt stained cliffs on Heanerath's southern half was the small village. Terraces bordered the town and separated it from the vast rainforest further inland. Grass was replaced by familiar dirt roads as Alden made his way into the irregular collection of clay roofs atop stucco walled cottages that was Mullentide. Every house was a home their magic family had been able to help. In the center of it all was the town hall where the mayor lived.

Alden twisted through the village until he finally arrived at the base of the hill which led to his home. Walking up the dirt path a building quite unalike the rest came into view. A striking white rectangle formed by spells. Blooming vines from Hemmoros draped themselves over the walls and the garden popped with colors uncommon in this part of the world. A fitting home for the only magical family in Mullentide as few mages ever actually lived in such rural communities.

Brushing open the picket fence gate Alden stopped in front of an oaken door. The beautiful flowing entrance was the creation of a local Nisuri craftsman. *If you want to sail on a ship you should find a Wekken captain and if you want wood worked then find a Nisuri carpenter.* Alden smiled at the warm yellow light coming from within which meant the cold night air would shortly be swept away by the warmth of his happy home.

Alden swung the door open and only managed two steps before he was stopped. Any adventurer should always be on their guard for traps when opening a door. Fortunately for Alden, the ambush in wait was somewhat less lethal and rather more loveable.

"Daddy!" shouted his lovely little girl, Amara. Alden swore she grew taller every time he left down the hill.

Alden fell back onto his bottom as the little girl crashed into his chest. Little brown eyes surrounded by flowing hair of the same shade gazed at him. He squeezed Amara tightly as his daughter buried her head into his shoulder.

"Ahh Amara! I'm already sore from the ruins, why are you helping the Crawpike?" he asked.

"I'm sorry Daddy, I just missed you all day! I got really good at Ventos. I actually polished a rock with it," Amara said.

"That's wonderful honey, but could you maybe let me get up? I want to show you something."

"Ooh, what is it Daddy? Did you find another spell book? I'm nearly through the last one you got me."

Like mother like daughter, all the books in the world would never be enough for them.

Climbing off her father, she stood up to start crowding her Dad in a desperate attempt to get a peek at the bag's secrets. He sat up and rustled around in the pack before pulling out the tome just for her.

You really are remarkable conch-head. Ten and already learning Arcanum level spells. Ventos on its own is a tough bit of magic to master, but you already have enough control to modify it for working rather than just unleashing. I still remember that devious little grin you got when you first learned it.

"Well I was going through the library and found a little volume I thought you might like. It's an old book on elemental magic variations. It'll show you how to do a lot more than just smooth rocks," he said.

Alden handed the beautifully bound book to Amara's outstretched arms and tussled her hair inspiring a giggle.

"Can you teach me later?" she asked.

"Of course conch-head. That is, I will if you've been practicing your spells like I asked?" Alden asked.

"Yep, I grew some daffodils and it only took me an hour this time, but they were all droopy."

"Hey that's alright, remember you need to try twirling the flow of magic when you focus. Curl your fingers and let them guide the spell, okay?"

"I'll try it, but can we still practice tomorrow?"

"Sure, but I better not find your clothes on the floor again or we'll be pruning the vines together tomorrow instead."

"Definitely, thank you Daddy."

Taking the book and running off to her room, Amara vanished nearly as quickly as she'd ambushed him.

Please pick them up, I hate pruning Amara. Why did I suggest that? I'm the parent I could've just threatened her with refreshing the Drentos spells on the toilet or something. It really has been a long day, hasn't it?

While he'd met one lady of the house, Alden still hadn't greeted the other. Searching around the central room, the sound of pots clanging came from the kitchen. Alden walked past their self-cleaning table and the glowing eternal fireplace Leonara had enchanted. Framed by a white stone arch was a woman who could step out of a portrait. Her hair was the color of chestnuts and she was wrapped in a fine green linen dress. As tall as him and sharper at least in her tongue; his heart still quickened even after all these years.

And I suddenly feel all better. Mmm, that stew smells so good. Does it still count as cooking if the tools do all the work for her? I suppose no magess would ever really do it manually when a wave of your hand will accomplish it just the same.

Knives and pans danced around the kitchen preparing what was unmistakably a stew by the savory smell of fish cooking in a red broth. Leonora hummed softly as she stirred her spoon, mixing the ingredients as they hopped into the pot. Sneaking up behind his wife, Alden wrapped himself around her like a blanket.

"Hi darling I missed you," he said.

"Oh hi honey I was beginning to wonder if you were going to find a nice little half collapsed roof to sleep under tonight. How did things go?" Leonara asked before pecking him on the lips.

"I ran into another Crawpike today. He actually tried to give me a kiss too, but I prefer yours far more."

"Really? I thought venomous overgrown arthropods were your type."

"Well why kiss him when I already have one at home-" Alden said with a big smile as she playfully shoved him. "Missed you darling."

"Besides flirting with our local lobsters did you manage to accomplish anything useful?"

"As a matter of fact, I got through the barrier today. I knew spending all that time in the library would work out."

"Truly? Well that's wonderful which spell did the trick?"

"Reserendum, it was an ancient hand pattern I hadn't seen before. Had to finesse the magic flow and it had a dozen hand signs, can you believe it? A dozen? Someone really wanted to keep that room locked."

"With a book that important it seems only natural. Nothing valuable is ever easily acquired."

"Oh really? You remember our first date and still want to say that?"

Leonara crossed her arms and smiled. "Well, you were cute and always knew how to make me laugh, even if it was on accident."

"Were?"

She put her hands on her hips and gave him a look that could only be described as incredulous.

"We've spent months trying to acquire that one incredibly rare book to expose an Ascendant high lord who's killed countless people and that's what you lead with? Have you even cracked open the cover?" Leonara asked.

"I may have peeked, looks like Cassara was right after all. It's even worse than she thought," Alden said.

"How? She told me about the experiments and all those poor people he'd killed and it's still worse?"

"Yes. I want to start going through it, but try to keep your voice down," Alden said looking over his shoulder before lowering his own voice. "I don't want Amara hearing about this. She shouldn't have to think about something like that."

"You're right, well even so we ought to celebrate. I'm making bask fish stew tonight. One of the fishermen was so happy with the

Venendum coated boxes I made him that he gave us some filets as a gift."

"I can understand why he was so happy, a box lined with vacuum will be cooler than any shade. Let me get out of your way 'Nara. I'm gonna go to the study, just let me know if you need anything dear."

"Will do honey and try not to kiss any more lobsters on your way over."

Alden smiled before walking over to the room on the other side of the house. Countless stacks of book sat on the shelves they'd overgrown like ivy. In the center was a mahogany desk they both shared. Placing his brown pack down Alden collapsed into the soft leather chair behind the desk. A room over, he heard only silence as Amara was no doubt digging into her spell book. On the other end of the house was the sound of soup bubbling. *I'm home.*

A few more minutes would be needed for dinner to be ready so he pulled out the book they'd moved halfway across the country to find. Its cover was bound with black leather and stamped with a single red symbol. Alden's hand ran across the book feeling the quality of the binding. Pictured in its center was a smoking skull in front of a simple sun. *Where have I seen this symbol? Damn this tired mind of mine. Perhaps a full stomach will bring my memory back.* Turning the page, Alden discovered the author's name and a short passage.

I H.L.D. wish that this book may serve others better than it has served myself. May you find this world's salvation in these pages and succeed where I have failed. Within I have recorded the hypothetical bridge between humanity and the Ascendant. My efforts by which a being of mortal life and magic essence could coexist in one. The fate of all things mortal and immortal rests within these pages. I only wish that you, reader, are a greater mind than I and can save this world. The things between the spaces are coming and they bring only death.

Cheery way to start a book. And here I was hoping for a comedy. Why do I always start the depressing ones before bed?

Inside the passages detailed bleak, bloody experiments. Pictures sprouted from the pages showing anatomy, magical systems he'd never heard of, and the writing of someone desperate for a solution. Alden now knew why the Order had been so interested in this book.

The spells in here could start another magical renaissance just like the Ascendant's ritual had four centuries ago and just as easily empower a monster. Every line is another person's life cut short. Who could toss away their humanity so easily? Oh right, Dreven found a way.

Every idea presented crystalized into a conclusion. *This ritual is a gateway to forge a human being's life with magic to create a hybrid from the pairing. Hypothetically the combination of these two elements would be like mixing paints to create colors undreamed of. Ascendant are already far more magically conductive, but anyone who underwent these rituals would be like the ancient Gray. If they survived it that is. Still think of the artifacts and cities that could come to life. Not a soul has been able to activate one of their relics in thousands of years since they require more magic than anyone alive can channel. Someone brutal enough to carry out these experiments would be a walking calamity if they succeeded.*

"Dinner's ready!" Leonara shouted from the kitchen.

Thank goodness, I need a break from this. Alden sat up and walked over to the dinner table as his mind tried to erase what he'd read. Alden found the stew hanging over the fireplace simmering with a rich red color from the tomatoes, garlic, and fish within.

"Thanks darling, how's it taste?" he asked.

"Wouldn't know I'm still waiting on you two," Leonara said.

Everyone sat down at the wooden table in anticipation of a wonderful dinner. No words were spoken at first as the only language at a dinner table with good food, is the kind one speaks with spoons and forks.

"Mmm it's good Mommy," Amara said.

"It's excellent, well here's to our friendly fisherman for being kind enough to provide this," Alden said.

"Daddy are we gonna be heading home, since you found the book?"

"Wait how'd you hear that?"

"You and Mommy were kind of loud. Is it true?"

"It is, I'm a knight and I have to go where the Republic needs me. We came here to get a book and now we've got it, but don't worry we'll still have a week or two here."

"Aww, I'm gonna miss the beach it's so much prettier here than in Krohfast. Will you take me tomorrow since you're all done, please?

"Alright but only if we can work on your spells there."

"Living in the capital again will be so nice, but I will miss how quiet life is around here. Would you two mind running some chores for me while you're out and about?" Leonara asked.

"Sure just leave a list and we'll get them on the way," Alden said.

They continued on for a time and many more bowls were had by all. After dinner, Alden and Amara cleaned up the dishes, although one may have contributed more to the effort than the other. After they finished it was quite late and the little one was beginning to have trouble keeping her eyes open. Alden scooped her off the floor with practiced precision. He carried her all the way to the bed before plunking Amara down onto the sheets with the softness of a falling feather.

"Alright conch-head time for bed. Sweet dreams darling," Alden said

With a goodnight kiss he closed the door behind him. *I can't believe what it's been like these past three months. The jungle hasn't exactly been a picnic, but getting to spend so much time home with her has been great. I hope duty won't call too soon after we get back, but I know that's just wishful thinking. There'll always be another fire for me to run into.*

Alden retired to bed with Leonara and as the night grew darker only one of them seemed to find any sleep. Any excitement over finally completing their mission was tempered by the book's warning. Eventually able to quiet his mind, Alden knew he'd do anything to protect the peace he'd found here in their little cottage by the sea.

Chapter 2: A Race for Lightning

Alden slowly opened his eyes to see Leonara sleeping beside him. She looked radiant in the sunlight even if her chestnut hair resembled a particularly poor bird's nest. *A few twigs and a pair of eggs is all you need dear. Good thing the window's closed or a robin might actually try to set up shop.* Smiling he planted a kiss on her perfect pale cheek. With practiced effort, Alden slowly lifted himself out of the bed leaving the mattress as still as a puddle on a windless day.

Rubbing eyes that seemed determined to stay closed, Alden slipped his clothes on before he wandered into the kitchen. Simply saying "Autendum," accompanied by a snap of his fingers the kitchen began to move. In no time at all scrambled eggs and toast had been made as the rest of his family joined him. Everyone sat down to a wonderful breakfast as the sun complimented the beautiful blue sky outside their window.

After breakfast had been cleaned up, Amara joined her Dad at the door. Dressed in a blue linen shirt, brown skirt, and wearing a beaming grin she was obviously giddy to go to the beach. Scanning down Leonara's relatively short list of errands Alden picked up the cloth sack off the counter which would help carry those items home. *Go down to the market to get some fish for dinner, pick up package from Cassara at post office, and practice spells with Amara. Hmm should've known she'd suggest the order we do them in without even saying it.*

"'Nara what's this about a package from Cassara? Does she just instinctively know when I've finished a job, because I'd honestly believe it," Alden asked.

"She is an ambassador for a reason, but no I don't think mindreading is one of her talents. Melcher just called me yesterday to let me know her gull had brought it in. I'm sure it's just a small comfort for us. You know how she always works herself up into worrying," Leonara said.

"I'm sure you're right, knowing her it'll likely be something worth more than our house. How much you want to bet she calls whatever it is plain?"

"Only a fool would take those odds. You should set off for the fish market while the sun is still rising. I'm going over to the terraces to refill the oxen's Autendum enchantments. Now get going or one of us will start to grow a beard."

"Bye darling I'll see you after we're done."

"Bye Mommy," Amara said.

"Goodbye sweetie, have fun at the beach," Leonara said.

Alden kissed his wife and started walking out the door before he quickly felt a small hand squeezing his own. Reciprocating in kind, Alden gently clasped Amara's fingers. *I have a feeling this is going to be the kind of day that goes by too quickly. Well best not waste another moment when we have so few left here.* Together they walked past the picket fence, out the gate, and down the hill's dirt road into Mullentide.

Breezes coming off the Otaton gently rocked the grass as the pair wandered through the village. The sea's salty aroma grew stronger as the wind's warm embrace caressed their faces. Brown clay roofs gently framed by a beautiful blue sky lined the twisting roads they walked along.

Good thing I've had three months to learn all these paths and switchbacks. I swear not a single plan was ever used to make Mullentide. I don't think I could make a more confusing maze if I had a month and the mind of a madman.

Experience finally brought the pair to the main road. Many of the villagers here bid them good morning as some were running errands while others were heading off to work. Most were farmers or fisherman, but Alden spotted the red robed alchemist who was one of the few people in the village who worked indoors like them. Mullentide had sprung to life like a dependable clock as it did every morning.

I suppose things aren't so different from Krohfast. Everyone gets up and commutes to work. Although I can't deny I miss the carriage trains. It's so much easier to be tired when magic is the one moving you instead of your legs.

Following the wide dirt path to the cliff they stepped onto the winding trail leading down to the beach. Carved into the cliffside rock it wound snake-like another fifty feet until it met the sand. Driftwood posts lined the side like dashes on a treasure map. A few fallen rocks were scattered across the path, each a victim of the sea's relentless erosion. Sand heated by the morning sun crunched underneath their shoes as they stepped onto the beach.

Mullentide's harbor lay before them; a collection of planks held together by nails where every fisherman docked to display their catch each morning. *They've done really well it's like every color, shape, and size of sea life is on display.* Most of the small fleet of boats were anchored just off to the left bobbing in the gentle waves. Amara's little hand unclasped from Alden's as she dashed off to one of the closer stalls to see what curiosities had been swept up from the sea.

The mind of her mother paired with my curiosity. What a terribly dangerous combination. Wait for me conch-head I want to see too.

The pair glided between stalls swiping up fish like greedy gulls. Each fisherman had stocked something different and beautifully bizarre which made it too hard not to try a bit of everything. A few spent kolos later, their cloth sack was nearly bursting at its seams by the time they'd gotten to the last few stands.

What a heavy sack, we may have overdone it. Well having fresh fish for the next few days isn't the worst thing in the world. Better cool it down before we leave. Inside the bag were fish who resembled flutes, gallant green groupers, rays studded with orange spikes, scythe finned sharks, and others shielded in silver scales. Alden ran his hand over the bag and said "Brumorta." An icy cold poured out from his fingers which would keep the contents inside perfectly preserved until they got home.

Looking up at the end of the dock they found a water blusher hanging from a hook. Thrice as long as a grown man and covered in crimson scales contrasted by black stripes along its body. Great black eyes the size of dinner plates framed the fearsome predator's head. A cavernous mouth held ivory white teeth as thick as fingers.

What a monster, I fear the pair of us would be little more than a snack to a fish like that. Whoever caught that had to be happy just to make it back home. No chance he's selling it, that's the kind of catch you hang on a wall.

"Have you ever caught one of those Daddy?" Amara asked.

"I have a lot of scars, but none of them came from one of those," Alden said.

"I think I want to catch one someday."

"Conch-head that fish wouldn't fit in our kitchen. If you tried to hook it with a rod it'd catapult you into the sea."

"I wouldn't use a rod."

"No? What then?"

"I'm gonna learn to use lightning spells and zap him from the water."

"That's a good plan, but that still wouldn't count as catching it. The fish would still be in the water."

"Could you teach me how you'd do it then?"

"Maybe I could. How about we head over to the beach and practice your spells? I think I know just the thing for us to do."

Alden led Amara across the planks and turned right towards the sea cliff once their feet hit the sand. He made for an overhang carved by the waves through the impassable wall of gray rock. Warm sea water splashed against Alden's shoes as his hands bristled at the much colder stone boulders they used as handholds to cross. Tide pools painted bright green by algae greeted them on the cliff's other side as the waves had just reached their low point. Amara couldn't contain her excitement any longer and sprinted over leaving him smiling on the sand.

"Come on Daddy let's find a few shells first. We can do spells after, I promise," Amara said.

Our days are running out here anyway, why not grab some souvenirs. We still have plenty of time for practice and picking up the package.

Alden dropped his bag of fish by some rocks and walked over to join in the hunt. Both of them pranced about the exposed tide pools hunting for any treasures stranded by the receding water. The first find went to Amara who found an iridescent shell that spiraled like a horn while glowing like a rainbow. Not to be outdone, Alden uncovered a great big clam shell that was clear as glass.

Amara raced ahead eager to scope out the next set of pools before her father. Unfortunately, she stepped too quickly crashing into the turquoise blue water. The splash sounded like a great drum as Alden began laughing at his drenched daughter. *She's gonna be a wonderful swimmer with how often she manages to slip into the sea.*

"You do know the point of low tide is so you don't have to dive for them?" Alden asked.

Laughing at Amara he failed to see his own mistake barreling toward his back. A giant wave rolled over the rock knocking Alden into a pool of his own.

"I don't think either of us know that Daddy," Amara said.

"You're not wrong conch-head. Still this seems like a prime opportunity to work on spells until we stop dripping," Alden said.

He pulled himself out of the pool before sending a helping hand Amara's way. With an iron grip Alden plucked her out of the water and the two laughed at the whole ridiculousness of the moment. Along the way back to the bag, Alden picked up a small collection of rocks in his hands. *Best way to teach is to make the lesson fun. Let's see just how much control you've developed little one.*

"Amara before we go up to the post office I want to play a game with you," Alden said.

"What kind?" Amara asked.

"The fun kind, it's a little trick my teachers back at the Arcanum taught me. If you want to control magic you need to learn control. So since we're at the beach I think we should have ourselves a rock skipping contest."

"Okay, but how does that teach me control?"

"Most rocks you find on the beach are alright, but the best rocks for skipping are smooth and thin as a kolo. So what do you do when there aren't any stones like that around?"

"You could make them. Like how I polished it yesterday."

"Exactly like that, but if you don't use the spell just right it'll crack since it's so thin. Make a few stones and we'll see who's better."

Alden placed his collection down for both of them to begin working on. Each said "Ventos," as an abrasive layer of wind magic channeled through their palms. Rubbing their hands over the stone smoothed the gray surface until only the rock they wanted to remain was left. *The test is so simple, but yet tricky at the same time. If she loses focus even for a moment the rocks will shatter in two. Looks like she's doing well though. First two are perfect, but that one's about to break.*

As he'd predicted the stone shattered into bits, but Amara simply picked up another one. She moved more slowly, but this time her little face scrunched up from concentrating. *Good conch-head. Our failures are only bumps on the path to our triumphs.* With only a few passes from her little hands a stone emerged that was simply perfect. After finishing five stones each, they walked to the water's edge just beside the tide pools.

"Now show me your best throw conch-head," Alden said.

Amara wound up and tossed her rock out onto the sea's mirror-like surface with a sweeping wave of her hand. Bouncing once, twice, and then a third time the stone stopped. As all her work sank beneath the water she looked up at Alden.

"How was that?" Amara asked.

"Pretty good, but let me show you how I like to throw them," he said.

Alden held a similarly perfect stone in his right hand. Winding up just like her attempt he said "Ventos," just before letting the rock go. *Sorry conch-head, but I think I'm gonna have to win this one.* Ejecting from his hand at lightning like speed, the stone began skipping across the water like a deer prancing through a field. His rock careened across the water until it finally struck a wave; sinking in a thunderous geyser.

"That was incredible Daddy! How did yours go so far?" Amara asked.

"That's what control does conch-head. I didn't simply toss the stone, but instead cushioned it with my air spinning in just the right way. Come on we have to get to the post office, but maybe tonight I'll show you a bit more okay?" Alden said.

"Okay I can't wait. Promise you'll show me more though."

"I promise. Now come on before some wave hits us so we have to wait even longer."

Alden picked up their bag of fish off the sand just as the sun was hanging directly overhead. Clambering through a rising tide they made their way back through the overhang to the village. Winding past the cliff road's fallen rocks and through Mullentide's maze of cottages they arrived at the post office after a few minutes.

Located on the opposite side of the village from their hill; the post office was one of the few unique buildings in Mullentide beside their own home. It's tall rectangular tower was made of the same spell-shaped stone their house was. The building resembled a chimney with an endless number of slits on its sides where gulls would fly in to deliver the mail they were carrying. *To think that those crescent shaped constructions carry almost all of Nisuroth's mail. A bit of shaped stone, two Ventos spells for the wings, and a compartment in the center to carry parcels. Veferothi inventions really are something else.*

Inside the chimney was a wooden counter with many cabinets behind it. Overhead were dozens of gulls perched on their shelves waiting to be called upon to carry something. Behind the counter and working on a particularly ornate gull was Melcher, Mullentide's dedicated postman.

"How's it going, Melch?" Alden asked.

"Alden and Amara, nice to see you two. Things are going well. I'm glad you stepped in I do have something from the ambassador for you as I'm sure you already know," he said.

Pulling a golden key from his pocket, Melcher inserted it into the gull's slot near the trunk. *I'm sure he's amazed he actually gets to use the diplomatic key. They may be standard issue, but how many village postmen actually ever get to dust them off? She may be our friend, but I suppose she's still an ambassador. I'd imagine most of*

her mail is far more interesting than the average bit of parchment.
With a sharp click, the key had disabled the construct's Telendum
spell. Popping open the trunk Melcher reached in and pulled out a
beautifully crafted wooden box.

The package was no bigger than a loaf of bread, but it was
covered in ornate pearlescent embossments. Each fine line glittered in
the afternoon daylight and its center was marked by a house sigil. *A
book sprouting wings pierced by a downward sword. That's the mark
of Cassara's house alright, the Ookborne. She couldn't know that we'd
just found the book so what did she send? Walking home won't make
me feel any less anxious about waiting to open it, but I'll endure it for
'Nara.*

"I'm sure she thought this was a drab way to package it,"
Alden said.

"I suppose you'd know, but I think that box may be worth
more than a house," Melcher said.

"Almost definitely, Cassara has never been one to disregard
appearances. If anything, she probably picked the package out herself
since she enjoys that sort of thing."

"I'm just curious as to what's inside. What could be so
valuable that you'd send it in something that is practically an
incredible gift by itself?"

"I guess we'll just have to find out what's inside when we get
home. Knowing her it's bound to be exciting. Thanks Melch, make
sure to tell your father I said hello."

"Course Alden."

Amara picked the parcel off the desk as Alden's hands were
still occupied holding the bag from the market. They began walking
back home as the sun began to dip closer to the horizon. Clashing with
the fields of cotton white cumulus above them was the smoke
billowing from Enten's forge. *Smithies can fashion almost anything
from the right metal, but the physical realm has limitations. Luckily
'Nara's spells are far less restricted. It hasn't even been a month since
she enchanted the forge with that spell I found at the bakery in the
ruins.*

Old goat doesn't know how lucky he is. That same spell would've required an Ascendant master enchanter all the way from Veferoth. It's quite the sight to see a forge flame as stubborn as the man who hammers its metal. We haven't been here long, but I'm glad our work will last long after we're just a memory for Mullentide.

"Come on Daddy, let's go home," Amara said.

"We're already walking that way Amara. What more could we do?" Alden asked.

"Well we could have a race. If I get home first you have to teach me one of the spells from that new book. I want to learn that lightning one. Also I don't want to help cook tonight."

"A race for lightning then. Alright, but if I win you have to help cook dinner tonight. That includes washing the dishes too, deal?"

Amara's little hand outstretched and shook his "Deal," she said. Not a second had elapsed before her tiny shoes started sprinting down the street. "Guess we started Daddy."

Well that is definitely Leonara talking right there. Of course she'll let Dad carry the heavy bag of fish while she takes a little box. That's not even taking into account the maze of streets I'm going to have to navigate to get back home. Quite the little tactician indeed. Not wanting to be beaten, Alden began running flat out on the dirt road. There was a little over a mile to make it back home and the task before him was clear.

He rounded the first house and saw Amara was only a little further down the street. *So much for that lead my little scamp. You'll need another trick to beat me.* Suddenly Amara did exactly what he feared she'd be smart enough to do. Vaulting over a neighbor's fence the little conch-head began sprinting through their yard.

Amara's gonna run straight home and I'm gonna be taking more turns than a snake in a maze. So much for a dignified jog. Almost feels like my days back in the Historic district. Sorry neighbors I haven't stolen anything; I'm just trying to beat my daughter at a race so she can do the dishes. Man that's gonna be hard to shout as I pass by.

Alden ran forth faster than ever. He passed one cottage, two, and then a third with a blooming garden full of lilacs. Amara had passed out of sight, but he knew she was bolting just as hard as him. He turned a corner before a smile painted his face. *This street leads right back to the hill. Sorry Amara, you'll have to help tonight.*

Neighbors looked on with curious expressions at their resident knight sprinting down the road. *Maybe it's a good thing we're leaving in two weeks. Could always pull out the old official Knights of the Abyss business line if I want. Eh, I'm sure they'll find out about the real reason for this later anyway.* Their inquisitive stares would have to be satisfied later. Alden's breath grew ragged, but no matter what he could not, would not lose.

Alden turned the corner at the hill's bottom as he finally saw their cottage at the top. All the weight he'd been carrying truly began to take its toll and glue him to the ground. *Why did I have to get extra fish? Of all the days I could get greedy why did it have to be today?* His breathing was heavy as Alden began the final push. On his right a little girl dashed out of the cottages before beginning to climb the green grassy slope up. Climbing the tremendous incline had slowed her down, but Alden knew better than to think his daughter would ever quit. *Sorry conch-head you're doing dishes tonight. I love you, but there's no way up that hill faster than this road.*

The front yard's picket fence grew closer with every strenuous step. Alden was nearly there and only had a few feet to go. He heard Amara only a few feet away scaling the hill, but the father had her now. It was all over, he'd won.

"Ventos!" shouted a voice just below the hill.

A great cacophonous explosive sound came from his right as Alden looked up to see Amara clutching her box fly over the road right into their yard. Each brown eye was sealed shut as she crashed onto the ground. The little girl rolled twice before stopping on the grass.

Alden stood speechless as he wasn't quite sure what had just happened. *Is she ok? That looked like a hard landing.* Looking over at Amara, she was face down on the ground, but still protecting Cassara's box. Before he could run over to check on her, Amara stood up straight as an oak. She raised both hands in the air and shouted triumphantly. Against all odds she'd beaten her father.

"How in a hock of ham did you manage that?" Alden asked.

25

"Well I was running up the hill and was nearly at the top. Then I noticed you were still going to win so I tried to concentrate like you showed me on the beach. I focused the magic so it would only push me out over the road instead of making a cone like normal," Amara said.

Alden pushed open the white wooden gate and walked over to Amara. *It's not about your power it's about how you handle it. She's always been a fast learner, but that was incredible.* He brushed the dirt off her somewhat stained blue shirt.

"Well I can say you really surprised me. Thought a deer had learned to fly," he said.

"Nope just me," Amara said.

The pair had a good laugh as they were both quite tired from their sprint. "Conch-head could you do me a favor?"

"Sure Daddy."

"If you wouldn't mind Amara, please go put everything away in the kitchen. I'll go grab the book. You won fair and square."

"Alright, but don't be late."

Amara pulled everything inside as Alden went to fetch the book from her room. *Well I think that's the first time I've been happy to lose to a little girl.* Alden couldn't help hiding his grin at the fatherly thought.

Not two minutes had passed until they both came out to the backyard to begin practicing. Facing the woods, Alden sat down on the ground as Amara plunked herself down on his lap. *Looks like I've been promoted to being a chair. I guess she should be pretty tired from our race.* Cracking open the book Alden began reading the spell to Amara. A swaying sea of green grass inspired by the wind danced around them. Jungle trees creaked and careened with their rhyme. Amara just absorbed every word Alden said without a word of her own. Instead she simply leaned her little head against his shoulder.

She's so cute just sitting here. I almost wish they never grew up, but then you'd miss out on how wonderful they become. I suppose I'll just have to enjoy it for what little time I have.

Once he'd finished they both stood up and Alden showed her the hand movements as well as the word Lumicendor which was the spell for lightning. Amara repeated each motion with ease and recited the words like a chatty mirror. She assumed a stance with one leg back and the other forward. His daughter raised her right hand stabbing it forward with her thumb, pointer, and middle finger thrusting forward.

"Lumicendor," Amara said.

Sparks fizzled, but the spell hadn't quite focused properly. Over and over again she tried until on the fifth failure Alden decided to offer some advice. "That's alright. This isn't an easy spell to grasp like Ventos. Try concentrating on your two fingertips until it seems like they're hotter than any fire. Only then do you want to stop channeling," Alden said.

"Lumicendor!" Amara shouted.

Lightning sprung forth from her fingers with a violent blue flash. While Amara had succeeded in focusing the spell, she'd forgotten about where it might go. An old hardwood with a charred black crater indicated just where she'd been pointing. Engulfed in flames, the tree began to belch black smoke.

Oh no she's vaporized the tree. I know there's no guidebook to children, but I feel like there should be a chapter on this. Well better put it out before the whole rainforest follows its lead.

Alden ran over to the tree and brought his palms together shouting "Drentos," to summon a burst of water which snuffed the flames. The old birch was a little worse for wear, but it was no longer in danger of becoming charcoal.

"Maybe I should go make dinner before we cause any more forest fires," he said.

"Sorry Daddy, I got so mad trying to make the spell work I closed my eyes," Amara said.

"It's alright, it was only one tree. Remember though you have to focus or your magic will get away from you. Quite literally sometimes."

"I will, thanks for teaching me."

"Of course and thanks for coming along with me for chores. It was a fun day together conch-head. I'll see you inside."

Although he'd have to explain this small calamity to Leonara, all he could feel was pride. *My little daughter is going to be a great magess someday. In the meantime, for the forest's sake I'll need to teach her to keep those eyes open. Now how am I going to explain this to 'Nara?*

As the afternoon began to fade the pair wandered back inside. Walking over to the window by the sink he gazed out over the cliffs and past the Otaton ocean. He couldn't help but smile over what had been a wonderful day and began preparing the last meal they'd ever eat in that cottage by the sea.

Chapter 3: An Unrecognizable Pyre

After dinner the sun had set over the ocean as orange ripples had been replaced by a dark blue that devoured any remaining daylight. Through the kitchen window, waves on the sea seemed a far cry from the splashes in the sink from dancing plates. *What a wonderful day together. Can't believe she figured out how to concentrate the spell like that in only six tries. Guess that was a better lesson by the beach than I thought.*

Leather-bound footsteps echoed off the tile floor behind him as Alden swiveled to meet their owner. Out of the corner of his eye he saw Leonara holding the package before she planted a kiss on his lips.

"Have you seen this box? It's over the top even for her. These engravings wouldn't be out of place at the Republic Assembly and I think this is petrified wood from the Stonholt Forest. Guessing you haven't looked inside yet?" she asked.

"Not even a peek. I may be curious, but I figured we should open it up together. Any idea on what's inside?" Alden asked.

"Not really, she called me on the vocalamitter earlier. Said she'd feel better knowing we'd have whatever's inside, but didn't want to give it away. Cassara thought it would still be useful even if we're coming back home. You know her; always worrying about us even when we're but a room over."

"I'm sure we don't contribute to that worry… too much."

"We? I don't explore monster filled ruins while fighting criminal conspiracies for a living. I can count the number of scars I've gotten in my entire life on one hand. You'd need to start using toes and may need to borrow a few of mine to finish."

"Hey if the claw marks all happened at the same time that should still count as one. Either way, let's agree that collectively we may cause her to worry occasionally."

"Fair enough. Well, no point in waiting. Let's see what she sent us."

Setting it down on the counter first, Leonara opened the box. Inside were four objects surrounded by a red velvet lining. A note from Cassara was suspended to the chest's top by a silver ribbon. Below it was three elongated triangular lockets softly humming. *Curious they each have a different engraving. The hand holding a staff will be for 'Nara, a conch shell for Amara, and I'm guessing the sword is for me.* Alden reached inside grabbing the locket emblazoned with a blade causing it to grow silent. On further inspection, he noticed the object was as ornate as the box itself with lines, runes, and ornamentation embossed into it. The metal necklace glistened in the kitchen light as its surface had a mirror-like shine.

I've never seen something like this, but no doubt that it's definitely enchanted. Rocks with runes carved into them don't just hum on their own. Why would it stop if I touch it? Is their connection to us more than surface level?

Leonara picked up the note before reading it aloud. "I hope this letter finds you three well, I know it's been some time, but I wanted to send you this little gift to make sure you stay safe. Especially you Alden, if I wasn't an Ascendant you'd have given me a heart attack a dozen times over. It's not kind to a young four-hundred-year old lady," Leonara said.

"Can Ascendant even get heart attacks?" Alden asked.

"Shush, let me finish. Anyway you're probably wondering what these necklaces are. They're soulenkets I had commissioned after I sent you off to Mullentide. They may be somewhat plain like the box, but I assure you they're no simple baubles. If you open them, you'll see three pearls with a rune next to each. Each one is bound to your well-being. As you've no doubt wondered since Alden has probably already picked one up without reading this. I won't bore you with the enchantment's particulars, but simply put the condition of the pearl is reflective of each of yours."

"Guess that explains the engravings."

"If the pearl glimmers blue it means the person is safe, but if it glows yellow then they are truly in trouble. Finally, if a pearl breaks it means that the person has passed on. Don't you even so much as crack those pearls or I'll have to bring you back and throttle you myself! Love Cassara."

30

"Is that really what these are? I've heard of them, but I've never seen one in person since they're supposed to be so rare. Supposedly only Ascendant master mages know the secret to making them."

"You're not wrong. Making them involves weaving several complex spells together while also carving perfectly. Only the most intricate and difficult magic requires runes to begin with. Even a single error or missed step would have made them worthless."

"Can't believe she got these for us. We'll have to do something nice for her once we get back."

Leonara embraced him. "Definitely, it was very sweet of her. I'll be sure to put mine on tonight. It will be nice knowing you're safe wherever you get swept off to next."

"As much as I'd like to stay with you two there's no way we're done with Dreven. If I know Cassara we'll use the book to hunt him down and stop his experiments for good."

"I know you will, but still make sure to take good care of that locket. I don't know if you even can, but please don't break your pearl on accident. I'm not sure Cassara would be able to save you from me."

"What a scary thought, two of the world's best magesses angry at me. I'd rather dodge creature claws than fireballs. Maybe I'll get Amara to shoot lightning at you two and defend her Daddy."

Alden's grin wilted as he felt nails digging into his back. *There are so many better ways to admit it and I chose that one. Well done.*

"Lightning? As in the extremely dangerous elemental energy which can explode a tree into splinters? I thought I smelled something burning walking up the hill. You taught her that today didn't you?" Leonara asked.

"To be fair she only put a crater in the tree, not quite splintered it. I put out the fire pretty quickly anyway. Honestly, Amara did pretty good for a ten-year-old," Alden said.

Come on I've got to do better, that excuse was flimsier than a rotting bridge.

"Was it now? I talked to Enten today and my hearing must be going, but I don't recall him mentioning the natural disasters Roesia was creating," Leonara said. Hands on her hips she sighed. "How long did it take her to get the hang of it?"

"Sixth try, I swear she's gonna be the best magess in an age. Besides she's not gonna be our little conch-head forever. A girl who can cast spells that well will be able to take care of herself. I mean it worked for you remember? When we first met at the Arcanum, I distinctly recall you animating a thorn bush to mercilessly slap that one pompous K.I.T.," he said.

There we go, the guilt carriage has left the station.

"Hey that's not fair, he didn't lose that much blood. Besides that jerk earned every scratch by deciding that he needed two women to warm his bedside. Anyway, I suppose you have a point, but just this once. I'm equally delighted as you when she learns something new, but can we at least keep it non-lethal until she's a teenager?"

"Deal, you should've seen the tree it looked like a meteor flew into it. Well here why don't you tuck our little elemental wielder to bed and I'll join you in a bit. I want a chance to study the book some more."

"Alright, but you better not keep me waiting too long. Don't you think a potted rose for the nightstand would be a simply lovely addition?"

"It did seem like kind of a light read when I think about it. Love you darling."

Before he left Alden gave Leonara a kiss. She smiled and went off to Amara's room while he went off to the study. *Still can't believe that I owe Cassara for meeting her, stranger still that she actually gave me a chance. Hope I'll get to stay in Krohfast for a little while at least. Maybe I can spend at least a bit of time with them before I ship off again. I know there's no way this book just ends up being something to put on a shelf. Anyway I ought to stop before 'Nara takes an interest in planting a garden on the nightstand.* Alden plunked himself into the chair and stared at the black book with a skull framed by the sun.

Wait, now I remember it. Knew I'd seen this symbol before. That's house Sunsullen. You know come to think of it isn't Dreven one of them? Is this a family legacy being carried on? They were the ruling family during the war after all.

Continuing to search for a solution in all the ink, Alden found his answer in the last few pages. The author claimed the Gray's ritual was a more refined process than the Ascendant's, but something held them back from succeeding. Oddly the last experiments recorded in the book involved far more people. Stranger still the author began to mention voices in his head guiding his efforts.

All but the mage was burnt to ash as the ritual consumed them? Whoever did this sacrificed hundreds of people, maybe thousands and yet they claimed it would save the world. What could frighten someone so much to commit this evil? One page left, maybe the answers I'm looking for will be there.

Alden turned the page over and discovered the final entry of the Ascendant mage. *I have failed. Every face of those poor people is burned into my mind. I shudder to think of the price others have paid for my research, but they will not die in vain. Perhaps another will succeed where I have failed. This link between our Ascendant birth and the Gray is undeniable for the voice guided my hands and with them I created our new race. Even still these achievements do not assuage my fear. Our only escape from the things between spaces is to uncover the Gray's secret. I believe them to be the only race to achieve a mix of organic and magical states of being. Humans are made of flesh and I am wholly made of magic, but these Gray wielded the strengths of both. My time grows short and the words in my head have fallen silent.*

Alden sat back in shock at what he had discovered. *To think that the war that split Nisuroth may have been started over this. Is Dreven hearing the same voice this person did? Who or what gave him the Ascendant ritual and why? I've found the answer to one of our greatest mysteries and yet I have even more questions than when I started.*

Dammit how can my time already be gone? As scary as the thing between spaces sounds I'd rather avoid getting my ass whipped by a rose. Rising from the desk, he quietly walked over to the bedroom. Opening the oaken door Alden prepared to explain what he'd just read, but his plan fell apart as he saw Leonara sleeping as still as a statue in the white sheets. *It's just like her to work until there's nothing left to give. I suppose my discovery can wait until morning.* Carefully clambering into bed, he kissed Leonara on the cheek and wrapped himself around her. She stirred if only a little as he embraced her.

"On second thought we don't need any more plants to garden, goodnight honey," Leonara said.

"Goodnight darling, love you," he said.

Her warmth surrounded him as Alden knew he'd have one incredible story for his wife in the morning. The night grew dark on the village of Mullentide as the clouds obscured the moon's pale specter in the sky. A salty sea breeze blew over each cottage in a village where no light was left unextinguished as the jungle danced to its own nocturnal song. Far out from the cliffs were only waves and ill-intentioned oars breaking the ocean's surface.

The night was calm as Alden and Leonara slept in their bed. No light from Mullentide pierced the darkness overhead. Only the ocean glowed with more than moonlight tonight. Piercing citrine eyes in rowboats stared out towards the cliffs and the homes perched above them.

Asleep in their bed, the parental pair knew nothing of the danger wading onto the shore. The night was dark and the approaching terrors were still far away from their warm cottage. A scream pierced the night's silence. Leonara shot up as she didn't know if a nightmare had made her imagine what she'd heard. Seconds passed and the night seemed to regain its silent hold over the town. Then another shriek louder than the first reached her ears. The wail stopped just as quickly as it started as if cut down by some cruel and silent blade.

"Alden get up, get up. Something's happening in the town! I just heard screaming and then it just cut out!" she yelled.

"Wait what? Are you sure?" Alden asked.

An explosion rocked their windows as the alchemist's house transformed into an inferno. Splinters of the building flew across Mullentide, painting the sky with piercing red debris. Flames began to spread to roofs and fields like the light of a terrifying sunrise. Embers choked the sky as the darkness of a summer night was stolen away.

"Something is very wrong Alden. Get your gear on in case they attack before we can leave and I'll try to get on the vocalamitter," Leonara said.

"Alright after you do that get Amara ready and grab the book. If they're here for us then we have to get it back to Krohfast," Alden said.

"Right, go and get ready. Good luck darling."

Leonara rushed out to the kitchen grabbing both Alden and Amara's soulenkets. Without hesitation she ran into her study to try the vocalamitter. The clunky stone instrument glowed blue as its runes came alive.

"This is Leonara of the Heanerath Mages Guild. Mullentide is under assault from unknown forces. Mobilize troops and send them at once," Leonara said. Only a faint buzz answered her desperate plea. "Can't be, but what else could do that? Alden whoever is attacking the village is using a vocalamitter jammer. We have to get out of Mullentide now!" she shouted.

"This isn't just some raid. They've got to be here for the book," he said.

Jammers are too complex for normal pirates to use. We have to prepare for the worst. Dreven may be making his move and trying to stop us from getting back to Krohfast. But why attack the village if he just wants to stop me? There must be more at work here tonight.

Alden donned his leather armor scarred from countless fights before attaching his ragged cloak he'd worn into his every battle for over a decade. These marks were a point of pride for a Knight of the Eternal Abyss. Each scratch and stain had a story behind it and marked Alden just like any medal pinned to a uniform. *I've fought monsters and even worse criminals, but never an Ascendant High Lord. Cassara said he's devious, brutal, and one of the best fighters she's ever seen. We'll just have to hope he hasn't come as well tonight or the road back home may be truly perilous.*

Leonara escorted Amara over to the front door as each of them had donned their outfits meant for dangerous situations like tonight's.

A battle robe was tied off around his wife's waist while she carried an elegant steel staff in one hand. While the striking red color was beautiful, Leonara was more interested in the padding meant for sliding swords away and deflecting magic. Amara had her own little robe which they'd enchanted to keep her safe from any stray projectiles.

I know the spells on that robe are stronger than any armor, but I don't think any protection could take my worry away. Hopefully we won't have to use it, but I still can't believe we're in this mess. The past pleasant months seemed only a distant memory as Mullentide burned in front of Alden. Kindling, smoke, and screams seemed to have replaced the quaint serenity he'd grown to love.

Getting down on one knee he placed his hands on Amara's shoulders. "Honey it's going to be alright. We're just gonna take a trip to see Auntie Cassara okay? Now remember stay with me and Mommy. We're gonna walk down the hill and make for the road north out of town. You're going to see some things that are scary, I need you to be strong for me and push through. We won't let anything bad happen to you, alright?" Alden asked.

"Alright Daddy," Amara said.

Damn Dreven for making me have to say this to her. I promise you conch-head I'll make sure they don't harm a hair on your little head. Cassara placed the soulenket around Amara's neck and finally on her husband's. He grasped the locket ensuring it was secure.

Alden hugged Amara to his chest. Rising up from the floor he placed his hand on the wooden door and pushed. As the door creaked open his face was stung by the smell of a burning village. An untouched garden of flowers lay at his feet while a horrifying nightmare lay before him. Ash fell from the sky as the fields they had helped sow billowed smoke like an endless sea of chimneys.

Mullentide may die tonight, but it might be avenged if we can escape to the road.

They walked over the cobblestone path to the fence and Alden pushed open the gate. The hinges creaked as even the wood seemed hesitant to press closer to the inferno. They descended down the hill as the air grew thick with smoke.

Their village had become an unrecognizable pyre. Buildings closest to the coast were charred heaps and the center of the town wasn't far behind as everything that could be ignited was now burning. Falling ash created a dense fog and nothing could be seen from inside the town. Only screams escaped to the hill through the impenetrable smoke. Alden drew his sword and Leonara raised her staff as they prepared for whatever awaited them below. *Close your eyes conch-head. I hope the smoke hides every horrid detail from you. Children should never see what I fear is lying in wait for us at the bottom.*

At the entrance to the village the cottages had already caught fire. Face down in the mud, two villagers were leaking life into the street. Standing above them were two Wekken pirates with bloody sabers in their hands. Each of them was over seven feet tall, covered in tan leathery skin, and had a single large citrine colored eye.

"Alden don't let Amara see this," Leonara said.

"Alright," Alden said.

He hugged his daughter so she couldn't see Leonara sprinting towards the pirates. "Brumorta!" she shouted.

A gale of freezing cold flew from her palm and painted the cyclopes in an inch-thick sheet of ice. *She didn't just coat them. Those two are frozen right through. Can't blame her for not holding back after what we've seen.* Leonara swung her staff at the right Wekken's midsection shattering the man into countless pieces. Her tool meant for enhancing magic carried into the second and obliterated him as well.

"It's okay to look now Amara. Good work darling," Alden said.

"They weren't even armed. What kind of coward stabs someone who's running away? I'm sorry we were too late," Leonara said.

"We caused this by being here 'Nara. I can't just let that go. Not after seeing this."

"What are you talking about? The road is right here. The book needs to go to Krohfast so we can stop this monster."

"Agreed, but it'll only take one of us to deliver it."

"No! Dammit, don't make me leave you in... in this death pyre!"

"We both know that book has to be delivered and we can't risk Amara in a fight. It was lucky that there were only two, but what if there are more next time?"

"Darling you can't possibly think you can beat all of them. Mullentide is gone and who knows how many people are dead already. I want to help them too, but you know what Dreven is like. If you go into that smoke, there's no guarantee you'll come back out."

"I know, but I won't leave them to misery and death. Look at those people in the dirt 'Nara. They may be gone, but there are still people alive in there. I'll save as many of them as I can and then I'll find my way back. That's a promise 'Nara."

"Don't you dare keep us waiting, don't you take a moment longer than you need to. I love you."

Tears filled her eyes as she hugged him to her chest and held on as long as she could. *I'm so sorry to do this to you 'Nara. I can't look away and run from this. You've always understood that and now is no exception.*

"I love you now and forever darling. Amara make sure you keep your mother good company while I'm gone. Also, if anyone annoys her you have my permission to zap them okay," Alden said.

Amara lunged forth and hugged his leg tighter than a vice "Okay I will. I love you Daddy," Amara said.

Releasing from Leonara's embrace Alden hugged his daughter. *You're not ready yet for this cruel world, but one day you'll be even stronger than your Mom or me. I can't wait to see it.*

"I love you too. More than you'll ever know. Goodbye my little conch-head," Alden said.

With that last word, Leonara grabbed Amara's hand and they both began running up the main road into the trees. Alden took a deep breath as he watched them vanish into the fog. Burning air danced on his tongue as he tasted the ash. The knight looked down at his sword and free hand.

I guess that's why they call us Knights of the Eternal Abyss. We're always the ones dumb enough to keep jumping into wherever it's darkest. A smile broke across Alden's face as he turned and ran back into the burning streets of Mullentide.

Chapter 4: The Billowing Blaze

Every house around him belched fire filling Alden's nose with the smell of ash. Dozens of villagers who'd escaped from their burning homes lay dead just outside them. *What kind of mind could justify this? How can you save the world by burning the innocent? Can this really all be just for a book?*

Pressing further into the smoke, Alden saw people running towards him. *Two people? No, there's a larger group behind them.* The first to emerge from the smoke was a bloodied Hansen carrying his boy, but they weren't alone. Four Wekken pirates followed with sabers raised and citrine eyes piercing the ashy veil.

"Don't stop, I'll take care of them!" Alden shouted.

Hansen nodded and kept running off towards the town's entrance. The pirates broke off their pursuit and began circling around Alden. *They're movement is impeccable. Not at all what I'd expect from some thugs; they're definitely professionals. Their armor is light, but I can tell it's deceptively strong and they're already trying to set up angles of attack. I'll have to pick them apart and use their lack of magic against them. There's no way I can parry seven feet of strength all night.*

The one on his far left rushed first thrusting his sword right for Alden's abdomen. He knew it was a feint in an instant. The real attack would come from his right. Swinging further left, he thrust his hand into the Wekken's guts shouting "Lumicendor!" The stunned assailant's mouth flung open as lightning evaporated his entrails. Momentum carried the pirate into the dirt as the next attacker glided past his comrade swinging his saber downwards.

Alden raised his sword upward to block. Sparks fell from the clashing steel as he pushed his blade to the right, pulling his opponent with it. His left hand flew towards the mercenary's temple as he shouted "Ventos!" Magic channeled from his open palm outward in a great blast as the wind shot through the pirate's head. The man's face disintegrated as all the power of a hurricane condensed into a mace collided with his skull. Headless, the brigand fell to the ground. Then Alden looked at the other two as they realized he was no easy prey.

The one on the right stepped forward, sword raised defensively and began circling him. Their eyes locked in an ocular dance as each knew that to lose their focus would mean certain death.

"Not so confident now when someone can fight back? You may be a professional, but I'm a knight. Allow me to illustrate the difference," Alden said.

Knowing the man was intimidated, Alden slashed forth from his right. The swordsman blocked and moved to counter him, but to no avail. He thrusted with his left hand towards the Wekken's legs and said "Nere Vendum." A smile painted Alden's face as his opponent's leg nerve endings were overloaded with electrical impulses. The Wekken's limbs tumbled toward the ground dragging their owner with them. Alden sliced downward parting the pirate's head from his shoulders. The third man crumpled into the ashes on the ground leaving only one attacker left.

The last Wekken tentatively took a step backward clearly terrified. Alden stepped forth, sword raised and with his palm open. Turning around, the last assailant sprinted back towards the town's center. *Oh no you don't. You lost the right to run away the moment you stepped foot on our beach. Wait did he just drop something?*

Clunk, clunk, clunk. Bang.

Piercing light blinded Alden as Mullentide vanished in a sea of white. *Agh! Who uses a Lumenator at night? I feel like my eyes are ringing. Now that bastard's gonna get help and something tells me he's got a lot more than three friends left.*

Alden rubbed his eyes as his sight returned to normal trying to study the area around him. Looking behind he noticed that the three dead Wekken were burning away to ashes. *I used Lumicendor on that one, but even what I hit him with shouldn't do that. Wait they must be using corpse immolation enchantments. No bodies mean even if you lose a man you don't leave evidence. Still who's crazy enough to risk burning to death? Is this devotion or insanity?*

Further down the street, Alden saw the blown out back wall of Enten's home. It was replaced by a burning red break in the stucco revealing the house's center. The ceiling had partially collapsed, scattering burning lumber around what had once been a living room. Flames danced about the interior consuming everything inside. *I've been in this home and I barely recognize it. These are good people. They didn't deserve this and we brought it down on them.* Suddenly Alden could make out a quiet cry emanating from deeper in the house.

Stepping through the blown out wall he tried to figure out where the noise was coming from. Listening carefully Alden figured out it was coming from Roesia's bedroom. Crouching under a fallen beam, Alden looked down to see a dead woman lying on the floor. The body was charred, but a deep slash across the chest was what claimed her life. It was Emmie; Enten's wife and a friend of his and Leonara's.

No, no dammit. Not Emmie. I'm sorry, I'm so sorry. Please let the others have escaped this horrid fate.

Alden stemmed his tears as he bent down and brought his hand across her eyes, closing them for the last time. Kneeling over her body he tried to stop choking on the smoke and listened once again. Another cry could be heard from the bedroom. *Roesia? Please be okay little one.*

"Roesia is that you? I'm here to help! It's Alden," he shouted.

Only more wailing answered him. Clambering under a beam that felt hotter than the sun he kept pushing deeper into the collapsing room. *This is definitely her's. Look at all the toys and dolls on the floor.* Alden heard sobbing coming from inside a wardrobe on the far wall. The wooden box was untouched by the flames, but the room around it was quickly being devoured by the fire.

Alden grasped the handle and pulled it open slowly. Suddenly the door burst open as a small set of fingers holding a knife jutted forward as he just barely managed to dodge in time. Wielding the blade was a little blonde haired girl, Roesia, the daughter of Emmie and Enten. Alden plucked the knife away and then embraced her. She pounded on his back while squirming to get out of his grasp.

"It's alright… it's alright, I'm here honey. It's alright I won't let them hurt you," he said.

"Why, why, why?" she asked.

"I don't know honey, but I'm gonna try and save everyone I can. I need to get you out of here okay?"

Alden rose from the floor holding her tight as he walked towards the doorway. Roesia dug her fingers into him as she buried her little head into his shoulder. Crawling underneath the burning wood he did his best to shield her from the fire. *Come on keep moving, I think my coat is starting to cook.* Pressing forward Alden emerged from underneath the rubble into the house's main room. *Can't let her see Emmie. Gotta distract her, uh I know.* Alden cradled Roesia's head so she couldn't look down at the floor.

"Honey what's your favorite flower? My little one's favorite is daffodils," Alden said.

"Roses. Daddy said he named me for them, because they're his favorite," she said.

"Well that does sound like your Dad. He must love you very much to give you a name like that."

Climbing out through the hole he'd entered the house through only a minute before; Alden placed Roesia down as he saw someone running in their direction. A few seconds later the ashen air revealed it was Melcher. *Thank goodness he's alright. Maybe there's still time to save the village.*

"Melch! Are you alright? It's Alden, I've got Roesia with me!" he shouted.

"Alden it's good to see a friendly face. What are all these pirates doing here?" he asked.

"I think they're here for me. We found a book in the ruins that we've been trying to get for months. You came from the center Melch, what's happening further into town?"

"They're rounding everyone up in the central square. Anyone they don't kill they tie them up and bring there. You have to stop them Alden."

"I'll do what I can, but Melch I need you to take Roesia out of town. I can't take her myself and every second I delay more people will die."

"Of course I'll take her straight down the road and won't stop for anything."

"Good, I'm going to go to the square and try to free as many as I can."

"Please save them Alden. Come on Roesia let's get somewhere safe."

The both of them ran off towards the town's entrance as Alden turned toward Mullentide's center. Everything around him was burning as after tonight the village would be nothing more than ashes. *I can't save these buildings, but maybe I can still save more people. I just hope I'm not too late.* Alden ran further into the billowing blaze before him.

The buildings here barely resembled the ones he'd run past just yesterday as thick gray ash fell like snow coating the ground. Their roofs had disintegrated and every wall had crumbled into rubble. Burnt corpses of his neighbors littered the ground like an upturned graveyard. *So many didn't make it. Damn you Dreven for being too cowardly to face me yourself. Siccing these monsters on innocents and you still think you're doing what's right?*

Within a few minutes Alden had arrived at the village square. Crouched behind an overturned oyster cart, he gazed into the town's square. It was shaped as it was named and edged by a dirt street around the exterior. An old Ascendant statue stood in the center surrounded by green grass. The limestone's brilliant white color was stained red by Mullentide's fires. Surrounding the center were more than twenty Wekken pirates standing about as if waiting for something or someone. Behind the circle of clutched spears and swords lay at least a dozen men and women bound on the grass. *They're just waiting for me. I see the one from before, but who is that one in front? Must be their captain since he's dressed so differently.*

The man wore a black leather vest stained with salt from decades of sailing. A bicorn atop his head was similarly weathered and cracked. Its tip pointing forward like a compass needle. His citrine eye scanned Mullentide's burning embers like a lighthouse.

What can I do against two dozen pirates? I'm good, but that's a lot even for me and what about the bicorn? Something about him is really unnerving me. It's almost like he's as calm as a rowboat in the eye of a hurricane. If I fail to beat them, I'll probably never see Amara

---

43

or Leonara ever again. If I don't fight, then every one of the villagers will likely suffer a fate worse than death. I'm sorry girls. I don't know if I'm going to survive, but I'm a Knight of the Eternal Abyss and I will not run. Alden swallowed his fear and stepped forth into the square.

"The guest or rather the knight of honor finally reveals himself. I must say you took longer than I expected, Alden," the bicorn said.

"You must excuse me I had to ensure the book escaped Mullentide tonight," Alden said.

"You don't strike me as the lying sort. A shame, but I suppose your usefulness isn't entirely exhausted. No, tonight we had two goals. One of them is tied up on the ground behind me and the other one has just saved me the trouble of finding him."

"Before I ruin that nice vest of yours I was wondering what guild you're from. I've never seen a group from Aetturus like you."

"I'm afraid the boys are a bit slow to trust strangers so unfortunately I'll have to deny your request. However, I won't be called an unsporting fellow so you may have my name. I am Captain Bojjer and I lead this band of salt swill. However, Alden I'm growing weary of words. Dreven says you're quite the talented fighter. I hope you last long enough to prove entertaining."

Alden tensed himself and prepared to fight. The group surrounding the prisoners disbanded and moved to either side of the square. *Only chance I've got to win this is to divide and conquer. I'll draw them to the street entrance and see how many I can thin out at the chokepoint.* Alden looked up as Bojjer raised his fist in the air. Every pirate's sword and spear stopped motionless in an instant. Each one of them looked to the bicorn and Alden realized he would be entering a near impossible fight. The bicorn's hand hung there in the smoke, almost a monolithic opposite of the soaring statue behind him. Alden's heart seemed to stop in anticipation. *Oh well that's not ominous. Guess they really are professionals.* Bojjer's fist dropped and every pirate descended upon him.

I can tell he's going to take the lead. Someone like Bojjer doesn't wait for anyone to start a scrap. I can't fight him yet or this will all be over before it even begins. Here goes nothing.

The spell variation that would save his skin was difficult and took time to build up the magical energies. Alden felt power surging within him and after a few seconds he released it as the bicorn was bearing down on him.

"Flammorta!" he shouted.

A wall of flame gushed forth from his open palm, blocking the pirates from the front. With the wall placed, he could now funnel his enemies through either side buying him precious time to even the odds. *That should keep Bojjer back for the moment. Gonna have to work quick.* Even with the blazing wall placed, a dozen enemies flowed in from the sides in moments. This was a different kind of fight from before. If Alden tried to take them individually, he would be unable to dodge their combined attacks. *Keep my distance and try to take out as many as possible with each strike. Time is precious and they aren't going to give me anything I can't take for myself.*

"Ventos!" he shouted.

Alden sliced with his left hand at the neck level of the soldiers. The three pirates closest to him had no chance to react as wind sliced straight through their necks. Each collapsed to the ground only moments before their heads followed suit. One just behind the first group lost his sword and the arm holding it. An older one with a scar from his eye to his chin ducked just in time.

"Close the gap. We can overwhelm him!" the older Wekken shouted.

Spurred on by their quickly mounting casualties, the pirates rushed forward. The Ventos spell had reduced their numbers, but Alden was still hopelessly outnumbered. There wasn't any more time to use large spells, but he could still overcome them if the whole group wasn't able to attack him all at once. Then inspiration struck just before the Wekken would have the chance to. *Not much time, but I don't see another option.*

"Umbros," Alden said.

He clenched his hand into a fist and then pulled it downward as a dark cloud began to spout forth. In seconds an impenetrable darkness enveloped the street and all of them with it. *It's scary how many times this spell has saved me. They can't see through the fog, but I can see them clear as day. One hand to maintain the spell and another to cut them down should be fine, but how long do I have? Bojjer isn't going to be delayed forever.*

Holding his left fist tight to his body, he readied his sword. The first thrust went into the guts of the pirate to his right who was swinging wildly from being blinded by the smoke. Blood stained Alden's blade and with one pirate dead he began carving the rest like a cake. *Not Dreven, not Bojjer, and certainly not you lot will keep me from my family.*

Alden sliced through the group like a butcher in only a few swings. Of the original nine pirates only one remained. As Alden moved to finish them off a shout from outside the darkness erupted.

"It was a good trick knight, but I will be delayed no longer!" Bojjer shouted.

The Bicorn leapt towards Alden from outside the darkness. Rolling to the right, Alden couldn't hold his fist closed. As the spell broke, the darkness dissipated leaving only himself, Bojjer, and the veteran Wekken behind his captain on the street. *How could he attack so accurately without seeing me? Could Bojjer really have figured out my position from just the sounds I made?*

Getting to his feet, Alden saw Bojjer staring down at him with his citrine eye aglow. The man staring back at him was scarred from countless fights and his teeth were as sharp as the blades in his hands. *Scars are a good thing. It means he can make mistakes, but the problem is none of them were bad enough to lose. I need to be careful or I'll just end up adding to his collection.*

"Stand back men this one's mine. If I lose any more of you I'll be sailing this ship all by myself. You're quite the skilled mage Alden, but magic takes time to channel in battle," Bojjer said.

His sword came swinging down as Alden dodged back to give himself distance. *Dammit he's right. That cold tone of his can only mean he understands his own skill. I'll just have to make an opening or I fear this fight is over already.*

"If you think I'm good you should see my wife. She'd have tossed your fancy ass back into the Otaton by now," he said.

"She sounds like quite a lady. Shame you'll never see her again," the bicorn said.

Bojjer then began showering Alden with blows. First the pirate thrust his saber forward towards Alden's heart, but as the knight moved to counter a second blow would fly from the left. With no time to counter the striking steel, he could only retreat. Each step gave Bojjer more ground as Alden tried to endure the blows. If he couldn't find a weakness soon, then he would be planted into the dirt just like his neighbors.

That calm attitude wasn't just for show. He may be the best fighter I've ever seen. It's only a matter of time until he finds a hole in my defenses and fills it with his steel. I've bought time with the blocks, but each moment isn't enough for a spell. I don't like it, but there's no choice left.

Alden held his sword tight to his chest and slammed towards his foe. The pirate seeing the change in strategy swung his saber arcing toward his head. Ducking downward he slammed his lowered shoulder into Bojjer's guts. Before the blow landed the bicorn swung his dagger towards Alden's center, but anticipating the second strike Alden tilted his blade to guide the dagger away from his body. The leather armored knight crashed into the pirate's chest knocking him back.

Bojjer was forced back as his sails seemed to have the wind sucked out of them. Swinging at an angle, Alden's sword rocketed towards the exposed shoulder of the Wekken. The brigand brought his sword up to block, but the knight would not be denied. With a vicious clang his blade carried the pirate's own sword into his black leather vest. The cracked clothing suddenly spewed forth crimson blood. A scarlet canyon had been struck into the pirate's shoulder above where the captain had blocked with his sword. *I'm going to make you swallow that big talk Bojjer. I have you now.*

The wound while deep was not fatal. Alden knew his next move and swung his left hand forth. Palm open he meant to dig his hands into Bojjer's body and obliterate it. No armor could stop his attack at this distance. Soaring through the air, victory seemed within reach.

Unseen by Alden, a dagger sailed towards his palm. Reaching within an inch of Bojjer's abdomen he screamed as pain shot through his arm. Bojjer's speed had saved him as the pirate had plunged his dagger through Alden's hand, pinning it to his torso. The bicorn dropped his sword. As the blade began to descend to the ground, his now free hand sailed towards Alden's face. Knotted muscle strengthened by decades of raiding plummeted upon the knight's chin.

Guess there wasn't enough time. I'm sorry Leonara and my little conch-head. I don't think I'll be coming back from this one.

Alden's vision blurred as the Wekken's natural strength struck him to the ground. His hand and Bojjer's slim dagger fell onto the hard dirt road. The metal's clang echoed around Alden as he reeled from the impact. I *just had to be the hero didn't I?* Then with only a breath in between, a second fist landed upon his face from above. Bojjer's clenched claws were the last thing Alden saw before his vision snapped to black.

Chapter 5: Six Days at Sea

What is that smell, ugh why does everything hurt? Salt filled Alden's nose as his eyes began to open again. A rhythmic roll swayed his head as the darkness began to recede. His every breath began to paint a picture as splotches of color appeared from the inky black. Wooden walls made of barnacle covered planks surrounded him and a wall of iron bars stretched from the floor to the ceiling in front. Water pooled around his feet, shifting with the waves. Thunder echoed from outside the ship as rain pounded against its exterior. *I lost so why am I still alive? What could that bastard Bojjer have meant by my usefulness isn't entirely at an end?*

Gazing past the iron bars, Alden noticed that he was not alone down here. Cells lined each side of the bilge with the villagers from the square inside them. *Looks like there's about two dozen of us down here. Hopefully everyone else escaped while I was buying time.*

Focusing back upon himself, Alden looked down at his hands noticing the pirates had left him a present. Without a word he knew just what they were, suppression restraints. *Bojjer really is a clever bastard isn't he? Gonna have to figure out a way out of these if we're going to escape. Even the strongest mage can't channel enough magic to break them and I definitely fall far short of that standard. Did they have to make them so tight?*

Turning his left hand over, he noticed that the wound from Bojjer's dagger had already been stitched back up. *Curious, they really must need every person for whatever they're doing. I would have killed me and I'm pretty sure I'm the nice one on this ship.* Even though the hole had been closed it was still quite sore. The white cotton stitching was clean and neat with each little loop lying perfectly in place. *I'll never understand how Wekken are so delicate with those giant paws of theirs. Good thing I didn't stitch myself up in even these gentle waves, I'd probably have ended up losing the hand.*

Standing up, Alden looked around the small cell he was in. A single wall separated him from the rudder. It's weathered wooden boards creaked constantly and were peppered with patches of barnacles growing out of them. An alarming amount of water sloshed across the floor as Alden tried to find a hole to peek through. Eventually he found a small kolo sized break in the boards.

Pressing his face up to the hole revealed the world outside his confinement. The sea surrounded them while above the sky was painted grey by storm clouds. Rain hammered the waves like a million tiny drummers. *No bird calls. We must have sailed far from shore already for there to be nothing at all.* As harsh as the storm was Alden could still see that the right side of the sky was darker than the left in the distance. Absence of light could only mean one thing; they were heading south.

Could it really be, Hemmoros? They burn my village down, kidnap us, and then take me back there. I've already had enough of that jungle for one lifetime.

Pulling up his shirt and armor, Alden began to remember the scar he'd received on his last visit. Running his hands across his lower torso he finally felt the large pink line. Although it was only one of the many scars he'd earned it was the one which had gotten him closest to leaving this life. *Amazing I didn't end up as one of the bodies littering that village. One second your nose is filled with that sweet smell, the next you're a smear on the ground.*

"Alden! Is that really you?" a voice asked.

"Wait I know that voice, Bakston?" Alden asked.

"It's me, I'd hoped you'd escape from these bastards. They caught me in my bunk on the docks. I never stood a chance."

"Would've, but I had to go back into town. Couldn't just let them take everyone. So many didn't make it."

"You're one man. How could you have saved them all? Did Leonara and Amara make it out at least?"

"They did. We came to the edge of the village and I told Leonara to take the book we found back to Krohfast. They should be safely shipping off to the capital by now. Hopefully their carriage has less water in it than ours."

"I don't know it does seem pretty rainy today."

Both men smiled as the joke pierced the gloominess of their present problem. As the ship shifted in the waves the mood seemed to work its way back into the both of them. *Can't give up hope. We're alive and that means we might still have a chance. If I despair so will everyone else.*

"Looks like we're headed to Hemmoros. Have you overheard what they want to do with us? Maybe some detail the crew mentioned? I don't remember anything after Bojjer knocked me out in Mullentide," Alden asked.

"I suppose it shouldn't be a surprise. You've been fading in and out since last night. After they dumped us in these cells I overheard one of them mentioning something about an isle. Talked about us like we weren't people, just things to be used for something. What did that pirate call it? Ah, he said we were going to be used in that damn Ascendant's spell," Bakston said.

"Hmm Ascendant spell. He was probably talking about Dreven. I think he's the one behind all of this. If this is about magic that means they either need someone to run experiments on or worse yet sacrifices."

"Neither of those sound all that pleasant. Not sure I see a difference from behind these bars."

"If it's a ritual then they'll kill us all at once, but if they're testing something they'll do it one at a time. Might mean we have more time to figure out an escape. Have to keep on the sunny side."

"It's hard to see the sun in the middle of a thunderstorm."

"We'll make it out of this somehow Bakston, I just don't know how yet."

"I'll keep these old ears open then. I'd hate for this to be the last tub I sail on."

Both men slunk back behind their bars before slumping onto the floor. *Can't blame him for not being positive about this. Our odds aren't exactly great and the mention of a ritual is worrying me. Does Bojjer want us to just be another failed experiment for Dreven or could this be something different? They could have just attacked me at our house, but they went after the village and took prisoners. Taking them would be pointless if the goal was to make it seem like this was just another pirate raid. Something more is going on I'm sure of it.*

Head aching from Bojjer's beat down, Alden rested against the planks. The waves rocked him to sleep as his mind raced to figure a way out of this mess. Any trace of sunlight was swallowed by the inky blue of night. It was likely to be the first of many as the trip across the Otaton was a six-day voyage to Hemmoros' northern most point and who knew how much further south they'd go. Outside his captive cabin, the storm roared around Alden. Their wooden ship bobbed and bounced as spray spewed onto his back from the holes around him.

The raging ocean surface no longer held back the water as it was thrust into the air to create a grey thunderous fog. Dark swirling clouds danced through the sky as lightning flashes appeared like flourishes in their performance. The treacherous weather lasted through the night and two others. *I'd forgotten how ferocious these storms can be. Half a trip can be spent without seeing the sun.*

The days aboard the ship during the storm were mostly uneventful. Every four hours or so a pirate would walk the cells. Alden studied his face and body for anything he could use to escape. Each time it was the same Wekken. His tan leathered skin covered a thin bony face bordered by two pointed ears of unequal length. A bright citrine eye sat in the center of his face lazily checking on them. His armor sat on top of a simple red cloth shirt above rough brown pants. His dark boots were still stained a shade of gray by Mullentide's ashes.

Each morning the pirate brought down a biscuit so the villagers wouldn't expire and refilled a fresh water flask assigned to each cell. The bread was harsh and hard, but without it they would all starve so no one complained. On the third day of this routine one of the villagers asked if they might have some more water as their throats were hurting horribly.

"There's water all around your feet. Drink up dog," the pirate said. The Wekken started laughing before moving along to the next cell.

Cruel and maybe even sadistic. This isn't a glorious assignment so I doubt he's very popular with the other pirates. Young, impulsive, and possibly my way out of this mess.

After the storm had passed on the third night the seas grew still. On the fourth day the same pirate who made the rounds came down the steps leading into the bilge and stopped. *Something's wrong, when has he ever cared about a prisoner enough to stare a second longer than needed? That's Enten's cell, after what happened to Emmie and Roesia I can't bear the thought of any harm coming to him too. He sounded so weak yesterday. Please be ok you old goat. Roesia still needs her father.* The Wekken opened the cage door and walked through the water on the ship floor. Alden heard a pause for a moment and then the silence was broken.

"Ugh dammit, old one passed away. The water must've sucked the life right out of 'im," the Wekken said.

Alden felt his heart sink deep into his chest. The pirate walked out of the cell and up the stairs to get another pair of hands. *Enten was a good man and he was so kind to us. Emmie always baked us pies even after they paid for our spells. Now they're both gone and Roesia, that poor girl will never see her parents ever again. At least Leonara will make sure she's taken care of.* Anger pulsed through Alden's veins as he bowed his head in pain.

Footsteps echoed from above as he heard shouting up top that was unmistakably Bojjer. A few moments later two Wekken returned down the steps. One was the guard from earlier who's flat nose was now broken. The other was an older pirate who couldn't hide his toothy smile. A scar extended from just south of his eye down to his chin. *I remember him. He's the old Wekken who dodged my attack back in Mullentide.* The pair held two large wooden buckets each.

"Won't get to do that again, Shruthus. You're lucky we're so shorthanded from that knight carving us up. If we weren't I swear the captain would've tossed you into the sea," the veteran said.

"Wouldn't matter. We're only two days from the isle, Turtan," Shruthus said.

"Not like you could swim that far anyway. Besides you're assuming the captain wouldn't turn ya to chum first. Anyways best to quit jabbering. Captain can't use a dead man, but he does want this old chub for bait."

Turtan looked uneasy as he stared into Enten's cell. Shruthus waved his hand dismissively as the pair walked inside. Out of sight Alden could only hear their splashing boots echoing off the wooden walls. Silence seemed to fill the bilge as he closed his eyes knowing what was about to happen.

Shlunk. Shlunk. Shlunk.

Knives began to hack through flesh as the ship's peace was shattered. Bone cracked and muscle fell apart as the sound of Enten filling the pair's buckets reached Alden's ears. Horrified, he covered his mouth desperately trying to keep down his biscuit. Looking down as he tried to endure his stomach, Alden saw the water sloshing around his feet turn red. The harsh reality pooled around his boots.

It took the Wekken an hour to finish carving Enten up. After the knives fell silent, the pair walked back out holding four blood covered buckets. Each container was overflowing as tears dropped down Alden's face. Stemming the tide from his eyes, he closed them trying to think of some way out of this nightmare. *I'll make these bastards regret letting me live. I will find a way home, but not before I make them pay for all the pain they've inflicted on these poor people.*

Over the next two nights, Alden had some conversations with the other villagers, but it seemed like the very air had been poisoned by Enten's death. Most of them feared the worst and few wanted to risk the wrath of their captors so the brig's only noise was the creaking of boards shifting in the waves. However, Alden had been listening to the conversations above their deck and had learned that Hemmarasp Isle was their destination.

While the key to their survival began to take shape in his head, another idea kept clawing at the back of his mind. *How can Bojjer hope to succeed in the rituals that Dreven failed at? Unless something has changed recently this should be just a repeat of his prior experiments and shouldn't justify the attack on the village. Could he really think this time will succeed where every previous effort hasn't?*

"Drop the anchor!" shouted Bojjer.

A great splash echoed as the ship suddenly came to a stop. The vessel he'd ridden across the Otaton stopped moving as the heavy iron anchor weighed them to the seabed. Birds cawed like trumpets announcing their arrival as Alden rose to his feet. The voyage was over and the search for their survival had begun.

Chapter 6: Some Unseen Danger

Once they'd anchored the Wekken crew grew restless like a particularly bothered beehive. Bojjer shouted commands as every pirate began scurrying about the decks. Alden heard a great splash as a rowboat was lowered into the sea. *At least I won't have to swim ashore in cuffs. Salt water never did play well with stab wounds.*

In no time at all Shruthus and Turtan came down to the bilge to unload the prisoners. One by one they attached a rope to each person's cuffs and led them upstairs. Each cell was emptied until the only person left in the ship's belly was Alden.

Finally, it was his turn as Shruthus unlocked his cell. Alden couldn't hide his disgust for the men who had defiled his friend as they tied the rope around his restraints. His wrists were jerked forward as he began taking the long walk to the stairs. They made their way through the bilge past each cell. Every empty iron cage was a person he'd failed and who'd joined him on this voyage. Alden passed eleven of them without pause, but at the last he stopped. Shruthus turned around to see a human statue with eyes as hard as granite.

Alden stood there, silently staring past the iron bars. His dark brown hair had grown matted from a week at sea and his chin was now covered in a coarse stubble. Centered between these features were eyes gazing down into the rotten cell where Enten had passed from this world. Irritated by the delay, Shruthus pulled on the rope once and shouted something, but Alden couldn't care to hear it.

I'm so sorry old man. Don't know if I'm going to make it out of this alive, but if I do I'll make sure Roesia is taken care of. You have my word.

The cell's wood was stained by a dark red rust that seemed to creep across every board. Splashing water and foam clawed upward at the stains as if the sea itself was rushing to swallow the memory of the man who'd once been there. Alden stared until a callous fist collided with his face. Shruthus had struck him to the deck.

"The stairs aren't through those bars dog. Did a little stormy weather shake you slow?" he asked.

Alden felt something warm start to seep down from his temple. Finding his footing, he stood up and glared at the young pirate. The Wekken froze as the knight's stare seemed colder than the deepest winter.

"The stairs are that way Shruthus. Are you waiting for one of us to carry you up? It'd be a shame if the captain had to break your nose twice," he said.

Turtan who had been uninterested until this point, grinned at the look in Alden's eyes. *Something's different about that one. I nearly took his head off in Mullentide and if anything he acts like I'm more of a friend than his crewmates.*

"Bring him up Shruthus or he can drag your ass up the steps. If the both of you don't knock it off, I'll carry each of you short stacks up these steps like sacks of grain. I'm not letting Bojjer ruin my nose over your spat," Turtan said.

"Ruin? It isn't that bad is it?" Shruthus asked.

"It looks like a cherry pie someone stomped. Now stop fooling around; we have a mountain to climb."

The old pirate started up the steps as Shruthus quickly followed suit while touching his shattered nose. Every stair creaked as the trio climbed from the ship's bottom up to the top deck. A ray of daylight shone down into the ship as Alden nearly felt blinded leaving the dark bilge behind. As his vision departed the darkness, his eyes adjusted and the world around him emerged. What had been a creaking musty mess below concealed an admittedly grand sailing ship.

The main deck must have been a hundred feet of rich dark brown wooden floors and blue painted railing. Two thick masts rose from the deck each holding weathered white sails. At the top of the middle timber a Aetturan flag identified it as a Wekken vessel, a bright blue flag with an eye above an anchor. *The one set of colors on the Otaton that strikes fear into the heart of every sailor. With most flags you know who you're talking to, but with that one you never know if you're looking at merchants or murderers. The other dead giveaway this is a Wekken ship is the sails with no engines. No magic means no Drentos motors to push you across the ocean.*

Alden saw they were moored just next to a sandy beach dotted by driftwood playing in the waves. Beyond the water's edge was a jungle that stretched far into the distance with a single peak rising out of the trees. *I suppose a dormant volcano is a fitting place for a dead civilization's ruins. Stunning from a distance and yet still so dangerous that no one will set foot near it.* Once his eyes had left the mountain they glided to the sapphire colored Turtamaw bay which lapped against their hull. A name it earned by resembling the mouth of a snapping turtle. *That must be Henaten. I've stood on that shore and looked towards this one, but I never dreamed I'd do the opposite.*

As the Wekken escorted him across the deck they bobbed and weaved past pirates preparing things for the long trek into the jungle. Sacks of food and crates of supplies swirled around him in a frenzy. Each armful was loaded into the boats on the sides of the ship. Every vessel was lifted up from the water and dove back down almost as quickly. One of them on Alden's right had popped up above the siding. In mere moments a worn wooden box, a brown bag of grain, and a small red stained barrel were loaded onto the boat by a hefty Wekken wearing a raggedy yellow hat. Simply seconds later, the boat glided down into the water and the sound of oars slapping against the sea reached his ears. *It's hard to forget they're the best sailors in the world. They're like automatons out here on the water.*

Shruthus and Turtan stepped into the back of an empty rowboat near the front. Shruthus motioned for him to enter the front with a terse tug. One leg raised he sat down on a bowing wooden beam and stared at the pair of eyes between the two pirates. Looking down he noticed that the only cargo aboard was himself.

"Drop 'er," Turtan said.

The ropes holding the little vessel next to the side relented and they sank towards the water. Grabbing an oar each, the cyclopes' pushed away from the ship before adjusting their course towards the shore. Their thin arms were deceptively strong and excellent for rowing. As they continued along Alden noticed that both of his captors seemed to grow serious. Any hint of their previous chatter was gone.

That's odd. Are they really so scared of the isle that they've both stopped talking?

Risking only a brief glance to hopefully avoid any more fists on his face, Alden saw just how serious they'd become. Interestingly Turtan seemed to be handling it better than the younger one. Shruthus' stared back at the ship as if his greatest regret in life was rowing towards the isle. Alden saw Bojjer on the ship's bow in his oppressive black bicorn staring towards the mountain as if searching for some unseen danger.

Why do I get the feeling that I'm not the only person on this voyage who doesn't want to be here?

Nearing the shore everyone jumped out to push the boat onto the sand. None of them wanted to risk tipping over in the swirling tides. Immense green trees leaned out over the beach casting shadows that contrasted with the white hot sand that stretched for miles in either direction. An ocean breeze soothed the sun's harsh heat as they began walking into the jungle.

Bird calls Alden had long since forgotten cried out in a chorus with other tropical oddities. Great green plants crowned with vast violet petals sprung from the ground. Sprawling giant trees whose roots wormed into the silt like wooden octopi soared far above them covering up the sky. Eternal jungle shade replaced the bright sunlight as the sprawling canopy stole the blue sky away.

The trio silently traipsed along a path of trampled plants that the other pirates had already cleared. *Their camp can't be too far away. They'll want to prepare for the hike up the mountain. Question is how far will we go up?* Grey silt ground crunched underfoot as it mixed with fallen leaves in various states of rot. After walking a bit further ahead they found a small clearing the pirates were using to camp for the night. A roaring fire danced under a black pot hung between two sticks. The aroma of the pot's mouth-watering contents seemed to banish the oppressive smell of the jungle and replace it with a fleeting reminder of being back at home. Surrounding the campfire were half a dozen pirates moving crates and erecting what appeared to be a red canvas tent, no doubt for Bojjer.

What I wouldn't do for a taste of whatever they're cooking. Biscuits and water falls far short of being a meal. It doesn't help the ones they've been giving us are more suited to being rocks.

"Place this one with the rest, I'm gonna savor the sunlight a little more before we camp tonight. I'd like to spend as little time between these trees as I can get away with," Turtan said.

"Alright, but only on one condition. While you're out on the sand see if you can scrounge up some abalones and you have a deal old man," Shruthus said.

"Only if you won't try and cook 'em like last time."

"They weren't that bad."

"When I spat the first one out it was so hard it sailed through a glass pane window."

"Must've been a soft window."

Turtan groaned as he pulled a cloth sack out of a crate. He wandered back into the jungle as Shruthus escorted Alden the rest of the way through camp. Finally, they stopped by the other villagers sitting around some crates. Each of them was tied to an iron post that had been struck into the dirt. After Shruthus had secured Alden to the spike, he shoved him to the ground and laughed as he walked away.

Groaning from his brush with gravity, Alden looked around the circle as a calloused hand landed on his right shoulder. Looking over he saw Bakston's battered old face greeting him.

"Welcome to Hemmarasp Isle Alden, how do you like it?" he asked.

"Rocks less than the ship. Shoves feel about the same. Is everyone alright?" Alden asked.

"Alive is more like it. It was a rough trip."

"Just glad not to be so damn wet, my bones were creaking more than the walls," said a coarse voice.

Alden looked over and saw a man with short brown hair and a hardened stone-like face. It was Amalric, the village officer. *Good to see I'm not the only one here who knows how to fight. Then again how good can either of us be if we ended up getting caught?*

"I'd hold the praise my friend. This isle has no inhabitants for a reason. Hemmarasp is a treasure hunter's dream full of Gray ruins and artifacts, but in spite of that no one ever comes here," Alden said.

59

"Kinda got that impression from the pirates. All of them seem so serious, but what's so dangerous about this place?" Amalric asked.

"There are a lot of Gray ruins on this isle and from what I've heard they're not all dormant. Step on the wrong stone or get near the wrong relic and you'll be turned to ash in an instant. Some of the spells are so powerful they've lasted for thousands of years."

"Oh is that all? You make it sound so inviting."

"That's not the worst of it. Hemmarasp Isle is home to Darters, Snare-Tails, and even Harvest Heads are supposed to live here. Catch the eye of the wrong tree, step on the wrong log, or get near the wrong burrow and you'll never take another breath."

"You make it sound like we'd be lucky to see the ship again," said Isolda.

She's the mayor's wife, but I don't see him anywhere. Best not to ask questions. I doubt many of the stories in our circle will be happy ones.

"I won't lie to you; we've come to a very dangerous place. If we have any hope, we must stick together and be careful. I'm not quite sure what they're planning, but I'll do my best to get you home," Alden said.

They all seemed to perk up as if bolstered by his words. *I make it sound almost like we have a chance. No one comes here, because no one ever leaves who does. Bojjer must really think this'll work. Maybe whatever ritual he's planning can only work with some unique ruin or enchantment found here? Our time is running out.*

The hours passed by as the sky grew dark and the trees seemed to close in around them. By now every pirate had finished up and pitched their tents in the glade. The camp itself was divided into one side consisting of the Wekken with a smoldering fire and the bubbling pot of stew while the captives sat in the dark near the tree line.

What evil bastards! It's not enough that you make us eat these rock hard lumps, but then you have the audacity to eat something that good in front of me. I hope you choke on it.

Bojjer was the last person to arrive at camp. The scarred and sea worn Wekken's face seemed irritated as if everything around him was distracting him from something far more interesting. *What is that he's holding? Looks like a stone cylinder carved with glowing red lines. Is that a Gray relic?* The bicorn barely said a word to his crew before he entered his red tent. As Alden stared at Bojjer he realized that another Wekken was doing the same to him. Turtan sat by the fire but his eye was looking straight towards him, but as their gaze met he quickly looked away. *Why is he so interested in me? Was he watching Bojjer too?*

The other pirates didn't seem to notice as they were too busy enjoying the plentiful food they'd been able to forage. Salted abalones that Turtan had carved off the beach rocks were passed to every pair of paws. A small fuzzy brown pig that hadn't been quite quick enough was served on juicy looking skewers. Finally, the cream colored stew was poured out of the pot one bowl at a time as the scent of onions paired with herbs wafted over the camp. Tonight was a feast for the pirates. The lost comrades in Mullentide were toasted and shanties were sung as the whole lot of them guzzled grog in great wooden mugs.

The party continued long into the night as every cloud seemed to vanish as the moon and stars took their places up above. Dim white light illuminated the clearing as darkness filled the jungle floor. Starlight seemed afraid to descend below the canopy as Alden stared into the inky black space between the trees. Like the night sky painted by celestial points, the jungle's lightless depths were illuminated by countless pairs of eyes.

Much later that evening after the party, all the pirates had drunk themselves asleep. Many had managed to find their tents, but more than a few had collapsed into the silt with their mugs not falling far from their hands. Alden noticed that not everyone had turned in for the night quite yet. The bicorn had kept a candle burning inside his tent as his silhouette hunched over a desk.

Maybe leaders are always the last to turn in for the night. Wait, is that a book? I think that might be the cylinder I saw earlier. He's chanting and moving his hands like you would for a ritual. Is he practicing? I've never seen that pattern before and those words sound so strange. This must be the Gray magic Dreven discovered. How can a Wekken who can't cast spells hope to use it though?

Alden continued to observe until Bojjer's tent grew dark. Now his only conscious companions were two Wekken guards on shift for the night. Unlike the two who had escorted him to camp the one closest to him was quite old. His aged face seemed to be permanently tattooed with a scowl. Eventually the guard took a break from his patrol and walked into the jungle to relieve himself.

Alden struggled to fall asleep knowing everything about the day ahead of them. The jungle's ceaseless chorus was as loud as ever, but then another noise was added to this mix. A sharp whoosh reached his ears. Leaves crunched as the man crumpled to the ground behind the trees. *No point calling for help. One less problem for me to think about.* Smiling, he closed his eyes as the stars shone overhead illuminating the guard's body just outside the clearing.

Alden awoke to the sound of shouting as his suspicions seemed to be confirmed. Parting his eyelids, he shook his head as pebbles fell from his hair. Twenty feet away all the pirates were crowding around a great big tree. He heard Bojjer shouting angrily at the rest of the crew.

"Stupid sod. I don't care if he needed to piss, he should have done it in camp. The trees have eyes on this damn isle and sometimes they do more than peep at ya! Who was on duty last night with this louse?" he asked.

"I was captain," a younger Wekken said.

"Ahh Crawdas. Come here boy, closer. What do you think happened to him, hmm?"

"Don't know captain. His mouth is foaming like the sea, but I can't see a wound on 'im."

"No? Well then take off his cuirass. I thought I heard rustling and I just remembered that you're on guard duty."

Alden could see Bojjer's venomous smile directed at the young Wekken. Crawdas hesitated for a moment and then began to undo the leather straps for the chest armor. His paws worked quickly unclasping each piece until only one remained on the body's upper right shoulder. Hands shaking like a ship in a storm the Wekken began to pull the armor away. Everyone leaned toward the body in expectation.

Clang.

A green slimy blur flew towards the young Wekken's face knocking the armor away. Crawdas closed his eyes lifting his hands upward, but the young pirate was too late. Whatever had leapt forth from the body was nearly on him. Suddenly everyone grew silent as the young pirate opened his citrine eye to see the captain's clawed hand holding some hideous green slug as long as a loaf of bread inches from his face. Quickly Bojjer slammed the slithering stranger into the dirt and stabbed it with his dagger.

"That is a Darter slug and if you weren't so slow he might've gotten you too. Look at his snout, looks almost like a flute doesn't it? The thing is, the only music that instrument makes is a sharp whoosh as its venomous dart flies into ya. Luckily for us they only hunt at night and are only a bother if ya stop moving for a while. Get the prisoners up, we're leaving," Bojjer said.

Alden got to his feet as the pirates turned around and began to get their packs for the journey. Some Wekken helped or more accurately dragged them to their feet and began tying them into one long chain. Others poured water on the fire to make sure it didn't set the beach ablaze. Bojjer entered his crimson tent and in only a few moments emerged with a brown leather pack.

Over the next half hour, the camp was taken apart and packed up for the long trek ahead of them. Eventually the whole group willing and unwilling alike were ready. Two Wekken guards led the front of the group with the villagers making up the middle. In the back Bojjer and the rest of the brigands made up the tail as they wanted to have the most warning of any danger.

Alden was near the front as they began marching into the jungle. *They want me to see the traps, but don't want me to be in front just in case we run into something. Guess Bojjer really does want me to make it all the way up the mountain. I suppose I'll take any advantage I can get. This place is really living up to its name. Hemmarasp Isle, the tongue of the great Turtamaw Bay. Just like a snapping turtle. If you touch it, you're sure to lose something in the process. Just hope there's something left of me to bring back home.*

Chapter 7: A Mutual Accord

Mud soaked into his leather boots as Alden trudged along just behind Amalric who seemed to linger on each precious breath. *I'm a prisoner being escorted by pirates up the most dangerous mountain in the world and of course it's during a thunderstorm. They took my sword, but at least they let me keep my clothes. Hiking through this muck in anything else would be intolerable. I hope the others are holding up better than Amalric.*

No one in their procession made a solitary sound as the sky conducted its deafening electric orchestra. *What's there to talk about anyway? We're all thinking the same thing. It's just a question of who will end up feeding the worms next.*

Hugging the thin path along the muddy hillside, dirt was replaced by great grey slabs which no plant dared touch. A geometrical pattern of right angles was carved into each of these rocks as all the lines seemed to converge on the center. Stranger still, the mud that ran over everything else on the jungle floor meandered around the stones as if some unseen hand nudged them away. Even the rain seemed to splash an inch above them as the droplets would run off to the sides.

Seems like you can always count on two things in this world: the sun setting in the west and Gray ruins to always be magical. Even after three thousand years their spells seem to scoff at the very concept of decay.

As if his thought had been too silent to express the seriousness of the change, a low hum became audible as one of the pirates in front stepped onto a slab. *Already? Dammit we've gotta move now!* Alden's pupils stretched to their limits as his experienced body recognized what had just been triggered. Grabbing Amalric by his shoulders, he flung them both to the ground off the hill side as they rolled over the rotting forest floor. The pair of guards in front of them looked back as the merciless trap's hum soared to a deafening level.

A great red flash of magical energy exploded from the slabs as lightning-like tendrils struck the Wekken. Armor, skin, and flesh evaporated as the spell wrapped itself around them. Each man screamed as they were transformed into charred piles of ash. As quickly as it had started the trap stopped humming. The rain pattered on the path as everyone in the group stood speechless.

"Dammit. What happened to 'em?" Bojjer asked.

"Some kind of Gray trap. They're just charcoal Captain, like a burnt out campfire!" yelled one of the guards.

Bojjer ran to the front and stopped just short of the slabs. Alden saw the old pirate's expression grew pained over the loss of two of his crew. However, it was only a brief flicker of compassion as the normal callous mask returned. Gazing out over the burning embers and unstained stones the old brigand was clearly studying the trap.

"Go around them. I don't care if there's so much mud in your boots that you could plant daisies in them. Just don't walk on the slabs! I don't think they expected someone to survive the trap so the jungle is likely our best option. Turtan! Get up here!" he yelled.

"Captain," Turtan said.

"Take the lead. No more disintegrations."

"Understood. Come on then, get them up out of the mud and let's get marching. We've lost enough time as it is."

Alden pulled Amalric out of the mud before noticing his escape hadn't gone unnoticed. A single citrine eye studied the knight as the grizzled pirate stared right at him. *Bojjer may be clever, but I fear this one is even worse. He was in the back and somehow still noticed me dodging the trap. What is he thinking in that bald head of his?* Alden spine's shivered at the veteran's stare. Turtan turned away from him as he began to order around the other guards. Ash mixed with the rain, wicked off the slabs, and continued sliding down the hillside. Once everyone had gotten back in line the march up the mountain continued.

The trail became a muddy ribbon as even the Gray's slabs seemed to have been washed away down the hill. Alden pressed his hand to the cliff leaning upon the soft greenery for support. Vines whirled about his head in the thunderstorm's harsh wind. Almost half an hour passed before the group arrived at a landing wide enough for two people to walk alongside.

As the road got wider the cliffs on their left side grew steeper. Immense trees which were as wide as tables looked like toothpicks from Alden's view. Rain continued crashing down upon them as the path emerged into a small glade surrounded by trees except for a massive cliff by the trail. No one wanted to sleep on the road and since night was already setting in Bojjer ordered them to set up camp.

At last I thought we'd never stop. I think even my bones are soaked through.

All the prisoners were tied to the spike in the ground as the rest of camp took shape. Tents sprouted from the grass like white sails in the midst of a green sea. Firelight painted everyone's faces as the grey sky stole any hope of sunlight. It was then that Alden heard a heavy pair of boots marching towards him. The Wekken wearing them walked into the tight circle and untied his binds from the spike. Looking up he saw the grizzled face of Turtan scowling down at him.

"Up. We're going to have a chat you and I," Turtan said.

Alden nodded as the old Wekken grabbed his back shoulder and steered him towards the trees. *Guess I'm going to find out what he's been thinking after all this time.* The pair walked quite some distance into the trees before they found a dry spot in a ravine under an ancient tree that was nearly sideways.

"You knew about that trap, didn't you? You let those men die and instead saved your fellow villager?" Turtan asked.

"It took me a second, but I've heard that hum before. Every time I've heard it, someone has died. Didn't see why it should be me or Amalric," Alden said.

"That's fair, I would've traded those blind sacks of meat for myself too. Still I suppose that's not really what I'm asking about. I could care less about these scamps, but I intend to walk down this mountain alive. Will you help me do it?"

I must have a concussion. Did I hear him right? Surely he's joking or trying to just see what I know.

"I am? Why would I do that? Way I see it; I'm being paraded through this jungle just to be Bojjer's sacrifice," Alden said.

"You're not the only one on this mountain who's been doing some thinking. I don't claim to be a good man, but cutting up your friend in that cell was a hard thing to manage. I've done things I'm not proud of; I steal from sailors for a living, but I've never had to defile someone like that. It made me sick."

"So, what you're just the one good guy in a crew of bloodthirsty pirates?"

"I'm just here to make money to send back home to my daughter. I mostly help with stealing Gray artifacts and smuggling them into ports. The Bojjer I knew never would've raided a village, but something's changed. Two weeks ago the captain announced he'd found us the biggest treasure haul of our lives. All we needed were some hostages as sacrifices and to silence a knight who'd found a book. Right then I knew I wanted out, but we were in the middle of the Otaton."

"So why not leave during the raid if you were so concerned?"

"My little Batara is still in Aetturrus. You saw the immolation spells in Mullentide right?"

"Yeah, I still can't believe anyone would use them. I've only ever heard rumors of spies using them since they have a tendency to fail."

"Bojjer isn't our boss. There's someone above him I've never met. All I know is that anyone who's ever walked away from the crew vanished soon after. I can't risk my daughter with someone like that."

"I still don't understand why we're talking then."

"This morning I stole into Bojjer's tent when he was looking at that poor sod with the slug in his chest. Inside was some black book with a skull symbol on the front."

Alden's eyes grew wide. *It can't be, but then again what else could it be?*

"This book, was it about Gray rituals?"

"Exactly, I think it was just like the one you were supposed to have in Mullentide," Turtan said.

"I found a copy not long before your crew attacked us. Inside it described a ritual like the one I bet your captain is trying to pull off."

"I knew I had a good feeling about you. If you read that tome, then you must know that only one person can become an Ascendant through it. Bojjer is going to kill everyone. You, me, all of us. But what if that didn't have to happen?"

"If you have a way out of this then I'm all ears."

"I'm worthless when it comes to magic, but I saw you fight in the square. You'll definitely be able to handle interrupting the ritual. The way I see it, if I run, Bojjer will execute me and everyone including you will die. Even if I escape and he kills you all then he'll hunt me down all the same. This little trip is meant to silence the whole crew along with you and running away won't change that. However, if I can help you use the ritual instead of Bojjer then I can slip away. Saw the soulenket on your neck. You'll get a second chance to meet up with that family of yours. Don't you want that?"

"If I did that then all of those people will still die. There's gotta be something else we could try."

"Can't see anything that'll work. If you try to let them all go in the middle of the night, he'll have the men hunt you down and recapture you. Maybe some of them escape, but you and I both know they'll probably just all end up dying on this mountain. If you try to fight, then Bojjer will just plant you back in the ground and we're back where we started. Either we help each other or we're both dead."

There has to be another way. I can't beat Bojjer in a straight fight and there's no way to lead everyone down the mountain unless the pirates are dead. 'Nara I promised I'd come home, but everyone else will never get that chance if we do this. With a sigh his decision was made.

"Dammit I don't see another way Turtan. What's the plan?" Alden asked.

"I figure it'll take us another day before we reach the temple on the summit. Stick in front with me and keep my ass from immolating. If we survive the road there Bojjer will want to make camp the night before we do the ritual. That way he can give the men a proper send-off. He might be stabbing us in the back, but the man isn't heartless. I'm sure his guilt will force him to make it a feast," Turtan said.

"Alright so where's the part where I go free?"

"I'm getting to it I promise. That night I'll come by and unlock your cuffs, but you'll have to leave them on so they don't get suspicious. In the morning we'll enter the temple and as they begin the ritual I'll sneak out. Let Bojjer start the ritual and during the final passage the captain will need to slam his hand down on the dais in the middle through a stone spike, but-."

"Are you seriously telling me this is going where I think it is?"

"What do you mean?"

"I'm going to have to get my hand stabbed again aren't I?"

"It doesn't have to be the same hand."

"Fine. So what'll happen after we pull this off?"

"After the ritual is done I'll meet up with you to make sure it worked and we can both head home I expect. Do we have a mutual accord?"

Turtan offered his large right paw to Alden. He hesitated for a moment and looked down at the hand. *If I do this there is no turning back. Everyone dies, but I get to see them again.* Amara's sweet face entered his mind as did Leonara's. *Please forgive me everyone.*

He shook the leather skinned pirate's hand as they both nodded at each other. Turtan turned to head back towards camp before pausing.

"Alden before we head back I just want to say I'm sorry about everything. I learned too late what kind of man Bojjer was willing to be. I've made mistakes, but today I can start to make up for them."

"It's alright Turtan; not everyone gets a second chance. Sorry I tried to decapitate you in Mullentide."

"Don't worry about it I was trying to do the same thing."

Alden and Turtan both smiled at each other under the overturned tree. Returning to camp, the newly paired partners grew silent once again. A bouquet of brown fallen leaves crunched beneath their feet as thunder roared from above. Just before they reached the glade a scream pierced their ears. Alden offered his rope to Turtan and the Wekken grabbed it. *We may be partners, but until we're done I'm still gonna have to play the prisoner.*

Running back to camp they found the pirates huddled over someone. It was a Wekken frozen into place without a hint of frost on him. His axe was planted into what seemed to be a knotted log curled around his arm. Upon closer inspection the truth dawned on them. This was no log, but a Snare-Tail. A giant centipede covered in a chain of chitinous plates. Thick as a hip and covered in moss, the bug seemed to be an almost perfect imitation of a log.

Only heard about them before. All those little green needles on its underbelly are sticking into his arm. He had to have been dead in seconds.

"Must've swung his axe into it. Poor lad," Turtan said.

"Aye. He was building the fire when he stuck this creature. What are you doing with that one?" Bojjer asked.

He motioned towards Alden whose ropes Turtan was still holding. *Dammit, come on smuggler think of a good excuse. If you can fool the port authorities, then you better be able to come up with something good. Our plan won't mean much if he just kills us right here.*

"Just had a chat with our knight in the woods. Told him he'll be in front of the line from now on so we can avoid any more of these Gray surprises. Seems to be quite the expert," Turtan said.

"Ah, very well then. Throw him back in with the rest and help with the fire. We're running out of hands to build it," Bojjer said.

"Captain."

Turtan brought Alden over to the circle of prisoners and gently bound him once more to the spike. Although his binds had been restored the knight had never felt closer to freedom on this torturous journey. Neither man made any visible expression of their pact, but something about Turtan made Alden trust the old pirate. His plan and the regrets he'd expressed seemed to be genuine. All the same, only tomorrow night would tell if Turtan had been telling the truth.

Scarlet flames from the campfire painted the entire glade with a red glow as every other light seemed to fade away. Bojjer was reading again in his crimson tent. Just like the last night Alden could see the captain hunched over his table studying something. *Two days left you scum sucker. Enjoy every breath of them.* Lying in the wet dirt, Alden closed his eyes and fell into a deep sleep.

Overnight the storm finally relented revealing fog thicker than the smoke from a burning saucepan. The morning passed quickly as Bojjer seemed eager to keep moving up the mountain. Each Wekken dug into their breakfast as the prisoners scarfed down their tack.

Once the camp had been packed up, the group reformed ready for the hike. Alden had been moved to the front right beside Turtan. *I'm glad good news can make even sleeping in the mud comfortable. Still I can't help, but feel like I'm failing the villagers. Perhaps someone smarter could conceive of a plan to save them, but I don't know what else to do.* At Bojjer's command they stepped forward into the mud. A great green trail awaited them and lying at its end was a ritual that would decide the fate of them all.

Chapter 8: Sight Turned Black

Muddy ground slipped beneath their feet as a twisted collection of curves led them higher. Impenetrable fog enveloped everything as even the sky seemed to vanish in the clouds clinging to the mountain. Wispy moss flittered in the waning breeze like green fingers reaching down towards them.

Alden was just behind Turtan observing his newest friend. Every sense he had was focused on the cyclops's survival. His ears perked at any noise out of the ordinary as his eyes scanned the path ahead for any stone or statue that could present trouble. Even his nose was employed in their protection. *Gray traps create ozone just like lightning so if we're careful I might be able to smell the magic before I hear it. I know it's only one day like this, but staying so tense really is exhausting.*

They passed by various shrines, statues, and houses which luckily were less incendiary than the stones they'd come across yesterday. Fountains carved from smooth square stones with strange lines at ninety degree angles carved into them were becoming common markers along the road. Strangely they emitted a flow of red magic instead of water that danced across the white rock like a scarlet ribbon.

Thousands of years and even these still work. Back in the ruins only the most masterful spells remained untouched by time, but here even the most frivolous use of magic seems eternal. Krohfast is equally enchanted in that almost everything uses magic. We have carriages that fly past stone towers that reach to the sky, streets that never grow dark even after night, and it all seems so quaint in comparison. Magic is woven into every stone here that's stronger than even the greatest Ascendant works created by masters of centuries of study. Whoever the Gray were, they must have been unimaginably powerful.

With every step these structures grew grander and more common. After two hours of hiking, the fog seemed to stop suddenly as a small Gray town emerged from around a bend. Alden looked behind at the wall of clouds which had ceded itself to clearer air.

The atmosphere altering spells are still active here? This is no normal Gray ruin. Could the main spell source still be working? I've only heard of a handful of places like that in the whole world. Guess it might explain Dreven's interest in having us come here.

A circular ring of single-story buildings surrounded a plaza where a stone obelisk stood monolithic. On the monument's left was a grand hall that carried as far as the cliff before it transformed into a cantilevered balcony. Stone cylinders rose like a sea of stumps around the structure. Each marble white rock was covered in glowing red patterns just like the slabs they'd stepped on earlier. A faint scarlet mist hung between them as an ominous hum echoed from the field.

We're surrounded by certain death and our only route forward is through that town. The air feels different here. There's no fog so the humidity has dropped and I smell ozone from the Gray magic, but I'm still missing something.

"Everyone halt. Knight come here," Turtan said.

"What are you thinking?" Alden asked.

"I'd go around, but we've gotten too close to the Gray ruins. I can see those cylinders, but I can't believe those are the only traps around this town. Going around means risking the jungle and hoping nothing in it will try to eat us. We need someone to chart a path through the ruin full of impossibly dangerous magic and who knows what else. If anyone can go in there without winding up as a pile of ashes, it's you."

"You might be right, but no Gray ruin is typical and this one is certainly no exception. Gray spells never seem to fade, but we understand so little of their technology. Those cylinders and this fog wall may be the only working ones of their kind in the whole world."

"Why am I surprised? Still you've explored more of these ruins than any of us. Ever find one that didn't want to try to kill you?"

"No not really. Anyway there's no sense in giving your comrades any more time to stumble into something we've missed, come on."

Nodding in agreement, Turtan unbound the ropes from Alden's cuffs before gripping them in his left hand. Stepping forward they scanned the ground to see if any of the plaza's stones looked similar to the ones before. While bearing the characteristic markings their patterns we're definitely different. Lowering himself onto the ground, Alden placed his head next to the plates to listen for even a hint of humming to give away the trap. Each stone in front of them couldn't have been quieter.

"Seems to be ok, here goes nothing," he said.

Alden placed his foot down on the slab. Muscles tensed in anticipation as he waited for the telltale hum.

One. Two. Three. Four. Ahh I think we're alright. This may not be suicidal after all.

"You're not dead. Does that mean the panels won't kill us?" Turtan asked.

"Well this one won't. I can't hear any humming from the other panels so maybe they're really just stones for the street."

"That's encouraging to hear. Even still Bojjer isn't going to let us go until you've found a path all the way across."

"Agreed, I'll try to find a safe way across. Let go of the rope, I know you want to keep up appearances, but if I'm wrong about the panels I need to be able to move."

"Alright, but be careful. Something about this place just feels off to me. Good luck."

Acknowledging the Wekken's gesture, Alden turned towards the courtyard as he looked around the circular market. Each little nook had likely been a shop as every building seemed to stock entirely different items. One had shelves of stone books inscribed with unlit runes, another had baskets in a variety of shapes, on the opposite side was a collection of odd musical instruments, and even an armory was just off to his right. Each stall was unnaturally clean as Alden noticed that a layer of dust was flowing over the stones towards the town's entrance.

I've covered ten panels and nothing's happened yet. If the inside of the town was really trapped I think something would have tried to kill me by now. If we do survive this ritual, I'd like to come back here. If for no other reason than to study this place and admire it. What a beautiful alien bit of architecture. As Alden's eyes studied the plaza he noted the obelisk punctuating the market's middle.

It's too thin for someone to live in, but then what purpose could it have? Is this the construct stopping the fog or is it the magic source itself? Glowing red lines were carved all across its surface distinguishing it from the rest of the sterile white structures. Alden's nose began to fill with a sickeningly sweet smell almost like ripe fruit. *Come on, no way I'm that unlucky. Dammit there's no mistaking it. Nothing can ever be simple, can it?* Alden froze mid-step as his eyes were wide from fear.

"What is it? What do you see?" Turtan asked.

"Not see, smell. It's a Harvest Head Worm nest," Alden said.

Turtan's face grew concerned as he realized what the knight had just said. *No chance we can find a way around and especially not with Bojjer in charge. That settles it we're gonna have to sneak past. The last one killed a whole village and it nearly killed me. What chance do I have cuffed? Gonna have to go around and hope it's content to stay warm next to its magic heater.*

"Do you think we could cross along the sides? If the worm hasn't eaten you yet then maybe there's hope for the rest of us," Turtan said.

"It's crazy, dangerous, and I'm afraid there isn't any other choice. Tell the pirates to get rid of any fruit they have in the provisions. Scent seems to be coming from the tower and the only reason it hasn't smelled us already is the lack of wind from the atmosphere spell. We should be able to walk around the town edge, but if it catches even a single whiff of us we're done for," Alden said.

"What's it even doing by the obelisk? Can it sense magic? I thought they were mostly drawn to fruit plantations."

"They are, but the only thing more enjoyable to a worm is a nice warm spot. That obelisk is a portal to a magical plane which it uses to draw power for the enchantments. Besides being a priceless relic it also makes an extremely good heater."

"So basically it's a horribly dangerous fifty-foot slimy worm that acts like a cat?"

"It'll swing like one too once awake so honestly that's not too far off Turtan."

"Now I'm beginning to understand why no one comes here. I'll tell the group and get them ready. Good luck plotting the route."

Alden felt the scar stretching across his stomach start to itch as his feet began to shift away from the center. *I've gotten one scar from these monsters already, I don't need two. I can't use my hands and I don't have firebombs on me like last time. If it comes to it then I'll have to run and let the dust settle. Anything else would result in my guts floating on top of these slabs. For now, one foot in front of the other.*

Alden stepped as softly as his mud soaked boots would allow along the clean white stones. Each time his foot left the floor, a dirty imprint of his sole was left floating above the slabs. Sweat dripped from his forehead and mixed with the soil now sailing past him over the ground towards the town entrance. Mercifully Alden reached the plaza's other side and a smile broke across his face.

There is a path to take. We can actually make it across. Also the worm's aroma is growing weaker. That slimy tree trunk must be curled right around the obelisk's base underground. I'm not dead yet 'Nara. Alden slowly retraced his steps until rejoining Turtan who stood a few feet back with a pile of confiscated fruit.

"Please tell me you've found a way," the Wekken said.

"The right edge along the plaza is safe. Well, at least the stones won't kill us anyway. Are you ready?" Alden asked.

"No, but Bojjer isn't going to give either of us a break. Let's do this."

Alden took the lead as the group followed just behind him. While there was the occasional creak and stumble, it all seemed to be going rather well. *I might finally catch a break on this journey. A few more feet and I get to enjoy mud on my boots and no monstrous worms beneath them.* Alden passed through the gateway once more. He hung back watching each pirate pass him. *Just a few more left before we're done. All the villagers are safe at least.* Just as the last few Wekken were coming towards the gate Alden heard his worst fears realized.

Thud.

A great horrible cracking noise erupted from the obelisk. The stone spike pointing to the sky began to crumble towards the ground as the plaza's center collapsed. *No, no, what happened?* Dust erupted from the emerging crater as a horrible shrieking sound pierced the jungle. Alden frantically looked for the creature he knew was about to attack when he saw Shruthus lying flat on the ground. *Clumsy fool must have tripped. Wait is that a banana next to his head? You useless dimwit!*

"Run!" Alden shouted.

A thunderous slashing sound emerged from the dust cloud, eclipsing everyone's panicked shouting. The slimy worm swung its massive hammer head sharpened to a vicious edge through Shruthus. In the blink of an eye the dimwit was sliced in two and flung into the side of the building, splattering the white stones with a crimson cocktail.

It's huge! Only hope I have is to run away. Please don't die Turtan or I may as well jump in front of that worm now.

Alden sprinted out of the cloud of death away from the rampaging monster. It was thick as a tree trunk and nearly as long. The head was wider than a desk with a great glowing line cut across the middle, marking the deadly edge of its hammer shaped head. Below the blunt instrument was a cavernous mouth filled with gnashing teeth.

As the dust plume raced closer from behind, the fog wall broke like a crashing wave towards them. Alden couldn't see further than five feet in front of him as he sprinted with the group out of the town. Still coughing dust out of their lungs everyone stopped after a minute when they realized the worm hadn't chased after them. It's shrieking called out hauntingly into the jungle as the sound of it demolishing the town continued.

Can't believe we didn't lose more people. That had to be the biggest worm I've ever heard of. Alden saw Turtan with his hands on his knees bent over and obviously shaken up. Sharing a glance, they both knew that nearly could have been the end of both of them.

Turtan walked over to Alden and placed his hand on his shoulder. "If you hadn't been leading us, we would all be worm food right now. Thank you," he said.

"You're welcome, but that's not quite right. Harvest Heads don't actually eat meat. They just don't like meat that gets near their fruit," Alden said.

"He didn't want to share a banana? What a prick! Well at least I won't have to babysit Shruthus anymore."

"Yeah real shame that."

"I'm very heartbroken, but we'll just have to manage. Here let me get the rope back on you. We still have to make it to the temple. I'm afraid we're not done yet Alden."

He held up his hands as they both shared a glance as the binds were restored and the Wekken led him back to the front. *I should be glad that he didn't die so our plan can work, but is he really growing on me? There have been stranger friendships than ours. Maybe after this is all done we can have a drink and both our daughters could play together.* After some minutes everyone had settled down and Bojjer ordered them back to marching. They must have been close to the temple now as the fog began to thin out.

At this elevation the tropical warmth seemed to vanish as the trees faded and the harsh winds returned. Waist high grass sprung from the dark black soil and brushed against their waists. The fog that had stolen the sun from them slowly disappeared opening up the sky to reveal the summit. Only the grasses remained at this altitude as Alden gazed over a field of boulders surrounded by swaying waves of green.

Hemmarasp's peak was in fact the top of a long dormant volcano. Three great black volcanic walls remained from its creation. They're looming slopes created the valley before him. Black boulders as smooth as glass were strewn about the interior and rose from the sea of green like little isles. Each rock was covered in a patchwork of verdant mosses facing south to bask in its cool shade.

It's such a strange sight and yet I feel almost calm here. How many eyes have ever seen this valley? Has it really been thousands of years since anyone has visited this wondrous place? Wait what is that structure further back into the bowl?

In the center of all the black boulders and the green grass swaying in the breeze was a mysterious Gray temple unlike anything he'd seen. Thick stone pillars rose from the ground at irregular angles like urchin spines around an enormous stone dome. Carved into the smooth white rocks were runes and patterns which Alden couldn't make out, but there was one thing he could see. They were glowing red.

Hours passed as they walked across the crater as every step moved the sun closer to the horizon. Night had finally fallen by the time they passed into the forest of stone pillars. Here the wind seemed to stop just like in the town far below them. After a few minutes navigating the spines they arrived at the dome itself.

It's shiny white shape was contrasted by the now slate black sky. Unlike the pillars around them this building's carvings weren't illuminated, but as they walked around to find an entrance Alden was stunned by a warm glow coming from up ahead. A grand carved trabeation shined a brilliant scarlet light onto the near motionless grass. The door's right angles were precise and surrounded by sections jutting in and out at random.

As Turtan had predicted; Bojjer told the men to get a feast ready to celebrate arriving. Preparation began for the party while the camp was built right in front of the dome's entrance. *What a kind way to betray your comrades. I suppose it's a bit like a final farewell where you make someone comfortable before they go. Shame it's a kindness I can't give the villagers.*

The Wekken brought out a few kegs of grog, ale, and any leftover rum to celebrate. Others who'd left to hunt returned having caught some rabbits which were now roasting over the new campfire. Drinking, singing, and something resembling dancing was done by all the pirates. Red fire light painted the stones soaring high above with shadows that dissipated into the starlit sky above. Even captain Bojjer seemed to spring to life with uncharacteristic merriment. Swinging about a constantly refilled mug, he boasted about battles long since passed and swung his sword in mock fights with the shadows. Carrying well into the night the party only died down when the pirates' enthusiasm was finally quenched by alcohol. Embers flittered into the air like fire flies as the red specks mixed with the white stars shining above them.

Everyone seemed to have gone to sleep as Alden alone kept awake. It wasn't hard to keep his eyes open after hearing the villagers make their last goodbyes only a few minutes before. *Well the night is late and I guess my time is coming too. Either I join them in death or I'll live by failing them. Damn you Dreven for forcing this awful burden on me. They don't deserve it and there's nothing I can do to save any of them.*

Alden kept listening for the rustle of his pirate friend approaching to save them both. The grass by him suddenly parted and a glowing citrine eye appeared in the darkness staring at him. It was Turtan clutching a small key in his massive paw.

"Guess you couldn't sleep either?" he asked.

"Not a wink. Tomorrow is coming and I can't stop thinking about it," Alden said.

"Well I saved you some of my special brew. Maybe that'll help dull your head until morning."

The pirate passed him a mug of something blue that smelled sweet as Turtan pulled out his own to match. They tapped their cups together before they both drank deeply. *Mmm. That may be the first good thing I've had on this whole journey. It's so sweet, but I can feel it already warming me like there's a campfire in my belly.*

"What is this Turtan? It's incredible," Alden said.

"A Strong Breeze. Old family recipe we make in Aetturrus. Truthfully I would have started you off with a smaller cup, but we're both gonna be sleeping soon anyway," Turtan said.

"I can feel it already. We better start talking before we both keel over eh?"

"I'm a pirate Alden. We'll need a lot more to get me tipsy. Still, I may have drunk a whole keg before, so who knows. Before I forget, here is what I promised my friend. The key to our salvation."

Turtan's clawed hand reached out and inserted the key into the cuffs. A faint click could be heard and they unlocked. *He actually held up his end of it. 'Nara I'm going to see you again. I can feel that little Conch-head tackling me when I enter the door already.*

"You'll want to keep those on until you're ready in the morning. Don't want to spoil the surprise until you're ready. I'm guessing you'll be heading home then?" Turtan asked.

"I will. I'm used to leaving home for a while on missions, but this can't have been easy on them. Every day away is another reason I may never come home," Alden said.

"I know what you mean. I think I'll find my way home to Aetturrus and see my daughter. Little shrimp ought to be getting past my knee by now."

"Problem is they don't stop there do they?"

"No, no they don't. Who knows, maybe she'll dwarf us both eventually. Give her a few years and she'll definitely beat you."

"At least I don't dent the door frame when I come to visit. To the strangest friends in Nisuroth."

Quietly clanking the mugs, the odd pair drank together beside the cool swaying grass on the mountain top. *How did I end up here toasting with Turtan on top of a dormant volcano? Talking about our daughters and chatting as if we'd known each other forever. Nothing like a little ritual sacrifice to bring people together I suppose.*

"After we're done maybe we can both get our lives to look a little more normal or at least less exciting," Turtan said.

"You haven't met my family, not sure less exciting is even a possibility at this point. My daughter is more rambunctious than that worm and my wife is the greatest magess in all of Heanerath. Boring isn't really how I'd describe most days, but I wouldn't trade either of them for anything," Alden said.

"Hope I get to meet them someday, they sound nice. You know it's funny I'm in my hundred and forties and I barely even know my family. All that time yet I've hardly been around my own little girl."

"Hey, you guys live to three hundred there's still plenty of time. I'm curious why'd you name her Batara? I kind of like it."

"Named her for being so beautiful just like the dance of a batfish's fins. It's a shame her Mom never got to see the little shrimp grow up. I was off on some voyage when it happened."

"Sorry to hear that, but I bet Batara will be thrilled to see you. Sounds to me like we've both got a second chance at this life. Maybe Amara and her can hang out someday."

"Wouldn't that be something? Ahh Alden we can't spend all night talking or someone will notice. Before I go I'm sorry about everything. I've never really been a good person, but I didn't try to hurt people if I didn't have to. Let's not keep our daughters waiting."

Both men nodded towards each other as they shook hands. Alden felt the rough calloused claw grip his hand tightly. After he released his hand from the pirate's, Turtan slunk back into the grass on his way toward to the tents.

I can feel that Strong Breeze starting to knock me over. Might as well get some sleep before the sun comes up. Stars drifted through the sky above him as the lime colored grass swayed around Alden. Morning eventually came and it's light ignited the tips of the field like a sea of torches.

I guess this is my last morning as the same man I am. I'll have to get used to wearing an Ascendant face after today. I wonder if the sun will feel any different or if the touch of the wind will change? At least I won't have to wonder for long.

Groggy pirates got to work rounding everyone up as Bojjer barked orders and moved them into the dome. Passing through the doorway a magnificently lit rotunda emerged before him. Each panel of the domed roof glowed bright red like a grid of scarlet bricks. Pillars lined the outer edges of the room; each of them were topped by a radiant red glow. Most striking of all was the center where there was an elevated platform above the floor with a dais in its center. A series of five increasingly smaller circular steps separated it from the rest of the room. On top of the dais was a spike glowing in its center that was brighter than any other light they'd seen.

The pirates corralled them around the circle and took their position just behind. Looking around Alden saw Turtan near the entrance walking back out of the temple as if he'd forgotten something. Only moments after his friend had left through the door, Captain Bojjer entered the room. Walking down the aisle into the center he had the book in his left claw, the strange cylinder from before in his right, but no sword or dagger were tied to his belt. *Cocky bastard thinks he's won. I'm sure this will be very disappointing for him then.*

Raising his hands above him Bojjer held the black tome aloft. Placing it upon the dais he opened it near its middle and held the cylinder above his head. Bojjer plunged the relic into the hole in the dais. The room began to glow far more brightly as a humming noise could be heard. Bojjer began reciting the ritual as Alden couldn't believe he was hearing the long extinct Gray language.

He can read and speak Gray? I guess that makes sense, but how can he know a dead language? That would mean Dreven knows how to speak it, but where could he learn how to? Better stop thinking about it. I need to focus on the here and now. If this is anything like the normal Ascendant ritual the spike should glow with magic. Only then can he put his hand through it and that will be my one chance.

As the spell passed around a minute Alden recognized the words leading up to the finale from when Bojjer practiced. *It's about fifteen feet between me and him. If I fail, we all die and I'll never watch Amara grow up. I'm sorry everyone, but I'm not going to miss that. It's not what you deserve, but it's the only thing I can do. I'll avenge you and live for Mullentide, for Heanerath, and for my family.*

Finally, the moment arrived. The spike's magical intensity exploded as a pillar of red light engulfed the dais and a red bubble formed over everyone. A thunderous hum rattled Alden's ears, but he knew his opportunity had arrived.

His right leg carried him forward as he stopped holding the cuffs closed. The weight left his wrists as the metal restraints descended to the floor. His second step brought him halfway across the floor before the stairs. One of the pirates shouted something, but he couldn't hear it. A few more brought him within a few feet of Bojjer as the Bicorn turned around to meet his gaze. He shoved his shoulder into the captain's body flinging the pirate to the floor. Alden raised his right hand high above him.

"No!" Bojjer shouted.

You deserved so much better than this everyone. I can only say I'm sorry I failed you. Goodbye.

Without a word or even a glance, Alden slammed his palm through the spike. Blood exploded into the air, but instead of falling back down it hung there floating. The red beam of light became blinding as the dome's humming became deafening. Alden watched as the bubble around the room became black as pitch while the floor was enveloped by a dark mist. Everyone began to scream except Alden. It had begun and they all knew it.

The pirates and villagers screamed as the fog clung to them like an angry pack of bees. Swirling around them like a hurricane, their bodies began to dissolve into the magical mist. Each person's flesh and bone turned black before falling away to join the swirling maelstrom around Alden. On the ground Bojjer's flesh fell away, revealing his skeleton as his screams were silenced. One by one each person faded into the mist and left him all alone.

I'm sorry. You deserved better.

Only the howl of the dark gale could be heard as the mist began to draw closer to him. Alden's flesh began to turn black as the others had, but it didn't fall away. A pale red light began to emerge as his bones became as bright as neon under his skin. His skeleton was the only light in the darkness and only then did he realize he'd truly become an Ascendant. *I will see you again 'Nara and Amara. I promise.* Alden's sight turned black and with it so too did his world.

Chapter 9: His Illuminous Companion

All light had departed Alden as each of his senses seemed impossibly numb. He heard nothing, felt nothing, and saw nothing. *Did something go wrong or is this just what the ritual does? Am I where I've always been or am I just drifting through the void? Wait what is that?* A small light appeared in front of Alden. It shined like a solitary star in the night sky at first, but then the point grew to illuminate everything around him. His dark body, scarlet arteries, and neon red bones were revealed as the light became blinding. Then a great humming noise began to fill his ears until it felt like his head was going to explode.

The blinding light vanished as quickly as it had come. Opening his eyes, Alden could instead see the stone floor of the glowing red temple. Laying on the ground Alden wheezed and choked until his lungs stopped burning. He looked at his hands and realized they were covered in black ash. Oddly the temple itself was pristine as ever, but the central circle was coated.

What is all of this ash around me? Oh. Bakston, Isolda, Amalric. That's who I'm standing in. It's fitting I ended up looking like a skeleton. My second chance at life was born from everyone else losing theirs.

Alden felt his new skin bristle as a cool wind blew across his face. It came from the doorway gleaming bright white against the dome's dark red interior. Slowly ascending the staircase up to the door, Alden placed his hand on the rectangular archway. Its warmth spread through his fingertips as he saw outside was the same lime green grass waving in the wind that he remembered.

The Soulenket! Are they alright? I haven't wanted to check it all this time in case they'd take it. Please be ok.

Alden curled his fingers around the small triangular locket and stared at it shining in his palm. The intricate silver lines covering the surface gleamed in the sunlight as he opened it with bated breath. Three pearls lay within and none of them were broken. Gazing at his own pearl it was blue, but now it emitted a red glow from its azure shell.

Didn't think that was an option in Cassara's notes, but this trip hasn't exactly been an ordinary one. How about 'Nara and Amara?

Leonara's seemed to be blue without the tint his had. *She's alright. Thank the source you're alright darling. Only one of us left.* Amara's pearl shined with a piercing red color. Alden saw the hue seemed identical to the glow around his.

Oh why didn't Cassara mention red? It's fine. Everything's alright. Leonara's is blue so she's probably there to make sure whatever happened is ok. Still what if the ritual did something to her? What happened to my little girl?

Alden shook his head to steady himself. Panicking wouldn't solve anything and if something really had happened he needed to get back to her. Just then he noticed the swaying green grass seemed as long as ever, but something else was out of place. The camp was entirely different. Each tent had collapsed into the dirt leaving only rotten rags in their place. Every crate was now a mound of splinters and as Alden looked around he couldn't find a morsel of food between them. A few of the pirates' swords were scattered about the camp. Each one out of its scabbard was pocketed with rust.

What happened here? Did the spell cause all of this? Shouldn't Turtan be here?

Looking down he spied a decent blade still in its scabbard which upon inspection was still well oiled enough for him to use. Tying it to his belt, Alden continued around the camp scavenging anything useful he could find. Looking through the debris revealed some Gray artifacts the pirates had pilfered. He helped himself to the small treasures while also pocketing a few stray bags of kolos.

If I ever make it back to town I won't have a problem affording a ship back home. Thanks for the treasure you awful bastards.

Alden frowned upon finding some tack in edible condition and his skeletal scowl was cemented by not finding any other food. *Of course nothing else is around. Perhaps I should find a shoe and boil it? Might be softer at least.* Fortunately, in the scarlet remnants of

Bojjer's tent he did find a flask of Aetturan rum which was quite tasty. *Only good thing that pirate ever did is leave this lying around.*

Content with the results of his rummaging, Alden stored everything he found in a leather rucksack he'd discovered. Finally, ready to set off for the beach far below he began to wade through the swaying sea of green. Once Alden passed the furthest stone pillars the wind began to pick up, chilling his onyx black skin.

Let it be cold I couldn't care less. I'm going to see both of my girls again and the sky is such a lovely blue. What a wonderful day for a journey home!

Alden left the crater's embrace behind as the tree line rose up from the ground to meet him. *I went up this mountain as a prisoner and now I'm coming down from it a free man. I must say I think hiking without hand cuffs is far more enjoyable.* Cool air turned warm as the jungle surrounded him once again. There were no clouds in the sky and more notably none on the ground.

Alden kept walking down the path until eventually the Gray town came into view. A giant crater had taken the place of the obelisk in the plaza while the red mist was nowhere to be found. Alden kept on his toes as he approached the shattered gateway.

Can't smell anything sweet, where is the worm? Could it really have left after the spell source was destroyed? No warmth means no giant slimy cat I suppose. Fine by me.

His shoulders relaxed as the worm seemed to truly be gone. Alden walked along the stalls looking for relics that might be useful. Most of the artifacts were little more than white lumps of rock, but in the armory there were plenty of exotic garments still sitting on shelves.

My clothes are pretty rough right now. The leather is barely holding together and I'm sure I smell rancid from all this time marching through the rainforest. Maybe there's something comfortable in all these outfits. Besides each of these pieces must cost fifty-thousand kolos since they're so rare.

Alden picked out an elegant asymmetrical brown and grey leather outfit. His shredded cloak was replaced with a striking white one which split into three ribbons running down his back. Packing his old clothes away in the rucksack, Alden admired himself in a nearby mirror.

These clothes are so simple and yet I feel better dressed than a Republic representative. In fact, I can already feel the enchantments woven into them. I'm in the middle of a jungle, but the air already feels more inviting. Well I ought to explore the main hall before I leave. If nothing else the view ought to be spectacular.

Carefully navigating around the crater Alden entered through a grand gateway into an enormous room. White stone was everywhere he looked, but it wasn't the architecture that amazed Alden. There were numerous treasures he'd only heard stories of scattered around the room. Beautiful black sculptures covered with dancing oils, paintings made up of several shades of light, and in the center was a floating fountain made of five orbs. Each spherical stone was covered in water that dazzled him with its elegant dance between the balls.

Incredible! Even for a Gray ruin this must be one of the most impressive collections in the world and I just stumbled across it. I have to go home, but I can't leave without seeing all of it. Surely I can find a souvenir to take home, but which treasure should I choose?

Alden noticed a bedroom and some other adjoining areas, but the balcony called out to him more than anything else. Floating above the jungle cliff was a smooth white platform that seemed to defy gravity. Shaded by the stone roof overhead he walked over to the siding and gazed out towards Turtamaw Bay's turquoise waters. After a few moments he turned around and noticed sunlight illuminating a large rectangular box on a table.

Drawn to it, Alden opened the hatch to reveal a magnificent white stone sword. The blade itself was twice as thick as his own and covered in beautiful ornamental carved lines. *Normally I'd think someone was crazy to make a sword out of a rock, but I get the impression this won't break easily or maybe even at all. I think I've found my souvenir.*

Strapping the sword to his belt next to the pirate one, Alden began walking back towards the plaza. Leaving the town behind him it didn't take long before the cliff road reappeared. Lightened by the lack of restraints, the path proved easily navigated and before long the trail widened back up. Even with his decent clip the sun had grown quite low in the sky, but Alden was determined to find his way to the beach before nightfall.

As the sun began to sink below the horizon he felt silt under his boots meaning the first night's campsite was close at hand. Ferns brushed against his legs as palm trees pirouetted above him in a wind willed dance. Soon the campsite came into view, but the clearing seemed overgrown from before and the knight swore some small trees had sprung up that weren't there before.

Am I losing my mind or did the spell affect more than I thought? The soulenket changing colors, rusty swords, and now I find an overgrown clearing unalike the one I saw just a few days ago. Hopefully the ship will have answers for me or I'm afraid all Hemmarasp will leave me with is questions.

Brushing off the oddities, he pressed forward into the final stretch to the beach. Silt was replaced by sand as the jungle began to grow thin. The tree line appeared before him and just past it was white sand painted by a fading sunset.

Waves crashed on scattered rocks along the shore as he spied the pirate's ship and a rowboat behind a boulder. However, this was not the same vessel as the one Alden remembered. This one's hull was littered with great gaping holes like a rotting skeleton run aground. *What happened to it? Something is very wrong here. The ritual couldn't have done this and yet I can't deny my own eyes.* Before investigating further, Alden grabbed a hearty tree branch that looked like it had recently fallen from on high. Holding it in his hand he felt the weight and knew it should work splendidly. The knight wrapped his skeletal fingers around the top.

"Lumendo," he said.

A flash of light burst from his fingers and the branch's tip began to glow bright green like a torch made of a thousand fireflies. *That should be worth a few hours for looking around this tub.* Alden started walking towards the rowboat first as it seemed to be the only boat still in workable shape. Hidden behind a boulder, the wooden craft seemed intact until his light illuminated its true condition. Like the tents near the temple, the rowboat had become almost unrecognizable. The coating had come off and with it so had many of the planks.

Strange I remember there being two rowboats so where's the second? Turtan must've made it back down to the beach too. Thought he was going to stay behind and wait. How long was I trapped in the ritual?

Alden traced his steps back around the boulder and made for the vessel. The ship loomed above him, it's ragged sails flapping in the breeze. The sun's light had vanished leaving only the low rhythmic rumble of the waves. Alden's stick illuminated the dark and as he approached the vessel a great grumbling could be heard as if the ship were twisting itself in pain. Light began to paint the ship's hull or rather what was left of it as Alden's face froze in shock.

It had become a wreck. It's once proud wooden frame had fallen into the sea and lay about him like the bones of some great beast's carcass. Every deck below the top lay bare and the cells he'd traveled in were being washed away by the waves. Splashing and trudging up to the side, he saw barnacles covering even more of the wood than last time.

Something isn't adding up. The ship looks ancient, but I saw it only a few days ago.

Looking about Alden noticed a rope hanging from the top deck down to where he was. He yanked it anticipating a board flying into his face, but instead it actually held. Putting his weight on the twine Alden began to climb up past the broken ribs of the pirate's once proud vessel. Clambering onto the top deck his leg brushed against some siding which simply cracked in half before falling into the waves.

That's not a reassuring start. Better be careful then.

Brushing off some rotting splinters, Alden gazed around the top deck and saw that several of the boards had fallen away. At the other end was Bojjer's cabin which if he was going to find anything it would certainly be there.

The spine of the vessel still ran down its center and that's where Alden figured the wood would be strongest. Rounding the first mast he heard the ship shifting below him. It groaned like a dying animal so each step forward was placed with care for fear of falling back into the sea. Carefully, Alden found his way around the first mast and made his way across the deck until he found himself soon passing the second. Finally, at the threshold into the captain's cabin he placed both hands on the twin doors and pushed with all the effort he could manage.

Come on you oversized floorboards. Move!

As the wooden doors swung open a great musty smell greeted him. Looking about Alden saw trophy cases of swords that Bojjer had presumably won from their owners on either side of the room. The back of the cabin was a wide iron and glass window caked in salt from the sea's spray. In the middle was a large desk with a nautical map sprawled across it, a compass floating between two ornate glass hemispheres, and a single piece of paper.

Alden laid his illuminous companion on the desk as he picked up the parchment. In the green glow of his torch he realized this was a note from Turtan. *Finally, maybe I can learn what happened to him. I knew Turtan made it back down here, but why didn't he meet in the first place?*

The note started with Turtan explaining that he hoped to deliver this message personally, but couldn't delay any longer after the red bubble holding Alden didn't dissipate after a week. The pirate apologized for not trying to get him out, but as he was useless at magic there wasn't a thing he could do. Instead the Wekken came back down to the ship and collected his things for him along with a few choice gifts.

How long was I in the spell? He doesn't seem to mention that the ship had rotted suddenly and there's no mention of all the strange decay on my way back down the mountain. If the spell didn't do this that would mean it was time. For a ship to waste away like this would take years. I have to get home.

After reflecting, Alden looked back down at the note and saw where Turtan had hidden his things. *Where the sea meets your shoes? Funny old bastard.* Finally, the note said that Turtan had headed home to Aetturrus and that one day if possible he would like to see the knight again. With a smile squarely across his face, he left the cabin behind him.

Plunging his feet into the waves Alden trudged through the surf until he came upon the iron cell which had ferried him across the Otaton. Its door swung freely in the breeze and only a few crates remained inside the decaying walls. Opening them one at a time Alden discovered a leather pack containing a sizeable bag of kolos, a bedroll, and best of all his confiscated weapons. The dagger and sword both remained impeccable as the enchantment surrounding them made them immune to any rust.

Oh how I've missed you two. Let's get you out of the surf.

Securing the swords and their scabbards to his belt Alden tossed the rusty Wekken sword into the waves as he waded back to shore. Once on the beach, he built himself a fire and chomped down on a piece of tack as the stars dotted the sky. With the horrid bread down his throat, Alden extinguished the fire before laying out the bedroll. He collapsed onto its pillow before falling asleep as the waves broke upon the sand.

Chapter 10: The Gentle Hurricane

Morning came and with it the expanse of Turtamaw bay's turquoise water bloomed before Alden's eyes. Fearing that the only thing he would ever eat on Hemmarasp was tack; he looked around for a palm tree. A tasty green bundle sat at the peak of one just a few paces away. Walking until he was nearly under it, Alden aimed his thumb, index, and middle finger right at a branch holding up a nice cluster of coconuts. *Just an easy little cut should be enough. Goodbye brick hard bread and hello breakfast.*

"Ventos," he said.

What was meant to be a simple snipping wind was a violent hurricane that smashed the palm tree in two. Its bark splintered into a million pieces as they were scattered all over the sand. Stunned, Alden suddenly remembered Ascendant could much more easily conduct magic than humans.

Apologies my palmy friend. I'm still new to this.

Picking up his prize, he walked back over to his campsite. Cracking them open with a nearby rock; Alden dug into the sweet white flesh savoring every bite. He quickly wolfed down two before stopping as his stomach's protests convinced him to quit.

I never want to see tack again. Not while there is still any other food left in this world to eat.

Content from his full belly, Alden looked over to the rowboat he'd seen last night and went over to inspect it. Unfortunately, the vessel was still perforated with holes and missing several boards. *She's two splinters short of a compost pile, but with this new conductivity I think I might just be able to make her sail again.* Stepping inside the rowboat, Alden raised his palm and applied it to the wooden siding.

"Telendum," he said.

Alden began running his hand across the boat's interior. As it passed over the boards an invisible coating began to form, enveloping the boat's inside and plugging even the largest holes. In no time at all a new invisible hull had been constructed that wouldn't leak. *Normally only Leonara could maintain a field like this long enough, but now with this new magical conductivity the task should only be taxing instead of impossible.*

Shoving the heavy wooden craft down to the water, Alden made sure to throw in his belongings. Oars and all aboard, he began pushing the boat into the serene sea. Foam splashed around his legs as sand shifted with each footstep. Once the water began to reach his belt he clambered onto the rowboat. Lurching forward Alden yanked as the wooden paddles obliged, pulling him further away from the white sandy beach. He continued rowing until finally passing the reef before making for the city of Henaten.

It feels like I'm leaving a part of my life behind on that isle. I wonder if the world has changed as much as I have? I suppose I'll have my answer soon enough.

White puffy clouds dotted the skies above him as the mountain shrank into the distance with each stroke. After an hour of paddling Alden's arms began to twitch from the exertion and the tropical sun had begun to melt his good mood. *Sailing is so much more fun when the sails are the ones doing the rowing.* While Henaten had grown closer he figured there were still a full day between him and his goal.

What if? Worth a shot. Sailing ships use Drentos engines so why shouldn't I? Shifting himself to the back of the rowboat, Alden opened his hand as if to hold a doorknob, dunked it into the water, and pointed back toward Hemmarasp.

"Drentos!" he shouted.

With the earlier experience tempering his efforts a continuous stream of water exited his hand propelling the rowboat forward at a considerable clip. Heartened at his ingenuity Alden flew across Turtamaw bay like a tuna chased by sharks. Zipping and bobbing the hull began to take a beating, but his spell continued holding the conglomeration of boards in place. Shifting his hand like a rudder, Alden adjusted the course to head straight towards town. A day would've been needed to row across the bay from Hemmarasp for most men; Alden made the journey in only three hours.

Spying an expanse of beach near the city he slowed down to guide himself in. Alden parked his magical pile of rotten boards on the beach as he spied the city of Henaten was only a short distance down the coast. Slinging the rucksack over his back, Alden planted his boots in the sand and stopped to look back at Hemmarasp.

It looks so much smaller now. I've already traveled so far and yet there's so much more to go. Well I don't want to keep them waiting, let's find a ship home. With all the treasure I've got in my bag surely I can afford one with less barnacles. I suppose the room doesn't matter that much as long as they have something to eat other than tack.

He climbed up a small hill off the beach and onto a verdant field. Palm trees popped out of the soft hip high grass waving around him. After passing through the clearing a road appeared ahead. The well-traveled path was made of crushed coral which looked like it would lead all the way to the city gate. After only a few minutes the trees fell away as the city of Henaten appeared before him.

Turquoise waters to his right framed the historic center of Hemmoros. It's coral colored stucco walls were topped by slate gray clay roof tiles. Chimneys belched smoke into the sky from nearly every two or three story structure. Many of the roofs were guarded by weathered stone gargoyles of various sea monsters.

Henaten, gateway to the southern seas and the city where the exotic is ordinary. It's still as beautiful as I remember. Think I see a few more gulls flying about though. How far have the Veferothi taken it since I've last been here I wonder?

As he approached the gate Alden joined a sea of people moving in and out of Henaten. Many of the passerby likely worked on some of the fruit plantations as evidenced by their tanned tropical skin and wide woven grass hats. Most were Wekken, but Alden spied several Ascendant and even a few other groups mixed in.

As he drew closer to the bright twenty-foot-high walls the path grew even busier. By the time Alden reached the soaring wooden gates he was nearly shoulder to shoulder. Like most cities there was no entrance toll for travelers such as himself, but merchants would need to register with the guards so taxes could be taken. On his right side a small area was set aside for such things. Traders exchanged papers with the guards as each cart was inspected for an honest accounting.

Surveying each cart were men in simple iron half helms and red cloth uniforms of the Veferoth Republic.

Interesting the guards aren't just Ascendant. It looks like Henaten really has become unified since I've been away.

Alden passed under the stucco arch which led into the magnificent city hiding behind the walls. Two and three story buildings more colorful than any bird lined the street. A baker's brick oven serenaded his nose with sensuous aromas. A general store's window held shelves of everyday items that anyone could want. An adjacent side street had an enchanting shop filled with racks of the obviously magical, staffed by an Ascendant magess weaving spells.

I'd nearly forgotten how much I love cities. All of the endless life, variety, and adventure all packed so tightly that every step is exciting. To think that every crumbling ruin I've ever been too once looked something like this is truly tragic. I hope the world is done with things fading away until all their wonder is forgotten.

While your average village's streets were covered in muck, Henaten's were made of spotless white coral bricks. Alden saw a ceramic sweeper cleaning them in one of the alleys off to his side. It's dark ceramic jug was held by two handles like a wheelbarrow as high pressure water cleaned the stones below it.

That's a young man's job. I swear it's a miracle they don't shake themselves to pieces from all the rattling they make. Don't remember Henaten having those when I was here last. I really do love the Veferothi obsession with enchanting everything.

Nearing the docks now Alden spotted an inn bisecting the street. The charming triangular structure was three stories tall and covered by a carpet of vines on its sides. Warm green walls highlighted an oddly tall oak door in the center. Above the entrance was a wooden sign denoting it as The Gentle Hurricane Inn. A great storm swirled around a citrine eye in the middle as it rocked in the light breeze coming off the sea.

It's past midday and I doubt any ship will be leaving for Heanerath today so I might as well get a room. This place actually looks quite nice. Still why is the door so tall? It must be ten feet high.

Pulling on the iron knocker, Alden entered the establishment. Inside was a cozy tropical inn with a standing bar on his right, a warm brick fire crackling to the left, and a check-in desk just ahead of him. A few people sat in chairs near the fireplace while others were ordering their lunch. The door to the kitchen just behind the counter had a hole in its top through which Alden saw several bubbling pots no doubt preparing for a busy night.

As Alden approached the desk to get a room, a young female Wekken with olive freckles turned around to look at him. She wore a simple brown coat with a lilac shirt and seemed quite tall for a girl even among her race as she towered at least three feet over his head. *Well that explains the door.*

"Hello I was hoping to book a room for the night," Alden said.

"Of course dear. We're not the only inn in Henaten, but I'd like to think we're the most comfortable. I believe I have a nice single room on the third floor, it overlooks the bay and is quite lovely. Would you like to see it?" she asked.

"That sounds exactly like what I'm looking for. It'll be a nice change of pace to sleep on something other than the ground."

"Wonderful, let me just get the room key and we can head right up. I'm Batara by the way. This is me and my Dad's little inn."

She pulled a large brass key from under the counter before walking toward the stairs. Alden sped up trying to keep up with the willowy lady's stride over to the steps on the main room's opposite side. They began their ascent up the staircase curving to the right. At the landing Alden stopped to admire the three story entrance as he could now see just how enormous it was. Beams of jungle hardwoods stretched across the triangular hall in an intricate grid as the whole room was illuminated by a majestic chandelier blazing with magical blue fire. While the flames were the same color as the sea the light they projected was more akin to yellow candlelight.

"Breathtaking isn't it? When I was a little girl I'd peer through the bannister at the crowd below. Imagining all the adventures they'd had and I tried to listen to every word," Batara said.

"You were a little girl?" Alden asked.

"A long time ago, but then I grew up. You think you'll ever get to do that someday?"

An enormous smile covered her equally large face as Batara looked down at him. *Damn it she got me there. Wekken never do play fair.* He couldn't help, but smile at her retort. The mismatched pair continued down the second floor hallway until they reached a large wall of windows marking the end of the second floor. A palm wood staircase greeted them as it curved its way up to the top of the inn. The ceiling stretched up all the way to the third floor. A crossbeam lay just over the steps reaching from the outer wall to just above the hallway entrance.

"Mind your head dear, the beam is quite solid if you don't duck," Batara said.

Looking up at the timber far above his head Alden couldn't imagine ever bumping into it. *At least I appreciate the thought. I wouldn't believe anyone could hit it, but she's standing right in front of me. Is everyone in her family this huge?*

"Guessing your parents had the same issue with the woodwork?" Alden asked.

"Not exactly, my mum passed when I was really young so my aunt took care of me. As for my Dad he's in no danger of hitting it. I was nearly as tall as him when I was just ten years old after he came back home from being a sailor. He'd probably need a box just to look me in the eye, maybe two," Batara said.

She smirked as only a daughter could before continuing up the stairs. At the landing the young lady stopped at the door just on the left, three hundred and one. Batara stooped down a little to put the brass key into the door even though the frame itself was even taller than her. The door clicked as the willowy young girl pushed it open to reveal something stunning.

Alden had expected a tavern inn with maybe a window staring at someone's balcony, but instead the room that greeted him was spectacular. Two sets of windows stretched across the walls revealing the north of Turtamaw Bay's blue waters. Cracking them open Batara let in a gentle tropical breeze as the soothing scent of sea salt filled his nostrils. Blue curtains fluttered in the breeze as a white comfy bed spread out before him. Topped with an almost excessive number of pillows, Alden held himself back from collapsing into them right then.

Walking around, he saw a dresser for his things and even a private restroom. Inside was a sink to wash his face along with a porcelain throne next to a spacious bathtub. Alden couldn't help smiling as he remembered the comforts of civilized life in the city. Even by Krohfast standards this was a lovely inn, but after his ordeal this was paradise.

It's perfect, after sleeping in a cage and in the muck I get to enjoy this. I'm about to be the most comfortable man in the world.

"It's perfect. This really is fantastic Batara, the decor is beautiful. I'd be happy to take it," Alden said.

"Thank you I did the curtains and fabrics, but Dad picked out the furniture," she said.

"Hey Batara if you don't mind me asking there's something that's been bothering me. How many years ago did your Dad come back from sailing?"

"Hmm about ten I think. Why?"

"It's nothing serious. It's just, what's his name? I had a friend long ago who said his daughter with the same name as yours was being raised by an aunt. Just wondered if there was any connection."

"Oh well I always call him Dad, but his real name is Turtan."

Alden stopped as if he'd run into one of the stucco walls. *It couldn't be, but how else could there be so many similarities.* His red eyes grew wide as the daughter of his pirate friend loomed over him seeming concerned.

"They don't stop there do they?" he asked.

Alden began laughing, holding his hand over his face. He bent over as his ribs began to ache as he noticed Batara wasn't quite sure what she'd said that was so funny. Catching himself, he wiped a tear from his eyes and couldn't hide his great big grin.

"Something your Dad said to me a long time ago. You are definitely your father's daughter; Batara my name is Alden. Your Dad helped me survive quite an adventure. In fact, the way he spoke last time I think he saw you as his second chance at a normal life. The funniest thing is he thought you'd be at his knee, but I guess that didn't pan out," Alden said.

"Wait you're Uncle Alden? Dad told me stories about you ever since he came back. He always spoke of an amazing knight who saved him from his treacherous captain. I thought you were human though?" she asked.

"I used to be. It's a long story, but one I'd be happy to tell you tonight. I don't suppose your Dad is in town too?"

Perking up and almost hitting the generously high ceiling Batara lit up. "He is, just went down to the docks to do some fishing. Dad has a fishing spot on dock forty-two. Think he was wearing a blue shirt, white shorts, and his straw hat today. I'm sure he'd be glad to see you."

"I'll do that right now. Your Dad did say he'd wait, but I can forgive him for not standing around for a decade."

Alden noticed Batara's eye begin to water. The mountain of a young lady got down on one knee and embraced him in her tree trunk like arms. Resting her giant leathery head on his shoulder she began sobbing as Alden tried to keep his feet from collapsing under her weight. *It's like being hugged by a dresser. Why is my back wet?* A waterfall of tears began cascading down his cape.

"I didn't really know him when I was just a little girl. Thank you so much for bringing him home, you gave me my Dad back," Batara said.

"Eh don't mention it. The only reason I'm here is because of him. Guess we saved each other in a way. I saved him from a monstrous man eating worm and he saved me from turning to dust," Alden said.

"No way, that's amazing. Promise me you'll tell me the story later tonight?"

"Of course, I won't skip a single detail. Even though I still can't believe what happened. Wait a minute. I've been gone ten years! That means Amara should be almost twenty! My little girl is going to be all grown up when I get home."

"Maybe you can ask my Dad for advice on that. I mean I'm definitely not a little girl anymore, but I'm still his little girl. I'm sure she'll just be as happy to see you as I was when my Dad came back."

"Thanks Batara I guess it's just a shock to think about. Best not keep your Dad waiting then. I'm so glad I got to meet you."

"Uncle Alden before I forget don't worry about paying for the room I'm just so happy to finally meet you. If you need anything at all, just say the word dear."

Batara towered over him as she stood up. Making her way through the doorway the freckled girl waved goodbye as she closed it. *What a small world we live in. Turtan must be really proud of her.* Dumping his bags over by the dresser Alden removed his swords and dropped himself right onto the bed. For the first time in a decade Alden was comfortable as he enjoyed its soft embrace. Closing his eyes, he knew that Turtan wouldn't hold it against him if he kept the old man waiting for five more minutes.

Chapter 11: You Old Pirate

After resting his eyes for a few minutes, Alden got off the bed and went into the restroom. Inside he found the sink and looked into the mirror. Staring back at him was not the face he'd known for thirty-four years.

His flesh had turned absolute black while his bones had become a glowing red neon color that shone through to the surface. A few arteries popped in and out of visibility as well, but they were almost completely absent on his face. Each of his pupils remained, but they had become glowing scarlet coals in his eye sockets. Marked lines had appeared across his jaw and forehead. They made up the unique pattern generated when someone became a mature Ascendant which was used to tell each other's faces apart as the skeleton underneath was little help. Lastly, a rather flamboyant neon stubble had been retained from his time in captivity.

It's like I've become someone else entirely. I suppose in a way this was always my face that no one ever got to see, not even me. I wonder what Leonara will think? Some wives have a hard time accepting you got a new haircut. How do you respond when your husband comes back as a glowing skeleton? On the topic of hair, this stubble simply must go. My chin feels like it's made of shark skin.

"Ventos," he said

Alden brought a single finger up to his face. A sharp wind emerged from its side as he ran it across his skin. Like a razor without steel, the digits glided across his jaw shearing the stubble from his face. Glowing strands of hair descended into the sink like embers fleeing a fire. After a minute spent trimming his face was as smooth as polished marble. Alden didn't mind his head of hair and instead just washed it with water from the Drentos powered tap. Sand, salt, and a few pebbles were washed into the purifying basin underneath the sink.

Ahh sometimes there's nothing better than water from the tap draining down your face. Almost like my problems were carried away just like all that sand. Well I think I've kept Turtan waiting long enough, let's see how the old scoundrel is doing.

Alden grabbed the room key off the dresser, opened the door, and then made sure it was locked. Going downstairs he passed under the beam which he still wasn't in danger of hitting before heading straight through the second floor hallway. On the landing he stopped once more to admire the walls of the Gentle Hurricane. Taxidermied fish lined the walls along with enormous monster jaws mounted throughout the main hall. In fact, one pair over the fireplace must have been large enough to swallow himself whole.

Wonder who caught that? Pretty sure I would've let go of that rod if whatever that came from was on the line.

Making his way down the steps Alden noticed a few more people had come into the inn since he'd checked in. Walking by the counter he waved at Batara who seemed much more at home in a room with three story ceilings. The graceful giant returned his gesture and smiled as he left through the mammoth door which didn't seem so odd to him anymore.

Stepping out into the sun, the tropical heat began bearing down on Alden even as the breeze did its best to relieve him. Turning left he began walking towards the docks and hopefully towards his old friend. *If I remember correctly Henaten has a few different districts. This should be the shopping district and I think this street goes to the harbor. Ahh I love these tall buildings, all the wind flying through them almost makes this heat bearable.*

As Alden walked past shops on the first floor a veritable rainbow of colors floated above him on clotheslines. Shirts, pants, and perhaps a few undergarments hung over the street on strings between buildings. Each laundry line led to windows where someone was likely doing chores waiting for the breeze to finish drying. A feature of the buildings in the shopping district were the endless vines growing out of porcelain planters left on each windowsill. Accompanying the ivy that swayed underneath the windows were a veritable garden of blooms. Each tendril sprouted gorgeous red, orange, and purple flowers that were as large as apples. A fleet of hummingbirds and bees flittered in the breeze hoping to secure a share of the sweet nectar for their own.

So many cities have gardens, but how many can boast theirs grow on the city walls? These pink coral buildings compliment the flowers so well. Would Leonara forgive me if the ship took two days to set sail?

Alden who had previously felt rather tiny next to Batara was nearly on the verge of only being short next to the average Wekken around him. *It's such a shame that most people only hear about them from war stories. Without magic they constructed one of the most beautiful cities in Nisuroth and nearly matched the Ascendant in war just from shear ingenuity. Well I suppose it's not all they overshadow with how tall they are. Air's growing saltier; the harbor can't be far now.*

As Alden passed around the corner, hundreds of docks and a simply staggering number of ships came into view. Small fishing boats meant for scouring the shallows were closer to his side with the larger trading and military vessels docked at the other end of the city. On each end of the port were fishing piers and in the middle was an enormous white sand beach.

Dock forty-two she said. Please let them start numbering from this side.

Large open air marketplaces lined Alden's left side as the piers started to climb in number on his right. Each bazaar was nearly ten city blocks long and to Alden's eyes it seemed almost every inch was devoted to fish. Ceramic magical constructs pulled heavy carts resupplying the markets at an almost endless pace. A veritable sea of Wekken crowded the stalls as even children knew that to make a citrine eyed girl happy, all you needed was a good day with a rod and reel in your hand.

Their fish market makes Krohfast's look positively uninteresting in comparison. I'll have to check them out after I talk to Turtan. I wonder what other Veferothi improvements they've made? Still I'm sure they're happy to let the constructs pull in the fish carts.

Alden quickly passed the fishing boat docks and reached those meant for angling off the piers. Each of them extended well past the ship docks out into the tropical bay waters. Wekken on top had evenly spaced themselves out hoping to avoid disputes. Alden noticed the signs had finally entered the thirties.

Looks like I'm nearly there. You'd think the area would be fished out, but with all the boats bringing in their catch it must attract quite a few critters. What do you even catch off the piers here I wonder?

After the docks had nearly run out, Alden found the sign for forty-two. Turning the corner onto the boards he expected a rickety pier, but instead he didn't hear so much as a squeak. *Is this magic or just their love of fishing at work? I don't think even Nisuri could craft wooden docks this nice. Ahh wait a minute, there is a spell. My feet feel cool and the air's become more mild, but we're in the middle of a blazing hot day. This is a Brumorta enchantment to cool the docks just enough so the sun doesn't cook our feet. The Veferothi really have been helping out.*

Enjoying his respite from the heat Alden scoured the pier for Turtan, but the old Wekken was nowhere to be found. Only the last section of the dock remained to be searched, but then he heard shouting coming from the end. There was a Wekken holding an enormous blue eel that was longer than he was tall. It was thicker than his leg and its snout was tipped with two hooked horns on either side of its mouth. He'd only read stories of them, but Alden knew it was a Geysergrab Eel.

That blue color is so vivid and the yellow ribbon running along it is majestic. What a beautiful fish and an even luckier fisherman. Wait a minute. Holding up the lucky catch was a man in an even bluer shirt and white shorts. On top of the Wekken's head was a simple straw hat and a face that Alden could never forget.

"Turtan, you old pirate," Alden said.

Looking up, the citrine eyed angler looked at Alden with a face squarely confronted with confusion. The man squinted trying to look at the stranger with the familiar voice.

"Alden?" Turtan asked.

"Hiding my stuff in the cell was a nice touch. You could've picked somewhere dryer though," Alden said.

"It is you. How can? How the? Screw it I'm just glad you're alive, but how'd you find me?"

The old Wekken embraced Alden in a gigantic bear hug crushingly similar to his daughter's. It seemed ten years had done nothing to dull the pirate's strength. Alden felt something slimy on his back as he realized in Turtan's excitement he'd not actually put the Geysergrab down.

"It's been too long my friend. Batara told me where to find you after I tried getting a room at the inn," Alden said.

"You've already met my little girl huh? Did she hit her head giving you the tour?" Turtan asked.

"Batara did mention something about it, but your little girl ducked this time I guess. She did tell me to mind my head though."

"Somehow I don't think that warning was all that useful for you."

"The thought was appreciated."

"You should check for a dent in that beam later tonight, you'll see it if you look closely."

"With how strong she is I'm shocked that wood hasn't been head-butted in half by now."

"It still surprises me to this day. I named the inn after her if you hadn't already guessed. She's gentler than a mother with a newborn babe, but if you cross her or her dear dad...well let's just say I haven't spent a kolo on a show since she's gotten old enough to handle the rowdier customers. Why pay for a concert when I can just watch her toss a few drunks through a wall?"

"I'm sure, her hug felt like a dresser embracing me. Can't imagine what happens if she starts swinging. Wait did you say through a wall?"

Does it make me a bad person that I want to see that?

"Gentle Hurricane isn't just a name, it's a warning. Thankfully it's one that's gotten around."

"It did seem awfully quiet. Wait, so how did you two end up back here in Hemmoros? I thought you lived in Aetturus?"

"After I waited about a week for you to come back I figured whatever happened was either taking too long or you were gone forever. So I left your things where no one, but you would find them. Then I went back to Aetturrus to get my life started over. Realized I was much more interested in being a father than a pirate. So I sold a few of the Gray artifacts I'd picked up, bought an inn here in Hemmoros, and we've been enjoying life here ever since."

"It all sounds so perfect. I'm glad it worked out for you although I'm a bit behind on the plan myself. I still have to get home and my soulenket says that both Amara and Leonara are alright, but something's odd about my daughter's pearl."

"Odd? Any chance you could be more specific?"

Opening the soulenket up Alden showed him the pearls. His still had its red glow around the blue and Amara's was entirely scarlet. "I think something happened to my daughter after the ritual affected me. I don't know how, but all I do know is that I've got to get back home."

"Well we've never had a normal friendship, why start now? I happen to know a captain who sails to Heanerath all the time. If you want, I can check when he's shipping off next?"

"Really? Thanks Turtan, you're as reliable as ever. I just hope they're both alright."

"I'm sure they're fine and if not, I know that won't stop you. I'll go sell off some of this catch and we can have the rest for supper tonight."

"Sounds good. I'll try not to keep you waiting so long this time."

Turtan gave him a last hug and returned to his pile of fish. Alden turned to walk back down the dock. Looking down the coast he saw that the sun had sunk quite a bit, but there were still a few hours left before it set.

I'll shop a little since I'm not going anywhere tonight even if he does find a ship. Really ought to get something for Batara and Turtan, but what would even make a good gift for those two?

Stepping off the docks Alden headed right into the endless stalls of fish. He'd thought that Mullentide had taught him a thing or two about sea life. However, that reassurance was obliterated as it seemed every creature under the sea was on display. Some were as small as spoons and others were gargantuan beasts being sliced into barrel sized chunks for restaurants.

Did they catch every creature in the Otaton? I've been around all of Nisuroth and I scarcely even know how to describe a tenth of what I'm seeing.

Some fish looked like frogs, others had beaks like herons, and stranger still some had iridescent skin like a squid. However, this was a market for seafood and there were many other creatures who were certainly swimming around with more than fins. On one table were crabs as big as watermelons painted with pink algae. Another stall had a polka dot patterned shrimp as long as a canoe. There was even a squid with as many eyes as it had tentacles. Which happened to be fifteen, he'd counted.

Within a few minutes the rows of sea life faded as they were replaced by stalls of endless merchants and their goods. *It's hard to forget that Henaten is the world's first stop on the journey to Nisuroth. There has to be something for everyone here. Are those stone statues bleeding? Those fruit look like blue wind chimes, but they're growing sideways. Did someone seriously make a floating eyeball construct that keeps reminders for you? This place is amazing.*

Browsing the stalls Alden couldn't seem to find a gift that was just right, but then one of the stands on the edge of the market caught his eye. A hooded Ascendant man robed in an opulent yellow outfit presided over the stall. A menagerie of magical items littered the shelves, but one in particular caught Alden's eyes. Stone horns with metallic cowbells at their ends covered in spell runes.

Wait are those vocalamitters? I know it's been ten years, but are they really so small now?

"Excuse me sir are those vocalamitters?" Alden asked.

"Why yes sir, I know they may look a bit strange to your eyes. This latest model is a particularly exciting improvement over previous ones. Now they aren't limited to only linking a few stones, but can work on an almost endless number of combinations," the merchant said.

"Actually I'm used to them just sitting in a room. Amazing they've gotten this small."

"Haven't been looking for a new one in a while huh?"

"Ha, something like that. Kind of been living under a rock for the last decade."

"Well glad you found your way out from under it. I think you'll find them to be an incredible improvement over what you're used too then sir. They're five hundred kolos each if you're interested."

"I'll take five. In my line of work these could really prove helpful. With all that's been happening these should buy a little peace of mind if nothing else."

"I've noticed a lot of families have been getting them to stay in touch even across the ocean. I'll get this bagged up for you. Have an excellent day sir."

Satisfied he'd found a worthy gift for everyone, Alden started making his way back to the inn. *Did he recognize my sword just by the handle? I'm sure it's only my imagination, he was probably just being nice. I've got my gift, time to get back to the inn. My mouth is already watering at the thought of eating that eel.*

Turning a corner further towards the inn, Alden noticed the sky had transformed into the beginnings of a beautiful sunset. Any laundry flying overhead earlier had gone inside for the night. Hummingbirds zoomed about the flowers on the building sides, dancing over each petal for another drink of nectar.

Time for me to get my own beverage. If there's any kindness in this world, please let Turtan still have some of that Strong Breeze. I have a feeling this will be a night to remember or maybe not depending on how many mugs I have.

Once he'd reached within a mile of the inn, Alden noticed the street had nearly emptied as everyone was starting to head home. Still he couldn't help but notice a hooded Ascendant wearing a mask staring at him from within a crowd. The stranger continued looking at him as Alden stared back. Unlike other Ascendant this one was hiding his face in a city where no one else was. The man's regal robes made him stick out like a sore thumb.

Did he notice I'm a knight too? Why does he keep staring when I've already caught him? Something's odd and I don't think I want to find out what it is.

Stepping more quickly now, Alden turned the final corner before arriving at The Gentle Hurricane. Its triangular stucco structure stretched three stories above him and each window room was now illuminated with a wonderfully warm glow. The beautiful vine covered walls gleamed in the ebbing sunlight. Putting his hand on the door's iron knocker, Alden pulled it open and entered with a smile on his face anticipating the night ahead.

Chapter 12: A Stiff Breeze

Pulling the heavy door open Alden entered the Gentle Hurricane. Unlike earlier that afternoon the whole inn was filled with travelers. The hall was brimming with all kinds of people drinking every variety of alcohol imaginable. A gentle strumming song came from his left where a set of instruments were playing themselves.

Whoa, I didn't know they had an Autendum enchanted band. It's not even a simple one either. I need to be careful or I may start singing along and Turtan doesn't deserve to have his pointy ears bleed because of me.

On Alden's right there was a barkeep with shoulder length brown hair framing a chiseled chin and short beard that he hadn't seen before. The man waved him over as if he wanted a word. Alden stepped up to the dark wooden bar and found a seat between two Wekken sailors drinking their fill. Before he could utter a single word the man passed him a wooden mug of a familiar blue liquid.

"Mr. Alden, I'm Roger the barkeep. Ms. Batara said you were a friend and that you might like a few free drinks along with a meal," Roger said.

"Hard to say no to that. Knowing her father, I should probably keep it to only a few mugs though. By the way I'm guessing this blue stuff is Strong Breeze right?" Alden asked.

With a mischievous smile "Almost Mr. Alden. Strong Breeze is the older version of the inn's special, Stiff Breeze. Batara told me you probably haven't tried this latest brew. It's a far stronger local rum mixed with banana and tinted by Blue Chimes. That's what gives our drinks their famous color."

"Stronger?"

"Well let me put it to you like this. That young lady drank a half barrel of grog and was as articulate as a poet. Four mugs of this will put her to sleep."

"Best take my time with it then."

"A wise choice. Also as I'm afraid the tables are all taken, might I suggest having dinner brought up to your room?"

"That'd be wonderful, thanks."

"Anytime Mr. Alden. Enjoy your meal."

How can it be stronger? Last time, one cup was enough to knock me out cold so what can this stuff do? Better be careful or I'll be a blubbering mess later tonight.

Grabbing the intriguing blue liquid off the counter, Alden made for the stairs. Weaving his way through the crowd, he saw a curious collection of people from all walks of life enjoying their time. Some Wekken near the fireplace were looking up at the trophies on the wall and arguing which of their catches was bigger than the already absurd specimens on display. Another cyclops in a strange black cloak was sipping on her own Stiff Breeze in the back corner. A Pekartan merchant in a stone gray tunic was stacking his empty drinks into a leaning tower of mugs.

Seven, eight, nine! The sun's barely gone down and he's already trying to drink the port dry. No wonder Batara gets so much practice as a bouncer. Then again maybe that's the whole idea behind such strong alcohol. Instead of it being a fight club after a few mugs the inn probably turns into a nursery for sauced sailors.

Above all of the commotion was Batara serving drinks and food to people sitting down. Alden noticed that she was now wearing a white apron on her front which must have been as big as a bedsheet. Her freckled faced could be seen from any corner of the room one ventured to as she towered over even the other Wekken.

Clambering up the stairs onto the landing Alden took one look back and could see why Batara enjoyed this view so much. Taking a sip of the Stiff Breeze Alden felt it's sweet and stinging flavor slide down his throat. *Are they downstairs just laughing at how I think this is such a strong drink? Something this good tasting couldn't be that bad, right? My mouth feels funny. Oh no.*

Finding his way down the hall, Alden stopped at the foot of the staircase. His legs seemed to have slowed down while the rest of him kept right on moving. *They weren't kidding! I just took a sip and I'm already starting to spin. Is it just me or are there more stairs than before?*

Alden looked up as Turtan had suggested and there was an unmistakably deep crater in the foot-thick beam. *I can't believe he wasn't kidding. Oh that poor thing, how does she manage to keep hitting it?*

After climbing the stairs Alden entered his room with a little help from the key. The sun had already set, but the Lumendo enchanted bulb above him helped keep everything brighter than any candle. Putting the dangerous rum on the nightstand, Alden went into the bathroom. Inside he found a little cup meant for thirsty guests, filled it with water, and drank to hopefully temper the alcohol.

Alden collapsed onto the wonderfully soft mattress as he took another gulp of the dark blue Breeze from his cup. Enjoying the taste and with no pesky stairs left to climb he began to drain his mug. A few minutes passed by until Alden heard some rather large sounding footsteps coming from the stairs.

Thud.

"Agh, ow. When did that get so low?" a voice outside the door asked.

After the noise the footsteps resumed their way up. Doing his best to hide his grin, Alden sprang from the bed and opened the door. On the other side was a surprised Batara holding a wooden tray just over his head. Noticing that he couldn't see the food she lowered it down to his height with a smile. It was a glistening golden Geysergrab Eel fillet with orange slices and a pint of ale.

What an aroma! If it smells that good, I can only imagine how tasty it's going to be.

"I know you want to dig in, but let me just put this down for you first," Batara said as she placed the tray on his dresser.

"T-thanks Batara. This looks incredible," Alden said.

"I'm guessing you've tried some of our new Stiff Breeze? I wasn't sure if it would be too much, but I did only give you one cup."

"Oh no, it's dangerously good. I'm just taking it s-slow is all."

"Don't worry Dad said you might have some trouble with it. I forget that we're pretty hardy when it comes to drinking. If the blue stuff is a little strong for you don't worry, the ale should be somewhat gentler."

"That's really t-thoughtful of you Batara, but I don't think I could face your Dad without finishing it. By the way Roger s-said it takes four of these to make you sleep. Any truth to that?"

"Oh well yeah, but that would be four of my cups. Yours is a bit too tiny for me, see?" she asked. Batara delicately picked up his full size mug in her massive claws. *It looks like a teacup for children in her paws. If that won't get her drunk what will?*

"W-wait so then what does your cup look like?"

"Oh it's just this one on my hip," Batara said. She motioned to an ornate wooden bucket with a thick metal handle tied to her belt. "Like I said mine is a big girl's cup."

She started to laugh as she saw Alden's expression of shock. *I thought that was a mop bucket or something. That's what she uses to drink?*

"You really are a pirate's daughter. Thanks for bringing this up Batara. I'm gonna dig into this before it gets cold. After I'm done all three of us should catch up by the fireplace tonight."

"Really? Oh I'm so excited. I can't wait to hear all of your stories!"

"Just make sure you don't drink too many buckets before then."

"No promises Uncle Alden."

Batara gave him a hug before heading back downstairs. This time her heavy footsteps weren't accompanied by another loud thud. Alden moved the tray over to his side table and began to dig in. With the first bite his nose had proved to be an excellent judge. The savory meat nearly melted in his mouth before he had time to chew. An orange sauce had been drizzled over top and its sweet taste was indescribably excellent. The sizable filet vanished over the course of an hour where everything including the orange slices was eaten. Eyeing the pint of ale, Alden downed the whole thing in a series of gulps.

If they-y ever opened a restaurant in Krohfast the line to get in would reach outside the city. I would've settled for a boiled boot after eating tack for so long, but this was a magnificent meal. I'll have to get them to make this again. I just want to take a nap, but I r-really ought to be getting downstairs.

Finished with his food, Alden picked up his dishes and held the mug in his right hand. Walking out of the comfortable room, he slowly ventured down the stairs and back to the main hall. The guests had mostly gone as dinner had already been served and most travelers had headed home. Alden plopped down at the bar where Roger was waiting to take his dishes.

"You're some cook Roger, that eel was excellent," Alden said.

"Glad to hear it, but I can't take credit for that bit of culinary artistry. Turtan brought that blue beauty back earlier and cooked up that filet especially for you," Roger said.

"Well I'll just have to thank him then. Where has the old pirate gotten off to?"

"Actually he's just behind you by the fireplace. If you don't mind could you take this refill over to him. Consider it a trade for your dishes."

"Sure thing Roger."

Alden took the second mug and walked over by the fire where Turtan was reclined in a comfortable looking leather chair with a twin by its side. He plunked himself down in it and placed the pirate's mug on a small table in front of the fire. Across from Alden's chair was an absurdly large couch which was undoubtedly for Batara.

"Ah I see you found my refill Alden, thanks. How'd you like the eel? It's been awhile since I've gotten to cook one so I'm sorry if it was a little overdone," Turtan said.

"Nonsense, I thought it was the best meal I've had in a decade," Alden said.

"Ugh, you really are a dad aren't you?"

"Takes one to know one I suppose. This really is an amazing inn Turtan and I still can't believe you were able to get an Autendum band. You haven't been trying to become a mage have you? I'm not sure robes are really your style."

"I'll stick to my coats for now, I like having pockets. Besides if I knew anything about spells I would've broken you out of that ritual a decade ago. No my talents fortunately lie elsewhere, Alden."

"I don't suppose you had any luck finding a ship home then?"

"Indeed I did, there's a vessel leaving for Krohfast tomorrow morning. An old business friend of mine, Captain Venik runs a trading vessel. Thanks to my talents you have a cabin waiting for you. I doubt it's as nice as our inn, but it should be a palace in comparison to your last voyage."

"Well then my friend here's to your talents." Alden said raising his mug as Turtan met it with his.

Clink.

Drinking deeply both men took a gulp of the blue liquor. The fire quietly crackled beside them as its orange glow painted both of their faces. Alden slunk down into the cozy chair as his body began to be pumped with a delightfully warm feeling. Looking above he saw the absurdly large jaw displayed over the mantle from before.

"S-so Turtan what's with the leviathan? What'd you hook it with, a broadsword?" Alden asked.

"No, better. Ship anchor," Turtan said.

"You liar, are you saying a fish tried to a-abscond with your anchor? Did you have some of your cooking skewered on it, because otherwise I find that very hard to believe."

"It went something like that. I was fishing in the bay a bit outside the city. Hovering over a huge sandbar and was just bobbing in the waves in my little fishing boat. I had been messing about with a rod and reel until I saw some big shadow show up below the boat. Only a second after it appeared, the monster darted faster than that worm on the mountain under my hull. Suddenly my anchored ship started sailing through Turtamaw Bay. Damn thing was strong enough to actually pull the whole ship. Can you believe that?"

"Maybe a little, but that jaw found its way up there somehow. So what'd you do to the ship stealing rascal?"

"Well a long story short I had more than hooks on that boat. Happened to have a store of harpoons and I speared the creature from the surface. He took over a dozen of them, but the fish eventually relented and that's how I got my favorite trophy."

"So what was it? I've seen some big critters, but nothing that could l-live up to that."

"It was a big old Sandmaw Shark Uncle Alden. That monster was as long as his boat was. You could stand him up in this hall tip to tail and he'd reach the ceiling," Batara said.

Walking up from behind them she sat down on the oversized couch. Apron off, it seemed she was done for the night and ready to relax. Batara's enormous head then tilted towards her father with a knowing grin. Alden saw Turtan look nervous as his confident expression had melted into a much more sheepish one.

She might not be my daughter, but I'd know that look anywhere. Dad just fibbed about his fish story and I get to hear the real version. This ought to be good.

"Would you like to tell him what actually happened or should I? Batara asked.

"Well I mean I didn't embellish that much. I did actually hit it with a harpoon," Turtan said.

"Yes, you did. Problem is that you used only one to bring the beast down. Care to venture a guess how he did it Uncle Alden?"

"Well there's always a b-bigger fish, but if that was the case then it would be hanging up there, so what did happen?" he asked.

"If only, that would've made a better story. No, the animal was so shocked by that one harpoon it ran right into an underwater boulder and knocked itself out cold."

"No!"

Alden sputtered before laughing uncontrollably. "To the best boulder a pirate could ever ask for," he said. Alden held his cup up for a toast as Turtan began to start turning beet red. Batara met it with her bucket as they both laughed.

Clink.

After taking another gulp from his Stiff Breeze Alden felt himself descending into drunken delight. *Well I'm never forgetting that story.* Still smiling at the tale a question began nagging at his brain until the only escape for it was through his lips.

"I l-love this drink you two, but there's something I'm dying to know. Who's the stronger drinker? Father or daughter?" Alden asked.

It's honestly a good question. He's got a lifetime of experience, but Batara's so big she uses a bucket to drink.

"Hmm, that's a good one. Honestly it's always a fair fight, but I'd say we're even most nights," Batara said.

"Ha! Even? You might be bigger than your old man, but I will not hear of my daughter being a better drinker under this roof. Roger I know you're heading out for the night, but would you mind pulling out a barrel. I need to put my daughter in her place," Turtan said.

"Just need a moment Turtan," Roger said.

The bartender walked through the kitchen door. Only a minute later a loud grunt could be heard as if someone was trying to move something very heavy. A few moments later Roger returned rolling a full size barrel along the floor from the inn's backroom. Alden spied a spigot on the barrel's front.

That's no ordinary container. What have I done? If I was still human my cheeks would be brighter than cherries already and we haven't even started the contest. Can Ascendant even get red in the face? If it's possible I'm about to prove it.

"Thanks Roger. Have a good night dear," Batara said. She rose up to her feet and gave the bearded barkeep an enormous bear hug.

"You too Batara. Happy drinking! Let me know who wins in the morning," he said as she released him before Roger made his way out of the inn for the night.

"You already know the answer to that one Roger," Batara said.

Reaching down with her massive paws the young Wekken picked up the barrel Roger could only roll right up off the ground. Gingerly she made her way over to the table in between all the seats and laid it down so gently that the wood didn't even squeak in protest. Heading back over to the bar she easily leaned over and stole a normal mug out from the shelves underneath.

Batara walked back and squatted down in front of the barrel. Spigot facing outward she filled her new cup and then motioned for the other two as well. Alden and Turtan obliged handing them over. Batara made sure each mug was on the edge of overflowing. Returning each drink to its owner she sat back down on the couch.

"Same rules as usual?" she asked.

"Wouldn't have it any other way sweetie," he said. Turtan then turned to Alden. "Don't get too worried, it's nothing fancy. Everyone fills their mug and then has to drink the whole thing. If you can't finish all of it, you're out. We'll do that until only one of us is left, which will be me," Turtan said.

"All I know is that I'm definitely gonna clinch third place," Alden said.

"Oh don't worry Uncle Alden it's not a big inconvenience. I'm sure you're very light, I don't mind carrying you back upstairs," Batara said.

They could at least make me feel like I have a chance. I suppose there's no point in pretending. At least the drinks will be sweet as I get my ass handed to me.

Turtan and his daughter had dropped their smiles now. Instead they both had become deadly serious. Alden tried to adopt the same expression, but already being tipsy his was more of a half grin than anything else. Raising his hand Turtan held it in the air. He looked around the half-circle and with a sudden smile he dropped his hand like an anchor getting taken by a shark.

All three of them began to drink their mugs. Turtan began wolfing his down while Alden's throat began to burn as he tried to keep up. Batara simply raised her head and the whole contents of the mug vanished like rain on a hot day. The father and daughter pair stared at Alden as they both tried to hold back their smiles.

"Doing alright Uncle Alden?" she asked.

"I think he might have lost his land legs," Turtan said.

Alden's head had begun to roll as he'd sunk into his chair. "I'm-m-m gooood. Just a bit of dra-inking. It's a bit early to be ad-mitt-a-n defeat don't you think? M-m-a-a-a-ybe I'm gonna take second a-a-after all," Alden said.

W-w-w-h-h-ooo am I kid-d-d-ing? I'm slur-r-ring my thought-t-s-s-s and I'm going to be-e-e-at them? I f-f-f-eel funny.

The pair smiled and everyone put their mugs in for a refill. The sweet blue nectar filled their cups in only moments. Alden hoped that the spigot would take longer so he could catch his breath, but there was no such luck. Raising his hand again Turtan looked to his friend. Alden's cheeks had turned a cherry red color. With a smile anticipating what was about to happen, Turtan dropped his hand once more. The two Wekken drained their mugs as if it was nothing, but Alden took his time. Once the last drop had passed his lips, he felt the room begin to spin.

"I think we've found our third place," Turtan said.

"I juust need a mi-i-minute. You know it's fuu-uny. Can't believe you'd think she'd be as tall as your kne-e-e-e. I miss-ed you my f-friend. I'm n-n-o-o-ot drunk. Just happy that you t-o-o-o-o-o are ha-a-a-p-py. Did the floor get taller?" Alden asked. Finally, his eyes closed as he slumped into his chair. Third place was now his.

"Is he ok and did he just say that you thought I wouldn't get any taller than your knees?" Batara asked.

"You make one joke, and no one will let you forget it," Turtan said.

"No not really, but don't worry, at least you're not the shortest one in the bar tonight," Batara said.

"He is quite tiny isn't he? Anyway to answer your original question, I'm sure he'll be just fine. Let him sit there a while, we still haven't found our winner," Turtan said.

Alden tried to listen to his competitors, but he couldn't really make any of it out. Though he wasn't quite sure, it sounded like the mugs were getting refilled almost endlessly. His slurred hearing worsened until after what seemed like two dozen rounds of mugs slamming on the table, someone conceded.

Shouting victoriously Turtan stood up from his chair stumbling. "This old pirate still has it," he said.

Standing up Batara began to jostle about like a palm tree in a strong wind. "Not bad Dad. I just had too many of my mugs before we started," she said.

"It looks like Alden did too," he said. They both giggled at the knight slumped over in his chair.

"Honestly didn't expect the little guy to make it through two. I'll get him upstairs, poor dear has to be exhausted," Batara said.

"Sure just don't drop him when you bump your head. I wouldn't have ever come home without Alden." he said. Turtan hugged his much taller daughter and rested his head on her shoulder.

"Hey I won't bump my head. I'm as twisted as a rope, but I'll still be delicate."

Releasing from the hug, Turtan stumbled up the steps to his room on the second floor while Batara came over to Alden and cradled him in her arms. He was utterly asleep and with a flash of her toothy smile she began the trek upstairs. With the grace of someone used to being this inebriated, Batara quickly climbed up to his room without a single bump to either of their heads.

Pulling her master key out, Batara opened the door and maneuvered Alden through the doorframe. With the utmost care she opened the covers and placed him on the bed. Sliding the sheets over him like a glove, the giant girl planted a great big kiss on his forehead.

"Thanks for bringing my Dad back Uncle Alden. I thought you did a really good job drinking too. Sweet dreams," she whispered.

Batara lingered for a moment and then turned to find the way back to her own room. Sleeping soundly in a drunken stupor, Alden was dreaming of what it would be like to meet his own family after everything that had happened. Smiling he faded into his sleep as the dark night carried on. Without a sound, the window to his right cracked open and a silent gloved hand pushed the pane inward.

Chapter 13: Only the Fates of the Few

The first thing Alden felt was the gloved hand over his mouth. He tried to shout, but no words escaped his lips. A masked Wekken stood over him restraining his arms while an Ascendant held his mouth shut. Staring at the second one, Alden stole a glimpse of his eyes. They were like a window into the mind of an unstoppable monster.

Who are these two? Wait I can't feel any magic. They're using suppression cuffs!

"Telendum," the Ascendant man said.

Alden felt an invisible magical cast being weaved across his body. *Dammit why did I have to get so drunk. No spells to surprise them with and I'm as trapped as a fly in a spider web. I hope they're in a talking mood.* The mysterious Ascendant squeezed Alden's chin and cracked his mouth open like a coconut. Without delay, the man poured a liquid down his mouth from a glass vial. *Ugh, it's so bitter. Did I just get poisoned? Wait, I feel so cold. It's like there's ice in my veins! What did he do to me?* The masked man got off Alden and sat down in a chair pushed forward by the Wekken.

"Sorry, it's not exactly Sweetwater I know, but getting answers from someone who's drunk Stiff Breeze is like pulling water out of a stone," the Ascendant said.

"That may be the worst hello I've ever heard. How'd you get in here without me hearing anything?" Alden said.

"The doors were always a little too creaky for my tastes so we used your window. You'll be relieved to hear that your hearing isn't going. Couldn't spoil the surprise so we coated all of our gear with Venendum. The vacuum it creates makes sure no noise can escape through the coating. For example, the walls of this room have a similar coating so no one will be able to hear our conversation."

At least he wants to talk, but who in the world is this guy? He's like a surgeon describing everything as so matter of fact. I'm completely at his mercy. Better tread carefully or I may never see the sun rise again.

"Most people don't need ropes and spells just for talking. As far as first dates go this is a little weird."

The red eyed man was serious, but Alden could almost feel a smirk forming under that mask. *He's professional, but still has a sense of humor. At least I know he's not some kind of Graybuilt. Maybe I can talk my way out of this.*

"I suppose it would've been polite to buy you a drink, but I came here on business tonight. Does the name Bojjer bring anything to mind?" the masked man asked.

"He was the pirate who raided my village. Always wore a big bicorn and was an annoyingly good swordsman. Why?" Alden asked.

"Well ten years ago I sent Bojjer on a mission and he never came back from it. Clearly something went wrong, but I never had any leads until you crossed the Turtamaw this morning. One of the eyes in my employ was stationed in the port guard tower and she saw you leaving Hemmarasp. Must admit it was interesting that you found your way here. Turtan was one of my men in a way. To answer your question, I was hoping to learn a bit more about you, Alden," the Masked man said.

How does he know who I am? Wait Bojjer was his underling? Can that mean that this man is? I have to be certain.

"Well usually when you trade names both people do it," Alden said.

"Ahh where are my manners. Sorry my name is Dreven, Dreven Sunsullen. Former high lord of the Veferoth Republic."

"It is you! Wait, but I thought the attack on Mullentide was to get your book back. If you wanted to turn Bojjer into an Ascendant why not just use the normal ritual?"

"How about a trade? You tell me about your adventure and I'll explain everything I can. In a way I'm the one responsible for all of your suffering, the least I can give you is answers."

What is this bastard playing at? I remember the file Cassara gave me. He killed dozens of people, burned Mullentide to the ground, and now he's trying to apologize to me?

"Generous of you."

Sitting back on his pillows, Alden recounted his tale including everything starting with that fateful day at the ruins. Throughout it all Dreven sat silently with the exception of the occasional head tilt or nod. Other than those scant reactions he was nearly as still as a statue. Alden concluded his story and Dreven leaned forward from his chair.

"Well that is quite a tale. For what it's worth I am sorry about Mullentide. It was a terrible situation I was placed in and it cost all those people their lives. It's a hard thought to stomach that my choice led to all that suffering. I trusted him too much even to the end," Dreven said.

"He butchered those people. Everyone who was too weak to survive the journey was murdered. I walked through the streets where my neighbors had crawled out of their burning homes only to die in the mud. Can you really sit there and justify this? I had to distract a little girl so she wouldn't see her mother in a puddle of blood on the floor!" Alden shouted.

Dreven stood up and placed his hand down on the dresser, the Ascendant couldn't look him in the eyes. "Cassara Ookborne forced me to Alden. Damn stubborn old woman that she is."

My mission, the book I found must have forced his hand. But what could that one book unwind? I suppose it just shows how smart that old mind of her's is.

"How can she be responsible? What children did she order to be murdered?"

"Alden, the book she sent you to find was my father's. I thought I'd erased every last copy, but it seems one survived. With it your wife helped Cassara expose me. I suppose she thought it was a heroic thing, but the experiments my father started had to continue."

"Your experiments were brutal! What value could there have been in them?"

"That horrifying research which created our race began in the service of a purpose my father discovered. The Gray's in their foolish arrogance created spells which were grander than any other race, but there was a hidden cost. Their bright beacon of progress attracted something in the darkness between the stars," Dreven said.

The book did mention something sinister, but what could scare someone so much?

"What are you talking about?"

"They awakened a thing between the spaces if you will. It feeds on life, devouring it like a cosmic predator. That doom has been coming for us ever since those days millennia ago. My father upon discovering this performed that research to devise a way to conceal this world from these horrors, but his experiments were revealed. The war they caused split the empire and killed Dad before he could complete his work. Every day since then this world's doom has drawn ever closer and we are running out of time."

"And I thought my story was outlandish. Still that doesn't explain what happened with Bojjer."

"He was one of my most successful associates who I paid to obtain artifacts which might allow us to understand the Gray. If I could complete my father's work, then maybe this world could be saved. Unfortunately, ten years ago Cassara discovered him."

"He was a loose end and you couldn't let him threaten your experiments."

"What is loyalty, friendship, and dedication in the face of oblivion? I had a choice to make. I could try to kill Bojjer, but he was no simple pirate. I feared he may sense the trap and in trying to save my operation I would simply create a very powerful enemy. Instead I decided on something less wasteful."

"You hoped the ritual would kill the crew, but make Bojjer better than ever. He would've killed me to stop Cassara from getting the book and you'd deny her a lead, all in the same masterstroke."

"An excellent albeit incomplete guess, there was a third purpose. I'd hoped the Gray temple would've turned him into something else, but instead it seems he would've become like you and me. Just another Ascendant failure."

Are we all just a stepping stone in his quest to save the world? Is there nothing he won't do to accomplish his goal?

"You make yourself out to be a hero, but you still wanted him to kill his own men. His friends, comrades, and innocents on top of it all. Good motives never justify those kinds of means!"

"Don't they? If the crew wasn't silenced, everything we worked for would be lost and with it so would all of Nisuroth. You know all too well what kind of decisions heroes need to make. What you did on the mountain was horrifying, but necessary. I think you understand me better than anyone Alden."

"I only had to make that choice, because your actions caused all of this. I tried to save those people and I failed. I jumped into the fires of Mullentide for those people. I bled to protect them, but it wasn't enough. Their names will never fade from my memory. Don't compare your selfish decision to hurt others to what I had to do."

"I'm selfish? No, I am a man willing to do whatever horrifying acts are necessary for everyone like you to survive. Tell me, did you truly try to save those people or did you just want to see your family again? Did you miss the warmth of your wife's embrace, the sound of your child's laughter, and the feeling of belonging somewhere in this world?"

Alden grew silent as he considered Dreven's words. *I tried everything. There weren't any other options and if I had clung to that foolish hope then I never would have seen them again. Did I kill those people? Am I really nothing more than a man who couldn't live without his family?*

"Carry that pain. It will make you a better knight Alden. As I said I truly am sorry for what I've done to you, your family, and everyone. I can't abandon this world for only the fates of the few and if that means I won't have a place left in it, then that's a sacrifice I can live with. You still have so much to lose and for that I am truly glad. May I ask what that locket you're wearing under your shirt is?" Dreven asked.

Get it together! He noticed it, there's no point in lying when he seems to know everything about me already.

"It's a soulenket, Cassara gave it to my family so no matter where we went we could all know each of us was ok."

"A most precious gift. May I see it?"

"Bound men don't typically turn down requests."

"True and yet the choice is still yours Alden."

"Fine, take a look."

Dreven's gloved hand reached under the knight's shirt and retrieved the locket. Opening it Dreven froze utterly still. The sight of the three pearls interred within stirred something or rather Amara's glowing red stone seemed to attract his gaze more than any other. Pausing for what seemed an eternity, the Ascendant closed the locket and placed it back on Alden's chest.

Why is he so interested in that particular one? Does he know why it's glowing red?

"It would seem your family is waiting for you still. A wife and...?" Dreven said pausing to let him answer.

"My daughter, Amara. I missed ten years of her life thanks to you," Alden said.

Dreven reached into his own robe and pulled an almost identical soulenket out. *Wait Cassara didn't mention that he has a family? Is that why he was so interested in Amara's pearl?*

"Alden don't beat yourself up over choosing your family, I would have chosen mine too. There is nothing more meaningful than being able to come home to them. Never let them go, if you can," Dreven said holding the locket unopened.

How could he do that to his family? What child could live with the shame of knowing their father has done what he has?

Getting up Dreven looked at the Wekken and nodded. The lady cyclops's citrine eye hovered above him as she opened his mouth. More liquid from a vial was poured down his throat. Alden began coughing from the revolting drink.

"That mixture will ensure you won't wake until the sun comes up. May your voyage home be swift Alden," Dreven said.

"You're going after Amara! No, not her you bastard!" Alden shouted.

An icy feeling surged through him once more as his vision began to fade. Alden lost consciousness as the weight of his bonds seemed to fly away into the night. Utterly disturbed and terrified he drifted into a dreamless sleep.

Chapter 14: Only the Beginning

Birds chirped as Alden's black pit of a brain woke up. Opening his eyes, he sprang up from his covers hyperventilating. The only thing around him was an empty room. The sun had just risen and the Turtamaw's waters glowed with a beautiful sunny yellow color in the cool morning air. Collapsing back down on the fluffy white pillows Alden caught his breath.

I survived, but that doesn't make me feel any better. Can't delay any more or who knows what that maniac will do to her? I'm so sorry Amara, what have I gotten you into?

Getting up Alden went into the bathroom and drew himself a bath. Pressing the stone button up top activated the Drentos spell built into the vessel's top rim. A stream of water flowed into the porcelain tub. Once the water had risen high enough, he pressed the heating button just next to the first one. With it the bath became a sublime temperature from the Flammorta enchantment.

Removing his clothes, Alden slid into the water and attempted to relax. His head oddly enough didn't feel groggy from the hangover he should be having. Still, while his muscles warmed in the water his mind remained cold and sober. *Maybe that wasn't just knockout juice. Last night still doesn't even feel real. Is he crazy, because he heard voices or is something real behind this? If I'm a failure, then is Amara a success? What does that even mean?*

Leaving the tub after soaking awhile, Alden grabbed the nearby turquoise towel and wrapped it around his waist. Walking out to a sea facing window he leaned on the room's corner pillar. Balmy morning air caressed his skin. Birds soared above the clay tile rooftops as the streets below were beginning to spring back to life. *Such an idyllic scene after a nightmare. I need to warn Turtan and Batara. After what happened last night they ought to know about it.*

Pushing himself off the wall, Alden closed the curtains as he gathered his clothes from the bathroom. Putting them on he felt ready to face whatever new dangers lay in wait. Alden grabbed his belongings and quickly made his way down to the main hall's landing.

Looking out he saw Roger, Batara, and Turtan all conversing by the bar. The wooden stairs squeaked in surprise when Alden's foot landed on the first step. Everyone looked up at the new arrival.

"Hey Uncle Alden. I was hoping I wouldn't have to carry you back down here too," Batara said.

"You know honestly I was really impressed you got two whole mugs down at all," Turtan said.

"You two we need to talk. My night didn't exactly end after Batara tucked me in. Turtan does the name Dreven mean anything to you?" Alden asked as he descended the staircase.

"Only as the name of someone I'd hoped to never hear of again," Turtan said.

"Last night he paid me a visit. He used magic to silence himself and a woman he brought with him. Ascendant bastard was smart too. Used Venendum to put a vacuum around the room's walls. No sound could get in or out so we wouldn't be interrupted."

"That must've been terrifying. Wish I could have been there to help. I would've tossed him out the window and let the fall do the rest," Batara said.

"What did he want?" Turtan asked.

"Dreven wanted to know everything about our journey. From when I picked up the book until now. Mentioned you too and how it was interesting that I met you in town. Then he asked to see my soulenket," Alden said.

"What in the salty seas for? Wait, did he know something about Amara's pearl?" Turtan asked.

He opened the locket up and held it close for them to see inside.

"It was almost like he couldn't help staring at it. While my pearl is only barely red, Amara's is practically scarlet. I think the ritual didn't just change me, but something else entirely has happened to my little girl. It's like I was only a conduit for the ritual's power. In any case that lunatic is out there and I have a feeling that he's going after Amara. He's already harmed my family once, I won't give him a second chance," Alden said.

"That settles it. We're coming with you and I won't take no for an answer," Turtan said.

'I can't ask you to do that. The road ahead is going to be dangerous and I can only imagine what Dreven's plotting."

"Exactly, we're involved already and I won't be caught flat-footed hoping peril will pass us by while my friend is in danger. All I know Alden is that he's extremely dangerous. Even Bojjer wouldn't mess about around him and you fought my captain yourself. If that old bicorn was scared of him, you ought to be too."

"Are you sure? I know Amara and Leonara will be delighted to meet you, but this could be dangerous."

"Uncle Alden if you're trying to scare us off it isn't working. Besides you brought my Dad back to me. It's only fitting that we'll give you the same chance you gave us," Batara said.

"Roger you have the inn while we're gone. If you could, get breakfast going while we go pack," Turtan said.

"Certainly Turtan, I'll try to not let the eggs get cool," Roger said.

"Hope your friend's ship has more than one cabin Turtan," Alden said.

"You better hope so too. I've grown used to sleeping comfortably and he hasn't met you yet. Shrimp come on let's get our things, I've always wanted to see Krohfast," Turtan said.

Batara gave Alden a hug before the father and daughter both ran towards the steps. Flying by Turtan with her endlessly long legs, the pair separated at the landing as Batara thundered down the hall to go upstairs while Turtan disappeared into his room. Smiling at the antics he'd just witnessed Alden found a chair by the fire.

I think those two have actually managed to make today seem a little brighter. I'm glad I won't be heading out alone. Dreven may have torn me away from my family, but it seems my friends are going to help bring us back together.

"Roger, need any help making breakfast? I'm not my wife, but I'm not entirely a stranger to kitchens," Alden said.

"Thank you, but a guest is still a guest. I promise your stomach shall not be left wanting. I am cooking for those two and frankly the pair of them can clean out an unprepared pantry in a single meal," Roger said.

"I don't think I've ever measured my meals in pantries, maybe that's just a unit for Wekken."

Alden looked around the room at the crackling fireplace, walls covered only in fishing trophies, and the barrel from last night. It was still planted on the table by the fireplace. Alden went over to it and noted the barrel had a few blue stains, but the table and floor were spotless. His hand bumped into the wooden vessel, but shockingly the container began to tumble towards the floor. Alden grabbed it in time to prevent it from falling over, but in doing so he picked it right off the table.

This was a full barrel when we started. I only had two mugs of this with them and they were able to drink the whole rest of the barrel trying to decide a winner. I don't think there's a drop left inside. They live by the sea, but I swear if the water was replaced with liquor they'd drink the oceans dry.

After some time, Roger emerged from the kitchen with breakfast. The bearded barkeep placed three meals on the counter. On the plates were minced piles of pork still giving off steam, scrambled eggs mixed with melted cheese, and some buttered biscuits. Accompanying each was a large glass of orange juice with ice cubes bobbing on the top.

Alden came over to the counter and was shocked. On the left was his plate which seemed perfectly reasonable and hearty. Turtan's had a few more eggs, but this meal was not the one that lay his mouth agape. On the right was a mountain of mixed eggs and pork accompanied by two buttered biscuits. If he had to describe its size and shape it was akin to a whole cooked chicken.

They really do measure in pantries. That is one big pile of eggs.

"This looks great Roger, thanks," Alden said.

"Happy to help. I'm afraid I won't be able to cook for you onboard the ship so I suggest you enjoy good food while you can," Roger said.

"I'll try to savor it, but I doubt I can resist digging in for long. Roger, is that really her normal breakfast?" Alden asked.

"You saw the bucket mug on her hip right?"

"I saw the bucket mug."

"Then I believe you have your answer. Pardon me, gotta clean up the kitchen. You would not believe what a mess all those eggs make," Roger said returning through the door behind the counter.

Alden picked up a fork and began to dig in. While not as impeccable as Turtan's eel the barkeep proved to be an excellent chef. The pork was succulent, but with a little crunch on its outside making it absolutely perfect. The eggs were fluffy and delightfully salted. Not more than a few minutes after he'd first struck the plate with his fork did Alden hear a loud set of footsteps getting closer from the second floor hall. Looking up he saw Batara on the landing making her way down the stairs. In a few short moments she'd plopped herself down beside him and began digging in too.

"Before I forget Batara I got these vocalamitters for you guys. Thought it might be good so we can stay in touch," he said handing her two of them.

"Whoa these are brand new! How did you manage to afford these?" she asked.

"Your Dad isn't the only one who found some treasure on that isle. Besides don't worry about the price just think of it as a thank you for everything. Honestly after last night they're going to be even more useful than I imagined."

Batara smiled and gave Alden a bear-hug that was on the verge of squeezing out bones. *She's so sweet, but I swear she forgets that she can throw people through walls sometimes.*

"Thank you, I still can't believe I'm going to get to meet the rest of your family. My Dad talked about it for so long that I didn't think it would ever happen," Batara said.

"You're welcome and I'm sure they'll be glad to meet you two. In fact, I haven't even told you all that much about my family since I've been here. Then again I'm not sure what it'll be like seeing them, it's been ten years. Who knows how much they've changed," Alden said.

"I'm sure they're still as wonderful as you remember. I mean time's gone by, but they're still your family. Bet your daughter is taller than your knee now too."

"I'm sure, but I don't know if she can get as big as you. I don't think she liked vegetables enough for that to happen. Still it's going to be weird seeing her after all this time. Amara may be a completely different person by now. It's terrifying to think my little girl is all grown up, but I'm excited too. I wonder if my dad jokes will still work on her?"

Both of them carried on conversing and by the time Turtan had come down the pair had cleaned their plates off entirely. He finished his eggs as well and within a few minutes the trio were all ready to leave. Each of them had a full leather pack filled with everything they'd need on their voyage. Alden pushed open the great wooden door of the Gentle Hurricane.

So much of my life has been about opening doors. Finding the book in the ruins, descending into the inferno that night, and now I'm walking through another to go home. I hope this time the door I arrive at is the one I've actually set out for. Not sure I could stand being swept off to somewhere else again.

Turtan and Batara followed behind him as they entered the busy Henaten city streets. A sea of Wekken, humans, Ascendant, a few Slolls, and even an odd Nisuri lumbered by. Turtan took point as the other two followed him down towards the harbor.

The morning air's soft caress while not as warm as yesterday's was still quite refreshing on Alden's face. Turtan guided them through the main street even though his path was quite clear. No bobbing or weaving was required by Alden to keep up, as Batara's massive frame carved a path through the crowd. This gave him a chance to admire the vines pouring from the flower boxes on each window and the songbirds serenading the passerby.

What a wonderful town. I'm sad to say goodbye to it, but we're needed elsewhere and I'll just have to enjoy the view while I can.

Within a few minutes they'd arrived in the harbor, but as Alden had learned yesterday that didn't mean the destination was nearby. The ship they would be leaving on would be docked in the merchant's section which was on the entirely opposite side of where they were. Since the morning was still young the docks were swimming with people. Fishing ships were bringing in their catch just as the merchants were importing their cargo. It was a frenetic explosion of life and they had to wade through its thick crowds like a river.

I know the old pirate is a good navigator, but this is like fording an overflowing stream in the middle of a downpour. It'll take us hours to make it over to the other side. Realizing the same thing Alden had, Turtan turned back to Batara.

"Shrimp could you take the lead. I wouldn't like to keep our friend waiting. I have to convince him to take you two stowaways and it'd help if we aren't late. It's dock two hundred and seven," Turtan said.

"Sure thing Dad. Try to keep up Uncle Alden, I can only leave so long a wake," Batara said.

With that she moved her nine-foot-tall frame into the front and began to carve a path through. Her considerable hips were twice as wide as Alden himself. With them she gently nudged her way forward past crates, carts of fish, and the much smaller people pushing them. With Batara's help they'd crossed in no time at all and within only a half hour they'd arrived at the dock Turtan had mentioned.

Alden looked up at the vessel parked in front of him. It was a merchant cargo ship with four decks and the same amount of masts. The back of the ship dubbed it the "Pearl of the Otaton". Its hull was painted in stripes of blue and white with accents of dark wood ornamenting the entire vessel.

What a beautiful ship! I wonder if it's as pretty inside as it is outside? Wait are those Drentos engines on the back? How can they create enough magic to push such a ship large across an ocean? My rowboat is one thing, but this is something else entirely.

Working their way down to the deck they passed by the crew loading cargo from Henaten bound for Krohfast. A short haired man stood right in front of the gangplank. His dark blue tricorn complimented his captain's jacket and white undershirt. In an instant the sailor lit up once he noticed Turtan walking his way.

I think we've found our captain. Judging by that look they must be pretty chummy. What business does an ex-pirate inn owner have with a merchant captain I wonder?

"Turtan how are you my friend? I didn't know you were bringing along the whole family. Good to see you Batara," the friendly captain said.

Reaching down, Batara gave Venick a bear hug. "It's been too long Ven," she said.

"Could be better, but it's just good to see you Ven. This is Alden. I know it was supposed to be just him boarding today, but we had a ghost show up last night," Turtan said.

"Oh? What specter is haunting you three? Most apparitions would be scared off just by looking at you Turtan," Venick said.

"Dreven."

At the mere mention of the name, Venik's face turned pale. "That spooky bastard. I know enough about that one to understand. Guessing all of you would like a cabin then? It just so happens that I have three reserved for only my favorite friends."

"Thanks Ven, I knew I could count on you."

"Only, because it's a mutual quality my friend. We'll be shipping out of Henaten within the hour so let me acquaint you with your quarters."

Turning about, Venik boarded the gangplank and bid them to follow. The trio climbed onto the top deck. A spotless wooden expanse greeted them that was overshadowed by the massive sails reaching towards the sky. Venik didn't waste time and instead led the group down a set of stairs. A red carpeted hallway of painted white walls greeted them as the sun's light was replaced by Lumendo powered candles.

It's like a floating palace at sea. There are hallways running so far I can barely see their ends. My shoes are still dry and I could swear the air in here is perfumed. Is that orchid I smell?

Venik chose a path toward the ship's rear as Alden noticed Batara began to hunch quite badly. *The ceiling must be eight feet in here. For most people that would be a luxurious accommodation, but it must be like entering a child's room for Batara. Hope she's careful*

135

or otherwise there may be white paint streaks on that bald head of her's. After marching all the way down the hall they'd arrived at the back of the ship as Henaten's harbor spread out before them through crystal clear windows.

Smiling, Venick opened one of the painted wooden doors nearby. Inside was a lovely cabin with a fluffy white mattress, desk, and private restroom. "All yours. There are two more just like this one behind us down the hall," Venik said.

"Your ship is the pinnacle of comfort as always old friend," Turtan said.

"Old? Didn't you just celebrate your one-hundred-fifty-first birthday? Wekken may live up to three hundred, but you're still ancient to me."

"You can call me old once there's a two in front of that number Ven. I think we'll get set up down here and be upstairs soon. After we're away let's talk. Had quite the time with Alden since he came back to town."

"If your ghost's reputation is to be believed then it will be hard for you to surprise me. I'd recommend getting above deck before we cast off, it should be quite a sight. I'll see you three soon."

Turning back to the hallway, Venik's footsteps disappeared as the sounds of the harbor drowned them out. With the captain gone the trio found their respective rooms and put down their packs. "Turtan what did you do for Venik that made him so nice to you?" Alden asked.

"I consult for him. If he wants to know the safest routes in an ever shifting sea, he just asks an ex-pirate who may know a few not so retired pirates. For a fee of course," Turtan said.

"Well whatever you did, good work. These cabins are quite an improvement over my last voyage's accommodations."

"Bit dryer I imagine. If you two want, we can go up to the bow and watch them take off."

"I'll take any part of this ship where I can actually stand up," Batara said head tilted forty-five degrees as she'd wedged it against the ceiling.

Seeing her point, they walked back up to the main deck. As they all walked to the front the vessel shifted and started to move. Hanging out over the rails they saw the harbor begin to grow further away as they glided out over the tropical water. The ship turned to the right towards the Turtamaw's opening. On the port side Hemmarasp Isle towered in the distance. Alden's now red eyes stared at the jungle covered mountain.

One last reminder I suppose. All the monsters, ruins, and even Gray magic couldn't stop me. It's funny that it takes a mountain to put a man in perspective.

Turtan and Batara were both leaning over the side gazing off into the horizon. Alden decided to join them as he fit himself between them. *On my left a courageous ex-pirate who started off as my captor and turned into my friend. On the other side is a nine-foot-tall barmaid whose hugs still bruise my bones and is sweeter than a kitten. I'm right where I should be.* Alden stared off towards the horizon where his 'Nara and Amara waited for him.

Chapter 15: The Pair of Ladies

A week went by and with it so did Alden, Batara, and Turtan in their comfortable cabins across the Otaton. There were a few storms and large waves along the way, but the voyage itself was rather pleasant. *Can't believe today has finally arrived. I suppose it will feel like finally leaving the past and stepping into my future. Can't wait to see both of them. If I stuck my hand out and added a little Ventos would the ship arrive sooner? Funny, I've kept them waiting for a decade and I'm pondering how to shear seconds away. We're almost into port; I should get my things.*

Putting on his Gray outfit, Alden equipped his weapons before heaving the leather pack onto his back. Gulls sang their songs in the morning's background as ship horns blasted over them. He opened his door and set off for the deck above. Both Turtan's and Batara's rooms were already empty. Looking up above her door, Alden noticed a rather large spot of paint had been rubbed away. *It's a good thing we don't use paint in most of Krohfast or I fear her head would leave a streak across the whole city's ceilings.*

Alden passed through the white hallways and along the red carpet floors to the stairs. He flew up the steps as the vast city of Krohfast greeted his awestruck eyes. Vast smooth stone pillars rose before him in almost every direction. Each one was a building escaping the sea of fog that often enveloped the city's lower levels.

It seems even the clouds won't sit above Krohfast soon! No doubt the new buildings are the Veferothi's handiwork. I can't wait to hear the details from Cassara. Hey, I can just make out the historic district. It's funny how every other area of the city is more advanced, but that's one of the most expensive. No one from my family would have ever come from there now, we've got too much sense to pay for nostalgia. I much prefer the forest of stone in the sky. Telendum windows letting you see everything and all the walkways look like branches connecting each tree to the rest. Trains to take you wherever you want and a million people competing with you for a piece of it, it's good to be home.

Through the fog Alden's destination shined above everything, a fitting symbol for the seat of Heanerathi government. *One crown and three spikes; I always did think it was a funny shape for a building housing a republic. We'll take a carriage, go up one of the trunks, and then Cassara should be able to help me find them. Batara and Alden will be getting quite the tour today I think.*

Alden spied his favorite Wekken pair over by the ship's bow. Batara leaned against Turtan as his bald head poked into her shoulder. They're pointy ears picked up Alden coming over so they turned around to greet him.

"I know you said it was a big city, but I can't believe it. Everything seems so different and strange. I actually feel small here, I'm so excited to explore it," Batara said.

"Krohfast is truly one of a kind. In a lot of ways, it is a crossroads to all of Nisuroth. Most people are Heanerathi, but they certainly aren't the only ones who live here. Every country and their people meet here in this city," Alden said.

"Alden I heard there were trains that fly between the buildings? Is that really right?" Turtan asked.

"I'm excited about them too. There's enough walking to do in Krohfast just to get around the buildings. We'd only reach the tower by sunset if we tried to get there on foot alone from the harbor."

"Walking a city this big would be torture. Although I'm pretty sure your legs would tire out first and we'd have to carry ya," Turtan said.

"We'll see who Batara carries first my old friend. This isn't a drinking game anymore and that mountain still hasn't cured me of hiking."

With that last jab the ship began approaching the dock. Innumerable ships sat in the waters around them. Each hailing from a different corner of the world and many had sigils representing the different companies that controlled much of the city's business. Within a few minutes the Pearl of the Otaton had been moored and the gangplank was lowered. Before they could depart, Captain Venik made his way over to the trio.

"It's been my honor to carry you three this far. Good luck to you Alden I'm sure your reunion will be wonderful. As for you Batara, it was good to see you again girl. Keep your old man in line for me. Lastly see you around my friend, may the waves be ever kind," the Captain said with a smile.

"Likewise Ven. Also I'd recommend you return home avoiding the Tidarean Spear. I might've overheard some unkind folk would be waiting there. If you must pass by it then make sure the engines aren't exhausted by then. Hate to make you embarrass yourself with that saber," Turtan said.

"I shall, goodbye you three," Venik said.

As the captain took his leave of them, they descended down the plank onto the docks. Stacks of crates and cargo from around the world surrounded them. Following the wide stone harbor path that ran along the coastline they quickly found a train station. A single metal rail ran through the platform before snaking its way into the city and disappearing into the fog.

Ah, at last. It's time we started flying.

Alden was the one person who'd been raised in this city so he led the group up to the platform. Underneath a stone overhang extending from the center was a lady Sloll in a city worker outfit. Her shiny green skin and big black eyes contrasted with the blue cloth uniform she wore. About three feet off the ground was her matching colored cap with a carriage service logo emblazoned on the center.

"Hello miss would you happen to know if this train goes to Solarsong Tower?" Alden asked.

"Oh, uh hello. Yes, the carriage will find its way there about half way through the route. Should be only a ten-minute ride over right now. Would you be the one buying tickets for you three?" she asked motioning to Turtan and Batara.

"Yes, but I'm actually a Knight of the Eternal Abyss. I have some business at the tower."

"Oh ho. Well I'll just need to see your blade then Sir."

"Of course,"

Alden withdrew his sword and held the handle out for her to examine. The sigil on the handle of the blade depicted a gauntlet grabbing a scroll in a sea of darkness. Beside it was his full name.

Glad to see some things never change. I suppose swords have always been a currency, maybe just not such a peaceful one.

"That's it no mistaking it. Very well Sir Brickborn, please enjoy your ride and of course no charge for your friends either. Have a nice day," the lady said.

"Thank you and the same to you," Alden said.

"Brickborn? Didn't know you had a last name," Turtan asked

"Never really comes up much I guess. It's just a common name in Heanerath. Our family is descended from the laborers who first built the brick buildings in the city's historic district. Speaking of which I don't recall you ever mentioning yours?"

"Azorai, Wekken last names are inspired by different colors of the sea, in my case azure. First names are for sea life. Mine as you probably guessed is for a turtle and as you know Batara was named after a Batfish for how elegant their fins are."

"I like it, honestly I think your system makes more sense. Ours is just a patchwork of people thinking something sounded nice at some point."

As they pondered over their names and where they came from a train rocketed into the station. Smooth and metallic, the vehicle was almost otherworldly. The carriage was nearly flat on its bottom, but the walls pushed a bit out from the sides before a canopy of metal created a roof over the top. Four large magical windows lined its sides along with one large one at the front and back. The side windows acted as doors for them to enter and exit the carriage. On top, the iron rail fitted into the carriage roof in a slot which guided them along to whatever the destination would be.

The doors faded as a group of dock workers disembarked to head off to the harbor. After waiting for it to clear they entered the carriage as Batara bent her head a little to get inside. However, upon entering she realized the ceiling was a whole foot above her in the middle where handholds dangled from the ceiling. *Now there's a shock for her. She probably thought the Gentle Hurricane was the only place with a roof high enough for her.*

"I like this city already. It's one I can actually stand up in," Batara said.

"They have to build it to accommodate Nisuri and the average one of them is almost as big as you," Alden said.

"Well whatever the reason I think it's wonderful. What will we-" Batara asked as she was interrupted by the doors reforming.

Before the girl could think of her question the carriage began to build up speed. Each one of them began to tilt as they left the ground far below. Fog engulfed them as only the endless illuminated windows of the surrounding buildings penetrated the dense clouds.

I'd forgotten how unreal this all feels. It's like we've entered an impossibly large forest from some fevered dream. Should be popping out of the fog soon thankfully.

Batara leaned into the windows as she gazed all around at the amazing sights before them. Turtan and Alden had both seen big cities before so they tried to restrain themselves, but they both couldn't help staring right along with her. *Ten years and it's more incredible than ever. So much is entirely new even to me. I can't imagine how overwhelming it must be for the both of them.* Staring up Alden saw walkways connecting immense structures as every kind of person walked along them. Enormous windows illuminated the thinning fog like giant fireflies.

Inside the stone structures were stores selling Heanerathi high fashion while others sold exotic ornaments that had journeyed from the world's corners just to end up here. Restaurants with food that could compete with even Turtan's cooking flew past their windows. Inside people gazed back at them as the carriage rocketed through the fog.

Shame we can't see the city streets right now. It's like a manicured jungle mingling with the world's largest stone sculpture. We may be failures in Dreven's eyes, but who can deny the magnificence and achievement of all this?

"It's amazing Uncle Alden. Everything's so different from back home. I only had to worry about the streets in front of me, but now it seems there's a dozen more above and below. This carriage is wonderful too; we've covered miles in only minutes," Batara said.

"Hold the praise Batara, you still haven't seen Krohfast's peak. Like any other mountain, the summit is the most majestic. We're going to Solarsong Tower, the seat of Heanerath's republic and where we'll be meeting with an old friend of mine," Alden said.

"It gets better? No way! This city is just waiting to be explored."

"Who's the friend?" Turtan asked.

"Ambassador of the Veferoth Republic and Amara's unofficial Aunt, Cassara Ookborne," Alden said.

"Really? I didn't know you had friends in such high places."

"We go back all the way to my days at the Arcanum and she's been laughing at my mistakes ever since. Though I suppose I shouldn't be so harsh since she's helped fix several of them too."

With the exception of the occasional stop at each new station, their carriage was soaring through Krohfast's forest until the tower's leg appeared before them. A massive stone pillar larger than any of the others loomed far into the sky.

As immense as ever and to think it's only one of the three trunks. Shame the elevators don't have windows on the way up, but I suppose the plaza at the peak makes up for it. It's finally time to get some answers.

Alden, Batara, and Turtan disembarked from the carriage and stepped into the station at the trunk's base. In front of them was a grand trabeation as tall as two stories which led into the heart of Heanerathi government. The road between towers here was as wide as ten streets put together in Henaten. Mist hung in the air as jungle plants were draped over their heads and smooth sculpted stone showed the path inside.

Entering the massive gateway, the Wekken were stunned by the plaza inside while Alden had seen it a thousand times and still smiled anyway. A dozen magical elevators stood in the back of the grand hall whose ceiling rose several stories above them. Each one was a circular platform with a panel of glowing blue buttons which took the passengers up or down.

All of this was carved by magic. I can't fathom the time it would have taken to make it otherwise. Some people don't know how lucky they are to have such a magnificent structure in their backyard when I'd have to travel half the world to find it's equal.

Alden stepped on one in the middle as the two Wekken followed his lead. Pressing the button for the top floor caused the platform to start rising. A magical Telendum field engulfed the elevator like a translucent blue bubble. In only a few seconds they entered a smooth tube rising up through the building's trunk.

Ahh the gust coming through the floor is so nice. Makes my skin tingle even if it feels a bit like the building is dusting you off.

Ding.

The little noise told them their floor had arrived. As the bubble burst the trio walked into a massive stone hallway which had a desk with an ornamentally dressed guard behind it. *Veferothi Ambassadorial Guard, definitely the right floor. Always liked that golden armor of theirs even if it is a bit showy.*

"Hello my name is Sir Alden; I was hoping to see Ambassador Cassara. I'm a Knight of the Eternal Abyss and an old friend," he said.

"Your sword is the genuine article, no doubt about that. The ambassador is in her office on your left. It's the first door by the windows overlooking the plaza," the guard said.

Nodding, Alden and the others went around as the man opened the door up. Inside was a beautiful office with a garden fountain in the middle topped by a blooming set of purple flowers as large as serving trays. Ascendant embassy officials lined the other wall working at their desks. A door on the left led to an office which took up almost half the windows on this floor. Opening the ornate black door Alden saw an Ascendant lady behind a rather large stone desk. Unlike the other officials she wore a stunning white dress accented by red ribbons and golden adornments.

"Cassara? You're looking lovely as ever," Alden said.

"I'm already happily widowed thank y-" Cassara said pausing before she could finish.

Cassara stared at an Ascendant man in Gray clothing who'd just spoken with a voice she hadn't heard in a decade. *I should probably just say it outright. Wish I saw that puzzled expression on her face more often.*

"I don't suppose you'd know where I could find Amara and Leonara? I might be running a bit late."

"Alden! What happened to you? Where have you been? Why haven't you given this old lady a hug yet?"

Cassara flew over from her chair to hug him as Alden met her embrace. The old ambassador squeezed him as she buried her face in his shoulder. Cassara began to cry as she wouldn't let him go. *Her tongue may be sharper than a needle, but she always did have such a soft heart.*

"Oh come on. Don't tell me you've missed me that much. I was really looking forward to hearing your insults again," Alden said.

"You haven't changed a bit you cocky bastard, oh I've missed you. Who are these friends of yours?" Cassara asked.

"This is Turtan, a friend of mine and ex-pirate. We worked together to escape his treacherous captain and that's the only reason we're both still breathing. We didn't have the best start, but it's been a good road ever since."

"Nice to meet you, ambassador," Turtan said.

"Well Alden always knew how to make friends under the strangest circumstances. And my goodness who is this young willow?" Cassara asked.

"I'm Turtan's daughter, Batara. It's a pleasure to meet you ambassador. This place is simply incredible," she said.

"You haven't met the people yet I take it and please call me Cassara. Alden and I share a disdain for such titles. I can't believe how tall you are. Have they invented new kinds of shelves for you to be able to reach?" Cassara asked.

"Cassara there'll be time for that later. Do you know where Leonara and Amara are? I've been waiting ten years just to see them again," Alden asked.

"Yes of course, I was going to meet them out on the plaza for lunch. Oh this is going to be so wonderful, come on what are you three waiting around for?" she asked.

Ten years they've spent waiting and it's all going to end in mere moments. I find it almost impossible to believe! How have they changed after all this time? What will they say when they see me?

The four-hundred-year old lady dashed out the door before anyone knew what had happened. Taken aback, but only for a moment Alden followed Cassara's lead. The whole group followed suit as the lively old lady took them to the elevator. She went up to the console and punched in a floor as they all stepped on.

"You know Alden you couldn't have had better timing. I know she'll be different than you remember her, but something has changed recently. Any chance it's related to the new you?" Cassara asked.

"I was stuck in a Gray ritual for a decade so that would prob... what happened? Is she ok? Please tell me she's alright?" he asked.

"She's fine you worrywart. Your little conch-head's actually grown into quite a wonderful young lady herself over these last couple years. Leonara really did a good job, with my help of course."

"Did she take after me or her?"

"What?"

"Is Amara more of a mage or does she still like exploring and getting muddy like I remember? It feels like I'm getting to meet her for the first time."

"Just ask her yourself. I'm guessing you've had quite the adventure getting back here, I think you can handle one family reunion. Remember to breathe and just try to say something clever. Oh, here's our floor."

The magical door disappeared and the group stepped through. Cassara took the lead and everyone followed. Her office at the embassy looked down into the beautiful green bowl of stone before them. Here on the tower's peak was a magnificent plaza filled with merchants, politicians, and people of all professions. Its multiple tiers made it one of the most ornate and beautiful structures in the known world. Giant stone statues of every race in Nisuroth stood triumphant guarding the tower's centerpiece in the middle. A massive marble globe covered with beautiful carved scenes from Heanerath's history where the Republic's representatives met.

It's as beautiful as I remember, but I couldn't care less. Where is Leonara and Amara? I feel like I'm about to collapse into a pile on the floor.

Cassara took them towards a balcony near the northernmost edge of the tower. Standing there were two ladies. One of brown hair and one of chestnut. Alden's heart fluttered after all these years at the sight of them.

"Leonara, is it really you?" Alden asked.

Turning around the pair looked at the Ascendant wearing that strange coat and using a voice they'd thought lost forever. *It's no mistake that's her, the same wonderfully sculpted face, piercing green eyes, and all the imperfections that make her just the best thing in this world. That scar on her cheek that she simply can't stand and all those little spots on her face that I wouldn't trade for anything.*

"That voice, Alden?" Leonara asked.

"It's me 'Nara. Your scar still looks beautiful on you," Alden said.

Tears began to run down both their faces as a decade apart was brought to a close. Embracing, they hugged each other deeply and Leonara planted a kiss on his lips that she'd been waiting to deliver since they'd parted. She simply held him in her arms for some time as neither wished to let the other go. Resting her head on his shoulders their time apart had ended.

"Sorry I'm late, things got complicated," he said.

"Dad?" another voice asked.

Looking up, Alden saw another lady who'd been standing next to Leonara. Her shoulder length brown hair and eyes seemed so familiar. Her face while so very different was completely the same. Wearing a beautiful set of blue adventuring robes and leather armor she stared right into his soul, in his heart Alden knew that face anywhere.

"How have you been conch-head?" he asked.

Her eyes widened as she sprinted towards Alden. Leonara let go of him as she saw what was about to happen. Amara tackled him in a hug, pinning him to the floor. *I never want to let you go again conch-head. Look at you! You're so beautiful and I'm not going to miss anything else in your life.*

"I missed you Dad, so much," Amara said as she hugged him tightly on the plaza floor.

"You're so different and yet you haven't changed a bit. I love you conch-head. I'm never leaving you again like that. I don't think my back can take it," Alden said.

After a few moments they both found their feet and embraced again. "What happened to you Dad?" she asked.

"It's a long story. One I have plenty of time to tell you."

Chapter 16: A Sea of Lights

"Well I'm certainly not letting you out of this hug until you do," Amara said.

"I promise to tell you every detail, but I have some friends I'd like to introduce you to first," Alden said.

He motioned to Batara and Turtan. Her bright brown eyes grew wide upon seeing the pair, especially Batara. "The one on the left is Turtan. He's one of the pirates who attacked our village, but during our journey we saved each other's lives. This young mountain is Batara, his daughter," Alden said.

"I'm Amara. Thanks for getting my Dad back, I hope he wasn't too much trouble for you," she said.

"I wouldn't be here without your Dad. Any fire he jumps into I'm happy to pull him out of," Turtan said.

"Don't worry dear, all I had to do was carry him back upstairs after he lost the drinking contest," Batara said.

"Dad, you lost? How'd he do?" Amara asked.

"Uncle Alden went down after two mugs. I know that may not seem like much, but he did put up a good fight for being so tiny," Batara said.

"Two? No! What were you drinking? Oh, I can't wait to hear all of this."

"I'm not surprised, Wekken are legendary for their drinking. Still I'm curious who won?" Leonara said.

"She might be taller than a bookcase, but I've been a pirate way too long to lose to my little girl," Turtan said.

"I know we've all got ten years to catch up on, but perhaps this is a conversation we could have over lunch? I still don't know how many strings I'm going to have to pull to get two tables instead of the one I asked for," Cassara said.

Only she could have to pull strings for something as simple as lunch. No doubt she's found the best restaurant in Heanerath and that was before I came back.

Everyone agreed and decided that any story good enough to tell would be better with food. All six of them walked to a nearby elevator. Alden clasped hands with Leonara and Amara never seemed to stray more than a foot away. They talked on the way down, but even as he answered each question Alden couldn't help but feel like he was in a dream.

I'm really back. Leonara should be in her forties now, but it's like she hasn't aged a day. I remember Amara as a little girl and now she's all grown up. I wonder how many trees she can accidentally light on fire now? Still I can't help but think if the small amount of magic I got changed me this much then what has she turned into?

Arriving at a middle floor they stepped out from the tower onto a walkway. High winds rushed between the buildings as the lush streets below were revealed by the dissipating fog. Carriages flew silently above their heads with only geysers of clouds erupting to show where they'd popped out of only moments before.

"Krohfast is incredible. It's nothing like what we have in the southern seas. It's staggering to stand in the middle of it all," Turtan said.

"Veferothi cities are more advanced, but nothing is quite like Krohfast. I grew up here and even still it doesn't seem real sometimes," Alden said.

"Surely you're kidding? I'm used to a self-heating bath, but here every window is made of magic and we can travel by metal carriages through a sea of stone trees that touch the sky. What could top this?"

"Even small Veferothi cities are like this. Their capital reaches not just into the sky, but below the sea as well and it's been a decade since I've seen it. Who knows what wonders they've built in the meantime."

"We have a floating waterfall in the middle of Vanadan now Alden. It's especially pretty during sunsets," Cassara said.

"How can a waterfall float?" Turtan asked.

"We enchant a sphere to oppose gravitational forces and then place a Drentos source inside. Just like that a river starts to fall out of the sky."

"Incredible! I thought our fish stories were outlandish, but it seems Nisuroth is far stranger than I could have hoped to imagine."

Veferothi architecture always sounds like a lie until you see it with your own eyes. I've seen enough to believe Cassara when she starts boasting. I wonder if the Gray always talked the same way about theirs? Oh a floating waterfall how quaint we just built our newest city a mile under the Otaton.

Only a few steps ahead were two daughters who Alden noticed seemed to be finding a lot in common. He smiled at Amara's six-foot frame matched against Batara's much more massive one. Each enjoying each other's company as they both craned their necks to converse.

"So where did you grow up Batara? I hope it had high ceilings," Amara asked.

"My aunt raised me in Aetturrus until my Dad came back a decade ago and opened an inn in Henaten. There is one beam that does give me trouble on the stairs though," Batara said.

"Aww I'm sorry. Still it must have been interesting growing up with all those different people around. What job do you do at the inn?"

"It was great; I grew up to be the best drinker in the family short of my Dad. Mostly I work at the front desk if I'm not serving food or throwing people out."

"Wait you're the bouncer? That's so cool."

"Some people just don't know how to find the door without help. Although growing up I was a little too strong for my own good. You can still see the patches in the walls from when I got a bit too eager."

"That's amazing, I've mostly done training matches at the Arcanum with the occasional mission. Don't think I've ever thrown someone through a wall before though."

"It's easy to do when you're as big as me. I just pick whoever I'm fighting up while they keep wiggling and then I set them outside. They're a bit like cats really."

"Cats? Is it wrong that I really want to see that now?

"Not at all, my Dad says it's a lot of fun to watch. He's never been the most normal parent though. Most just tell you how your new dress looks pretty."

"Honestly I don't think either one of us have even remotely normal parents. Mine taught me how to electrocute people when I was ten and I guess it makes sense that I like to use spells so much since my Mom is a magess."

"That's awesome I never could figure out anything with magic. Usually I like to use an axe and shield when things get serious. I'm a much better basher than I am a dancer, these big feet always trip me up. What spells can you do?"

"Not as many as my Mom, but I can wrap up someone's legs by messing up their nerves, blind them with darkness, and blast them away with a gust."

"You'll have to show me sometime, I'm so jealous. Do you have a favorite one?"

"It'd have to be lightning. In a way it was how I always remembered Dad since he was gone. It was the last one he taught me before everything happened. Although I've had to be a little more careful with it lately."

"Careful?"

"Oh, it's nothing. I've just been having some trouble lately. I'm sure it'll pass. I've always been a little too proficient at magic for my own good."

Further back a long awaited couple held hands and smiled at the friendship emerging in front of them. They gave each other stares which communicated more than most people could manage in an entire conversation.

"Ten years alone… I'm so sorry 'Nara I just had to play the hero didn't I?" Alden asked.

"Wouldn't have married you if you were the kind of man who didn't. You did what you thought was right. If it makes you feel better everyone you helped rescue before you got caught survived," Leonara asked.

"Really? Hansen, his son, Roesia, and Melcher. They all made it?"

"Every last one, I made sure myself. In fact, Enten's daughter is a good friend of Amara's. You should see her clay sculpting spells, that girl's probably gonna end up making the updates to these buildings when she graduates. They're all living quite happily now and it's all thanks to you."

"It almost doesn't feel real you know? Just a few weeks ago we were sitting around the dinner table and I was teaching our ten-year-old how to burn down the forest. Then I look at my hands and reality sets back in."

"Well you do make a very handsome skeleton if you ask me. Besides things may not be the same, but we're all back together again. Who knows maybe you'll like things even better than you did before. Amara puts her own clothes away now and you should see the apartment we have. It looks out over the harbor and at night Krohfast looks like a sea of fireflies."

"That does sound lovely. Here enough of my rambling let's catch up with the others and have some lunch. I'm excited to see what Cassara thinks is reasonable."

"Oh you'll love it. You know how she likes to have only the best so we're going to the Fogtop Cafe. All of the Republic officials regularly stop there."

Passing across the bridge the group entered through a grand doorway. Inside the stone tower was a soaring hallway consisting of several high end shops and restaurants. Cassara immediately turned right into the nicest looking one. Fogtop Cafe was adorned with a white granite interior complimented by rose colored wood accents and illuminated by chandeliers of scintillating fire. Dancing oil statues from Gray ruins like the ones Alden had gotten his clothes from lined the room's walls. Once inside Cassara walked up to the manager and apologized for asking for two tables, but unsurprisingly a second one was shortly found.

All six of them sat around gazing out at the city. It's modern wondrous majesty perfectly complimented by the sound suppressing magic windows and the self-playing string instruments in the corner. *I have to hand it to her, this place is pretty incredible. I wonder who's cooking is better though? Turtan or the best restaurant Cassara could find?*

Everyone began talking, but first Alden was asked to explain his adventure. He was happy to oblige and recounted the incredible tale from start to stop. Every fight was explained with arm motions, all the creature's appearances detailed, and finally the events of the ritual were played out. Everyone but Turtan seemed shocked by the story as he was quite familiar with it already.

Did I really do all that? It sounds like an epic tale for why a constellation is named and it's just been my last few weeks.

After Alden had his fun with the story it was Leonara and Amara's turn. The ladies discussed what all had happened after the raid and what they'd been doing in the time since his disappearance. After escaping Mullentide, Cassara had helped them get an apartment as her family was somewhat enormously wealthy. Leonara had raised Amara to be a magess just like her which led to his daughter being accepted at the Arcanum. During this time Leonara had become a premier magical architect for projects around Krohfast. The new spells she wove and things she built helped improve the Republic along with their own fortunes.

I'll have to thank Cassara for helping them. I'm sure it must've been hard without me around. I still can't believe Amara's already in the Arcanum and she's nearly about to graduate. I'm so proud of 'Nara. I knew she was the best magess in the country.

By the end of everyone's tales the afternoon had become a distant memory. The sun was beginning to dip into the clouds and it was decided that they'd all have to meet up again soon. Cassara offered a diplomatic suite to Batara and Turtan while they were in Krohfast which was readily accepted. Liking their company so much she decided to show it to them personally. The old ambassador quite liked Turtan's stories and was simply delighted talking to Batara as she had taken a liking to the curious young lady.

The Brickborn family hugged everyone goodbye and decided to retire to their apartment overlooking the bay. Taking the train back towards the harbor, each building had turned a golden hue as the sunset reflected off their smooth stone sides. Alden sat in the back while Leonara rested her head on his shoulder as they both found peace in each other's company. Amara leaned forward with a smile from a nearby seat.

At their stop Alden smelled the harbor's salty air grace his nose as the doors opened. Leaving the carriage, everyone stepped onto the stone platform hundreds of feet above the ground. A blue Telendum wall surrounded the sides as Alden marveled at how high up they were.

This is where we live? I always used to look up at places like this and hoped we'd make it there someday. I'm so proud of her, even with me gone it looks like she did such a great job.

Leonara took the lead as Amara and Alden followed her inside. Like the other buildings in Krohfast the floors were made of a long hallway with rooms that branched off of it, but here instead of shops were apartments overlooking the city. In the center were two elevators with blue glowing consoles on either side. They stepped on one as Alden noticed Leonara chose the button at the very top. *We can afford the top floor? We really must have the best view in the city.* Wind fluttered around Alden's feet as the elevator rose all the way to the top.

A stunning stone cylindrical room surrounded them which opened up to the sky. The walls were covered in waterfalls that adhered to the stone as they descended to the floor. In front of them was an exquisite wooden door that looked oddly identical to the one back home in Mullentide. The wood was polished smooth, but now great patches were a dark charcoal black which clashed beautifully with the unburnt sections.

"Is that our old door?" Alden asked.

"What's left of it. Our house burned down and most of it was destroyed. We found the door and I had it restored. It seems silly, but I hoped that if we didn't change the door then maybe you'd walk back through it one day like it was just another adventure," Leonara said.

"That's awfully sweet of you. No matter how much we change, I'm glad some things about us never do."

"You didn't turn into a poet during your ship ride did you?"

"I thought being clever with words was more your talent."

"Only most of the time. Welcome home darling."

Leonara unlocked the door and as the charred wood swung away a wondrous home was revealed. The entire circular building's floor made up the immense apartment. A stone kitchen with magical appliances sat on the right with plenty of cabinets for cooking. In the middle was a selection of leather seats and a central table to gaze out over the city. On the left was a guest bedroom and on the right was the master. Alden spied a spell laboratory on the same side which he could tell was stocked with every kind of magical implement imaginable. A grand Telendum window stretched from the floor before arcing up onto the ceiling. Orange tinted clouds hung overhead and colored the apartment in a welcoming glow. In front was an expansive view of Tekau Bay. It's dark blue waters were framed by the endless lit windows of Krohfast.

It really is a sea of fireflies. Can't believe she thought I was the poet out of the two of us.

"It's incredible. I've been gone awhile and we weren't exactly living in a hovel ten years ago, but this is ridiculous," Alden said.

"I wasn't sitting on my hands for all that time. I passed my master magess trial and that meant all new projects opened up," Leonara said.

"It suits you, guess I should've known you two would manage even if I was gone."

"Even still, I'm glad you're back Dad," Amara said.

"Me too conch-head. Maybe we can have our own little adventure tomorrow together? I'm really excited to see what you can do."

"Really?"

"Really, but before we do that I need to catch up with your Mom. It's been a wonderful day, but I'm exhausted so I think we're gonna go to bed and we can start tomorrow morning alright?"

"Well it is getting kind of late. I've missed you so much Dad, goodnight."

Amara hugged Alden before she went toward her room on the apartment's other side. Both parents held each other's hand as they watched their young daughter close her door. Finally alone their eyes met. No words were spoken, but everything was said. Alden grabbed

Leonara tight and planted a kiss on her lips. *Cherries, I'm so glad they're still her favorite.*

"You are certainly worth the wait. Should I grab some wine so we can go into the bedroom or should I let Batara know to come by to pick you up off the furniture?" she asked. Leonara returned his affection as their time apart had only sweetened their reunion.

"I made it across the Otaton 'Nara, for you I can stumble far enough to make it to the bed."

Leonara's face lit up with a smirk as she went behind the counter to retrieve the wine. She held up a dark red bottle in one hand and two elegant glasses in another. They made their way to the bed covered in fine red fabrics surrounded by dark wooden end tables. Beautiful paintings from local artists adorned the walls along with even a few Gray relics. A large Telendum window showcased the harbor and the splendor of its spectacular nocturnal lightshow. Sitting down on the edge of the bed Leonara handed the glasses to Alden.

"Winus Uncorkum," she said. As her hand pulled the cork from the bottle, a wonderful aroma began to float through the air.

"Not sure I'm familiar with that spell," Alden said.

She's one of the most powerful magesses in the world, a master architect of spell craft, and a complete dork. What would I do without her?

"It's just a little bit of magic I came up with. The effect is subtle I know," she said.

She poured the sweet red solution into the intricate glasses one by one. Handing the first to him and keeping the second for herself, they clinked their cups together. Alden sat down beside Leonara and laid his head on her shoulders. A thousand lights painted the city below them and a million more stars had emerged to light the night.

"You know every day I thought about you and Amara. Every punch I took, all the traps I dodged, and don't even get me started on the monsters. You never once left my thoughts and now here I am beside you sipping wine, sharing terrible jokes. I just feel guilty I had to wait a few weeks and you had to go it alone all this time," Alden said.

"It wasn't all bad. Without you here Amara burned down far less of the countryside," Leonara said.

"Guess I'll just have to make up for lost time. I think I saw a shrub near the elevator she could start with."

"You'll need to think more ambitiously than that. Whatever happened in that ritual didn't just affect you."

"I hoped I'd borne the worst of it. After I got out of the spell to check the soulenket mine was tinged red, but her's was entirely scarlet."

"It's like she's become a Gray Alden. Her body has become almost immeasurably more magically conductive. Even with my staff I'm not half as good as her. It's like magic has no resistance to her body. If you were a six on the Drenik-Abathon scale I would be an eight without my staff, but with it I'm a twelve."

"So then what would Amara be now?"

"Like a thirty, I'd be proud of her if I weren't so damn concerned Alden. She's more magically conductive than even the most skilled Ascendant master by far. I just don't know what it all means and she's so scared that she might do something terrible on accident."

"She masks it really well, but I did pick up on her apprehension. Wait, Amara's training to be a knight too, right?"

"She's a K.I.T. and need only complete her trial, but what are you thinking?"

"I'll ask leadership and see if I can train Amara directly. Help control her powers and get some time to bond with my daughter. I could help her undergo the trial mission and that may help her get some confidence back."

"I know you have a lot of sway with them, but do you really think they'd allow that?"

"Definitely, after what's happened with Dreven I think it's the best choice. I'm afraid finding that book was only the beginning for us."

"I'd nearly forgotten about all that. When I delivered it to Cassara she tried to arrest him which stopped the experiments, but that monster was still able to escape. Ten years later and it feels like we're just starting this nightmare all over again."

"Well I'm not going anywhere so one way or another we're gonna make it out of this. I'll make sure Amara gets what she needs, I promise." Alden said as he planted a kiss on her lips.

"I missed you darling. Please never leave me again like that. Venendum."

One of the enchanted statues by the wall began to paint the room with a sound silencing coating. *She really does think of everything.*

"Never, now come on we still have the rest of this bottle to finish," Alden said.

They filled each other's cups and embraced, holding one another as close as they could. Their clothes were discarded onto the floor just like the wine glasses. Outside a sea of lights shimmered through their window as the city competed with the stars. She embraced him and there in the darkness their love burned brighter than any night it had ever existed.

Chapter 17: A Bad Combination

Only a hint of the morning's light had arrived before Alden opened his red eyes and looked down at the matching sheets. The sea of scarlet fabric twisted as he began to gently peel away the covers trying to not disturb Leonara. There was something about waking up next to her that was like a sunrise that would soon appear. It didn't matter how many times he saw it, but each time managed to be magical. The way her chestnut hair flowed over the pillows and those silky sheets was almost indescribable.

She's always thought her nose was too big, but I don't see the problem. Every imperfection is just part of what makes her perfect. I could lay here staring at her all day, but I need to see just how strong my little conch-head is. Maybe I should ask for a mission where nothing's flammable? No, that'd just make her feel awkward and also anything burns if you're stubborn enough anyway.

Giving her a kiss on the cheek, Alden effortlessly got out of the bed without disturbing it as he'd practiced so many times before. Sneaking over to the bathroom he turned on their shower and reveled in its warmth flowing down his shoulders. *I feel like my mind is melting from some deep frost. Everything's just better than it's ever been or at least that's what it feels like. I wonder how Amara slept?* After he'd finished, Alden got dressed and went off toward the kitchen. Cracking open the wooden door he saw Amara was already awake and waiting for him.

"Dad! How'd you sleep? It's really something seeing the morning from up here right?" Amara asked.

"It's incredible. I swear I got the best sleep I've had in ten years," Alden said.

"There's your bad jokes I remember. It must've been easy to find sleep when there wasn't anything to do for ten years except float through the void."

"It's the strangest thing, but it honestly felt like only a few seconds passed."

"Well we've got all today to catch up since I don't have anything at the Arcanum."

"Actually me and your Mom talked about it. She said that you might be a little shook up from whatever the ritual did to you. What if I could pull some strings and say we try and tackle your trial today?"

"Really? Can you even do that? I haven't known what to think after I changed. Imagine waking up one day and everything you do just became immeasurably more powerful. What if I hurt someone because I can't control myself?"

Agh, I want to say she should just uncontrollably point them at the bad guy, but that's not helpful right now. Might save that one for later.

"I can understand how intimidating that must be. That face you made nearly burning down the backyard is something I'll never forget."

"Oh, don't remind me. That hits a little too close to home after what happened."

"I'm here now and I'll help you make it through this, I promise."

"I was almost ready to graduate, but after my change I knew I needed some time. If I've got you around then I'm sure we'll be ok, but don't make too much fun of my swordplay Dad. Mom leaned on me a lot harder to learn magic more than clanging steel around."

"That's alright, I make fun of her sword fighting skills too. Let me just write her a note and we can get going."

Amara nodded and waited by the door while Alden picked up a quill and parchment from the table. The metallic rod was a self-filling ink pen that would never run out until the enchantment expired. He composed a message explaining where they were going and when they would be back. Signing it with *Love you darling* he returned the pen back to where he'd found it and placed the note on the table.

"Come on. Let's go see what Berik can cook up for us. I'm hoping for a monster hunt; nothing better to help unwind than that," Alden said.

"What kind of creature lives in Krohfast that's ferocious enough for it to count as a trial?" Amara asked.

"I could ask Cassara to spar with you."

"Dad!"

"Just joking, besides she's not just good at fighting with words. No, odds are good that someone shipped something in that they shouldn't pretty much every day. So the possibilities for creatures are only limited to the entire world."

"That really narrows it down, maybe they brought in a Harvest Head Worm Dad? We can still go sightseeing if you want."

"Amara for you, I'll fight even one of those today. If we find two, then I hope your Mom taught you about cardio."

Alden smiled as Amara smirked at his sarcasm. Opening the door, they stepped next to the Telendum shielded elevator and Amara pressed the button opening up their ride. With another tap on the other console they were away. *Our first family monster hunt, oh I need to be careful or I'm gonna cry. It's still so hard to believe it's really her, but I'm so proud of what she's accomplished.*

The platform descended down the stone tube as Lumendo powered lights marking every floor passed them by. Finally, their stop appeared in front of them and they entered the hall. Turning left they once again stepped up to the platform to ride back into the city center. Their metal carriage had not yet arrived and so Alden decided to slake his curiosity.

"Still haven't told me the details. Guessing all that new conductivity didn't come with a warning?" he asked.

"I'd woken up in the morning and decided to heat up my tea with a little Flammorta spell. Whoosh," she said. Amara pointed her finger at an imaginary cup. "Next thing I knew I'd lit the tea, the couch, and a rug on fire. Took me and Mom ages to scrub out the ashes even with spells," Amara said.

"If it makes you feel better I forgot that Ascendant have a higher conductivity. Tried to get myself breakfast and instead of cutting off a coconut I killed a palm tree, blasted the poor thing in half."

"Oh no I hope you said sorry at least. Just glad I didn't make it to the Arcanum before I found out. Probably wouldn't have gone well if I singed the instructor instead of my drink."

"Wouldn't worry about it honestly. I did worse than that and they made me a knight. They'd probably make you a representative for that performance."

"You can't be serious?"

"Amara I may tell a lot of jokes, but that wasn't one of them."

This is so great. She's finally at the age where I can stop lying about how many mistakes I made. Never claimed to be perfect, but I think she may realize me and 'Nara weren't without our own issues.

The carriage arrived and the pair stepped into the metal box. Amara found a set of seats near the front so they could see the city ride unobstructed by other passengers. Remembering that he'd not explained just what was worse she gave him a curious look.

"So what was worse than that? You're supposed to make me feel better and I think that story was working," Amara said.

"I'd been dating your Mom for a while and we were great together. I wasn't all that much of a mage, but I was a damn good swordsman. She was a magess who only comes around once in an age. Naturally my instructor paired me with her for a training exercise," Alden said.

"Doesn't seem so bad so far. You did something didn't you?"

"We were doing spell and counter spell exercises. I was supposed to use Flammorta and she was supposed to counter with Drentos to put out the flames. She was so pretty in her armor that I might've forgotten which spell I was supposed to use. So it's possible I used Ventos instead," he said. Alden winced at the memory.

What a wonderful screw up. I hope Ascendant can't blush, because if they can I'm about to turn into a beet.

"No! Dad you didn't!"

"Yep. The gust hit her at full force spraying that puddle everywhere. Laying there on the floor, soaking and sore she shot me a look like I was about to be decimated. Scary thought when you're dating a lady with your Mom's talent. Instead she just burst out laughing at how scarlet my face had turned."

"Haha that's really cute. I guess you two have always made a good couple. You know I always thought you'd come back someday.

Some people thought you were dead and Cassara had just made us a broken bit of jewelry."

"Guess that makes me a not so dead man then. I've never heard of a soulenket lying and if I know Cassara she probably got the best mage in all of Veferoth to make them. Still wish she'd included an instruction manual for what's happened to us."

Would that have even been possible? It seems like we're the first people to survive a Gray ritual in a couple thousand years. You turned into an Ascendant and I turned into a well, whatever I am now. We're both different, but what matters is we've got you back Dad," Amara said. She leaned her head on him as the carriage began to enter Krohfast's center.

"I missed you too conch-head. The world's gonna have to try a lot harder next time to get rid of me."

As the carriage glided along, Solarsong Tower began to loom over them. To pass the short time left they both decided to stare out the window. A sea of nearly a million people had been set into motion just like Alden and Amara had been. *Architect weavers, enchanters, and farmers. I guess everyone has to figure out some way to get to work in the morning.*

Within a few minutes they'd finally arrived as the harbor wasn't far from the city's ever-beating heart. Unlike yesterday, they were packed like a school of fish as thousands of people worked in the government offices here. *Let's try and slip through this crowd and find a way up to the plaza. Should be easy enough to cross over to headquarters from there.*

Finding their way to an elevator, the pair flew upwards as the floors passed by in a blur. *I know it's fast, but I swear we're stopping at every floor. Don't some of them work in the same department or does everyone get off at different departments?* Finally, at the last stop on the elevator's track they got off.

The plaza which yesterday had been relatively calm was now a seething sea of bureaucrats, politicians, and business people all competing for a voice. Behind them was Cassara's office in the Veferothi embassy which sat several floors above them. Far across the vast peak of the tower was their destination. *There's the third spike, I wonder how the Arcanum and headquarters have changed? Will I even recognize it?* They made good time crossing the plaza and arrived at the enormous spike of the tower's crown.

Entering through the magnificent stone doors they arrived at the main hall. Looming twenty feet above them was a magical mural sky that ebbed and flowed with enchanted blue colors. The floors here were made of smooth black stone and keeping a brisk pace they came to the Arcanum's checkpoint.

"Hello we're here to get Amara and myself working on her trial," Alden said.

"Do you have your identification, sir?" the guard asked. Alden anticipating the question had already unsheathed his sword for him to examine. "Sir... Alden Brickborn. Very well and who is the young lady again?" the guard asked.

"Amara Brickborn, my daughter and a knight in training. Was going to try and help with her trial."

"Oh you're quite a nice father, then best of luck young lady." The guard motioned for the next group in line.

Walking towards the elevator up into the Arcanum "Dad, if you're called Sir, why don't I ever hear you say it? I've never heard any of the other knights go by their normal name," Amara asked.

"Never liked titles. They always made me feel like some kind of snob who always points out how much better they are than everyone else. If you're any good at what you do, you'll have other people to say it for you," Alden said.

This platform was much less crowded than the one into the tower as only a select few could enter here. A much shorter ride up later they'd arrived at the main entrance. Inside were two sets of doors on either side of a massive stone hallway. One led to the Arcanum where K.I.T.s and mages were trained on the skills needed to serve their country. Amara first started walking towards these doors as habit stole her mind for a moment.

She really is nervous isn't she?

"Any other day you'd be right conch head. You get to start going through the other doors today," Alden said.

"Right. Just never gone this way I guess," Amara said.

"They're just another set of doors, you'll be fine. Besides, you've got me beside you, they're not going to beat you up. Whatever we're going to hunt will do that," Alden said. He put his arm around her shoulders as she gave him a nervous smile.

Before them were towering ornate glass doors which glistened in the morning sunlight. Alden held up his sword and suddenly they creaked open with an almost ancient groan. *Never gets old, I still remember my first time seeing that. Feels like a whole new world is opening up to you.* As the glass parted the headquarters of the Knights of the Eternal Abyss appeared before them. Its walls were lined with metal panels that gave off a ghostly blue mist. Each of them covered the cylindrically shaped entrance's walls and ceiling making the headquarters noticeably darker than anywhere else they'd been.

A circular desk with racks of magical vocalamitters was in the middle of the room. In its center was a pony tailed Ascendant lady. *Tyreen! Well some things never change, but man am I glad to see her. I don't have enough fingers to count how many times she's saved my butt out on missions. Couldn't have asked for a better person to start the introductions with.*

"Alden! Cassara let me know ahead of time that you were back. I was beginning to think I'd never see you again. Like the new look by the way, red suits you nicely. Oh and who is this darling you've brought along?" Tyreen asked. Her glowing ponytail bounced as she stood up to give him a hug.

Alden returned her embrace. "It's good to see you Tyreen. Last adventure was a bit much, but we'll have plenty of time for stories later. This is Amara, my daughter," Alden said.

"Oh you are definitely your father's daughter. That beautiful brown hair and eyes to match. Spitting image of what your old man used to look like. You're a K.I.T. at the Arcanum right? Think I've seen you walking to class," she asked.

"I am, only have the trial to go and Dad thought it'd be something fun to do together," Amara said.

"You would Alden, I've missed your enthusiasm for jumping into Nisuroth's muck. Well I'm looking forward to working with you darling. So what can I help you two with?" Tyreen asked.

166

"I don't suppose Berik is still muttering over his desk like he used to? Figured he'd know a good mission for Amara's trial," Alden said.

"Oh take the hall on your left and it's the third door on the right. That strapping young one's got a window view now."

"Young? Berik is almost going on sixty isn't he?"

"I'm four hundred and eleven darlings, you're all young to me. Besides my house has nearly stored up enough magic and we'll be able to get him the ritual in a year or so. I'd be a wreck without him so I'm so happy we'll always be together."

"Wait you two got married? Man I have missed a lot, that's wonderful Tyreen. I'm so happy for you two."

"Thanks, but you're about eight years late. Rituals always take so long to get arranged. Anyway I shouldn't keep you waiting, we'll have to catch up later."

"Sure, thanks again and have a good one."

With that they took their leave of Tyreen and started down the left hallway. *They're married? Ten years away and all this happens. Everything's different and somehow so much of it still feels the same. I'm almost glad that 'Nara hasn't changed a bit.*

Walking through the dark hallway they couldn't help but peek into the other rooms they passed. A few were armories containing only the best equipment the government could requisition, another was full of ingredients which when combined with spells could create advanced enchantments, and the final one before Berik's room contained a library of collected texts which knights used to prepare for missions. Finally, they came to a door opening up to an enormous balcony. The walls were lined with boards of parchment nailed all across them. Inside an old man in plate armor without a hair on his head was stooping over a desk brooding.

Looks like he finally shaved that awful clump of hair on his head off. Old man still takes as many notes as he used too though. Good thing we have a budget for parchment or I swear he might just go into the library and start ripping out pages for his scribbles.

"Damn fool! Lucky he didn't have his blood watering their gardens after that stunt," the old man shouted.

167

"Things still going as well as they usually do old man?" Alden asked.

"I know that voice, but I don't recognize your face. Who are you?"

"I'm hurt, don't tell me a decade away was all you needed to forget me. Tyreen guessed it first try and she's got you by a few centuries. Leonara is doing well by the way."

"Alden! What happened to you? It has to have been a decade since I've seen you last."

"Tried to save a village. Ended up in a magical ritual for a decade and had a few side effects."

"You always were the first one to find trouble. Guess I shouldn't complain too much; you did make it back after all. Who's our guest?"

"This is my daughter, Amara. Actually I'm here because of some of those effects. The ritual I got trapped in was a Gray design. Someone named Dreven Sunsullen was responsible for all of it, but long story short it turned me into an Ascendant and I think it affected my daughter even more than me."

"Dreven, he was exiled because of the book you found. Feels like ages since Cassara sent you out to Mullentide. Anyway, I'm no doctor and I doubt that's what you had in mind. Guessing you want to help her with the trial?"

"Actually yeah, she gained more magical power than I've ever seen and I thought we could do her trial to ease her into training to control it. Besides I don't think we're done with Dreven and we need to start preparing."

"Easy for her or for you? Also when you say new power what do you mean?"

"Her magical conductivity is apparently registering as a thirty now on the Drenik-Abathon Scale according to Leonara." Alden's face had a smile painted on it in anticipation of what would happen next. *Here comes the fun part.*

"Thirty! That's twice the highest number I've ever heard of. Amara do you know the spell Lumicendor?" Berik asked.

"I do, it's one of my favorites. Dad taught it to me after I beat him in a race," she said.

"Really? Now that's a story I wouldn't mind hearing another time. Would you mind showing me what a full blast looks like. Just shoot out the window, it'll be safe. Five fingers to a point so you can concentrate it, if you would be so kind."

"A-Alright, but step back a little. Don't want to make your hair stand up."

That's my daughter. I think I'm dying even more than Berik to see what she can do. What does thirty even look like? I've seen masters at work and it's hard to think she's more than twice as strong as they are.

The two men stood by the boards as Amara came up to the balcony. Hesitating for a moment and then taking a breath, she readied herself. With rising anticipation from her audience Amara thrust one hand forward in a cone shape.

"Lumicendor!" she shouted.

Suddenly, a lightning bolt thicker than a tree trunk erupted from her hand flying almost half a mile forward. Wordless, Alden and Berik stood dumbfounded as the smell of ozone created by the thunderous power filled their noses. *Did she really just do that? That was so cool! How do you even block something that strong? No wonder the conch-head's worried about controlling that.*

"Girl that was incredible! An Ascendant master couldn't hope of approaching that display. Did you really use all you've got?" he asked. *Course he's excited, old man likes to play grumpy, but he's just a big kid when the magic show starts.*

"Actually I held back. Last time I tried this on my own I caused the grass around me to light on fire since I couldn't control all the magic from arcing around my hand," Amara said.

"That settles it, we'll get one easy for her. Good luck keeping up Alden. Let me see, how about something local so we won't have to keep you away from Leonara. You two want to do an escaped creature hunt right?" he asked.

"That was what I had in mind actually," Alden said.

"Should've known. At first I thought it might be a bit tough for the girl, but with you there to keep her safe you should be alright. Ever heard of a Tadammer?" he asked.

"Amphibious tadpole looking thing with an armored head and claws? Jaws that fly out of their mouths to spear you before dragging your corpse back into their teeth? Can't wait to hear how one ended up in Krohfast."

"Arigar ship came in a week ago. Some jackass thought he'd sell it to some criminals as a guard dog. Naturally it had other plans and broke out of its crate. Creature went into the storm drains and now I'm worried it could end up getting people hurt. Those things are known for being hungry and not very picky eaters. A bad combination for a crowded city full of people."

"Scary monster to hunt down and a maze of twisting tunnels to explore. I'm game, Amara?"

"Seems an almost perfect trial. I don't want anyone getting hurt and if we're in the storm drains I doubt I can injure someone with my magic," she said.

"Just remember I'm in there too conch-head. It's settled then Berik."

"Can't wait to hear about this one after you're done. Speak to the contact on the document. Good luck you two and Amara if you succeed consider your days as a K.I.T. over," Berik said. He tore a piece of paper from the wall and handed it to her.

"Almost can't believe it. Well then what are we waiting for let's go, thanks Berik!" she said.

Alden nodded to his old friend as he joined his daughter and left for the elevator. *She really is my daughter, not too many girls her age would want to jump into a sewer just to fight a monster. I almost feel bad for the Tadammer.*

Chapter 18: A Once Very Red Room

An hour after their meeting with Berik, the pair found themselves in Krohfast's harbor with a very irritable Sloll. His smooth blue skin was mottled with black dots which complimented his dark apple sized eyes that were glaring at them. *He's got a lot of bandages and they're not just for show. Some of them have turned burgundy with how much blood they've staunched. Why couldn't the Tadammer have just finished eating him?*

"I said it was an accident. It only ate three pigs. That lunatic was lying about the fourth. Just trying to take me money by lying!" the Sloll shouted.

"Actually I asked you where you last saw this thing," Alden said.

"Oh right, after my creature got out of its cage I thought I'd never hear of it again. On the off chance I was wrong, I left a lure to hopefully bring it back. Last night the trap I placed near that grate over there actually bleedin'' worked. Big hunk of pig meat on the bear trap was gone after I came back in the morning."

"You left a bear trap out on the open street? You could have cost someone a foot or killed a pet!" Amara yelled.

Easy Amara, I'm thinking the same thing, but we need some clues on where it went. Let's hope we can get something useful soon. I'm getting tired of his yammering.

"Do you know how much blood I lost getting that damn thing here. If I hadn't been as careful as I was I would have been a snack girl. Who cares if someone's dog goes missing," the Sloll said.

"You're lucky I don't knock you into the bay for that comment. Come on Dad. We have what we need," Amara said.

She stormed past the bloodied pig cages and stopped at the storm drain entrance. Alden could see her right fist was clenched.

"We do?" Alden asked.

"The creature was here within a day and in one week hasn't left the area. That suggests it's chosen the storm drains around here as its

---

new territory. The trail of pork blood should be easy enough to find and that should take us right to the Tadammer," Amara said.

The attacks only happening in this area paired with the recent sighting mean she's right about this being its new territory. Blood trails can be difficult to follow, but it should still be fresh and there's no weather underground to erode it. Concise, decisive, and more importantly correct. That's my little conch-head.

"Guess the Arcanum didn't just teach you spells. Good thinking, but remember that even with all that magic we're both basically made of pork if we mess up. Don't forget to communicate and be ready for anything, let's go."

The thick stone walls of the harbor framed the giant slate gray pipe before them. A steady trickle of water flowed along its belly into the harbor. An earthy stench emanated from within as they both could see smatterings of red pork blood lining the pipe on the areas out of the water's reach. Branches, leaves, and soil had drained onto the floor from recent weather.

Moist, maybe even slimy. As far as creature lairs go it's almost cozy. Problem is that means we'll have no room to move if it attacks us. I'm gonna have to be careful with her. We're not collecting seashells anymore. Can't think of a better time than this. She'll need every advantage and this just may be it.

"Amara before we get any further in I have something I want you to have," Alden said.

"What Dad? A good luck charm? Some secret monster killing oil?" she asked.

"Close, but forget the oil. I found a Gray blade in some ruins. If what Dreven said was true about you, then maybe... well let's see."

Alden unsheathed the white stone blade and handed her the sword. *Moment of truth, is she just another failure like me?* Amara grabbed the handle and the blade's carved lines began to glow red. Alden quickly relinquished his grip as scarlet magic engulfed the sword and her hand.

What's it doing to her? Looks like a Telendum field, but something is different about it. It's like the sword has created a gauntlet around her hand that runs to the blade.

172

"Amara are you ok?" Alden asked.

"Yeah I think I'm fine. What does this thing do Dad?" Amara asked.

"I don't know. No one does, it's a Gray sword. The last person who could still activate it died thousands of years ago. Maybe hit the walls with it?"

"I mean it is a sword, but are you sure that's a good idea?"

"No, but I think you're covered in some variant of Telendum. Question is what does this variation do? The Gray could use any spell imaginable so I doubt it's some magic to obliterate something. It's probably to enhance the wielder's fighting capabilities against someone who could even get close enough for them to need a sword."

Amara nodded and then looked at the wall. Lightly she tapped the glossy red sword against the stone.

Dink.

At first they both just stared at the practically inert weapon, but then Amara tried to pull it away. Her blade wouldn't budge as she tried yanking harder, but still it wouldn't move even a little. Alden cracked a smile at his daughter whose arm was now glued to the pipe wall.

Is it stuck? What use is a sword that doesn't cut anything, but can grab something else? Wait that's it! Gray didn't need weapons to cut through someone when their magic would dispatch almost anyone. This blade is meant to grapple the opponent and leave them open to an attack! Still if it can be stuck there must be a release word.

"Amara try Relendo," Alden said.

"Relendo," Amara said.

As she tugged the blade suddenly lost its grip and released from the rock. Amara smiled and gave Alden a hug. *Well not sure what I expected, but that isn't it. Still it should prove to be an excellent tool for her. Doubt anyone will expect a sword that can steal your blade right out of your hand.*

"It's perfect! As long as I can connect with someone then I should be able to get them off balance and then blast them. I can't wait to see someone's face when they go up against this. What should I call it though?" Amara asked.

"Hmm, well if you use Telendum again the field should dissipate, but then it's just a sword. How about the grapple sword? It'll let you disarm opponents or pull them off balance so you can hit them with spells," Alden said.

"I like it, if nothing else it's a unique name. Thanks Dad."

"You're welcome, try not to rely on it too much for this mission though. You'll still need strength for it to work and there's no chance you'll be able to yank a Tadammer around, but you should start practicing with it. A weapon like that will be hard to counter and that's even if someone knows what it does. Come on we should keep moving, the Tadammer isn't going to just wait around for us," Alden said.

Light began to fade as they ventured further underground. An all too familiar musty smell had begun to chase away all others as Alden kept his eyes trained on the darkness ahead. After about a hundred feet they came to a bifurcation with their route splitting off into two different paths.

"Alright since this is your trial, how about you tell me which way he went, while I make some torches for us. No reason we need to stumble around in the dark," Alden said. He started looking through the sticks on the ground for something suitable.

"Can't really make out the blood trail it's all been washed away and I can't smell anything other than this stench," Amara said.

"That is quite the quandary."

"The smell is too faint, but the blood should still be here. I've got it!"

"Lumendo. Oh? Well how do you track something you can't see or smell?" Alden lit both torches in his hands. The tips began to glow a bright green color like a pair of oversized fireflies.

"The blood can still be seen, but only if it's in the right light. Would you mind giving me one?" Amara motioned for him to hand her a torch.

Nodding, Alden gave it to her before she starting whispering the idea just soft enough that he couldn't hear. Looking down at a few flecks of red blood illuminated by the green torch she placed her hand on the now glowing tip.

"Lumendo Vuhema!" she shouted changing the light into a soft brilliant blue which penetrated the darkness of the storm drain. The glow from her spell illuminated both paths forward for several dozen feet.

"I Didn't think you'd make it as powerful as the sun." Alden said as he shielded his eyes from the blindingly bright torch.

"Agh sorry, didn't mean to. Still getting used to this," she said draining some magic from the torch by putting her hand to it. "That's better, damn it I still can't quite control all of this. How do you do it?" Amara asked.

"If you want to get better control then try to start small then use more and more of your focus. Most people have a hard time expending enough, but well that's not really your problem. Although your little sun has blinded us it has actually shown us where to go, look."

At their feet were bright blue blood splotches that continued further down the pipe. A trail which with any luck would lead to their creature. Suddenly a chattering sucking sound could be faintly heard from the left. Then scraping noises pierced their ears as something scurried deeper into the maze.

Chit. Chit. Chit.

"Well if there was ever a here be monsters noise that would be it. Time to work," Alden said.

"Guessing that wasn't the pigs," Amara said.

"Relax, I'm right here with you. Before we go any further I want you to do something. Try casting Telendum on your chest and arms. You just might be able to maintain it with all that conductivity of yours."

"Telendum," she said. Amara applied the coating to her chest and upper arms as an almost imperceptible magic sheen hovered above her armor.

"That ought to protect you from its mouth. I'd do it too, but if I try to maintain it I'll weaken my spells too much. Remember to always use every advantage you have. It's the only way you get to go home when you fight things like this. You alright conch-head?"

"A bit spooked, but I'm better now. We shouldn't delay any longer."

Only natural, monsters are something that should scare you. If they don't you're either crazy or stupid. Guess I shouldn't be surprised that it'll take more than a few noises to unsettle her.

Nodding his head, Alden charged first into the darkness with his daughter just behind. Their torches worked together in combination as her's highlighted the blood trail and his let them see everything else clearly. A rank odor emerged from the darkness assaulting their nostrils with its pungent scent that overpowered everything else. From the inky black ahead of them a large shape was revealed by the torchlight. Laying on the ground motionless, it was a pig or rather what remained of one.

Its body had been shredded as if something large had been gnawing on it like a dog does to a bone. A large two pronged wound could be seen on its neck over a foot across between its edges. *Lacerations are deep, must've severed the spinal cord with its tongue. Damn this one must be huge.*

"Seems we've interrupted someone's afternoon lunch," Alden said.

"Kind of a messy eater isn't it," Amara said.

With a smile at her jest he bent down to the crimson pile of pork. *Definitely one of the pigs that Sloll mentioned. Ugh, forgot the skin secretions. Ugly thing rubs itself on its kills which means the only thing that would want to eat it is the Tadammer.* Turning over the pig's stomach Alden noticed something troubling.

"Dammit. Well it couldn't be easy could it?" he said.

"What's the matter?" Amara asked.

"It's an adult. Was hoping for a juvenile, because once they grow up the Tadammer reproduces asexually. Meaning that every time it eats something it lays eggs in the body. See?"

Alden shifted the pig's underbelly up for her to see. Inside the wound were glowing green olives with black dots inside them. Clustered inside the crimson canyon there had to be dozens in just this one pig. Undoubtedly the hunt had just become more complicated.

"How long does one of those things take to hatch?" Amara asked.

"Two weeks give or take. We really can't fail now or we'll have a plague of them in Krohfast and Tadammer's aren't picky about what or who they eat, come on."

I know this is her trial, but why do the stakes have to be so high. I'm really glad I came along now. We'll burn the body later, but I just hope I'm not too late. It's only been one week so we should still have time.

Alden continued down the tunnel quicker than ever. Staring at the walls he saw the great thick gashes made from the creature's claws they'd heard only a minute ago. His eyes followed them as they ascended up the sides and onto the ceiling into the darkness. Following the blood, they went through seven intersections as layers of caked blood began to appear.

These stains are getting older. Nest has to be nearby.

Chit. Chit. Chit.

The noises had returned, but they were now coming from a junction up ahead. Daylight filtered down into the chamber illuminating a collection of meat, sinew, and bone sprawled across the floor. Red lichens carpeted the cold stone walls and floor making the room seem a vibrant scarlet in comparison to the rest of the stone maze they'd explored.

No wonder the smell is so strong here; the floor is covered with carcasses. Need to be careful or we're going to be added to this disgusting pantry. I should go first and clear the room. Who knows where this thing is hiding?

Alden stepped through the threshold first followed shortly by Amara. He saw three grates above them which led to the surface, each just large enough to hold the beast if it was determined to evade detection. Water dripped onto his face as Alden scanned the room.

"Drop the torch Amara, it's here somewhere and you'll need both hands for this," Alden said.

Each of them dropped their torches as the blue and green lights echoed off the stone creating a scintillating color palette inside the junction. They began circling with their weapons raised. Both had their sword in their right hand and an open left palm ready for firing off spells. A minute passed as they waited, but only the continuous drip of water from the grates above could be heard. Each drop of water splashed to the ground forming small puddles around their feet.

Enough of this torture. If it won't make the first move, then I will. Let's see it sit around after this.

"Flammorta!" Alden shouted.

He pointed his palm at one of the pig corpses. Meat began to blacken as his flames lit one corner of the room ablaze. Small olive green eggs inside began popping as the pig turned to charcoal. A bone chilling screech emerged from another pile behind him.

Scraaa!

"Roll away Amara!" Alden shouted.

The Tadammer burst out from its cover underneath the corpse. Amara rolled towards the entrance as Alden dodged towards another tunnel. Just in time they both avoided the creature as it careened through the center. Unable to stop, all eight slimy feet of the Tadammer crashed into the wall just next to the burning pig. The stone crumbled from the creature's hard as steel head. As it turned around to continue its onslaught they finally got a good look at the beast.

The Tadammer looked like a tadpole balancing on two massive claws with talons as large as steak knives. Its body was a slimy green color mottled by great black patches meant to hide it in a marsh. The tail was thicker than a man's leg and the tip was shaped like a paddle. Thick tan bone covered its massive head which framed four beady yellow eyes on top. Razor sharp teeth were tucked behind a crooked plate smile, but just behind those weapons was a tongue which could skewer plate armor.

"That head is too hard for spells and sword strikes. Try for the limbs Amara!" Alden shouted.

The creature turned toward him as its legs began to bend for the next attack. *Gonna need to distract it so Amara can damage the back. Hope you like Ascendant you big ugly beast.* Before he had a chance to play bait though Amara made her move.

"Lumicendor!" she yelled.

A bolt of blue lightning whizzed towards the creature, but the slimy monster was faster and jumped onto the wall next to Alden. Making that same haunting sound it's jaws suddenly opened as it tried to spear him with its tongue. Alden moved to the right and brought his sword slicing down.

Clang.

The bone was too thick and Alden's blade merely bounced off the creature's spear-like appendage. Clawing at him, the Tadammer began striking from the wall as he rolled away to give himself some room. Jumping onto the floor, the Tadammer's vicious assault continued pushing Alden back to the other side of the junction. It's spear-like tongue thrust forward once more creating the opportunity he needed. Alden stabbed his blade into a slot of muscle between the tongue's bones as the wound began to bleed profusely.

Now's our chance. Come on conch-head.

"Hit its back now Amara!" Alden shouted.

Running to the creature's rear she yelled "Flammorta!"

A massive jet of flame engulfed the creature's back as it shrieked in pain. With a shrill cry the Tadammer spun around quicker than any creature that size ought to be able too. Alden couldn't hold onto his sword as it was knocked away while the creature's head slammed Amara into a wall.

"Dammit don't you dare hurt her!" he yelled.

The beast flung itself towards Amara, trying to skewer her. Alden sprinted, but he didn't have the time and she couldn't dodge out of the way. The Tadammer's tongue thrust right into her chest as Alden screamed. Covering the distance between himself and the creature, he swung his hands towards its head.

"Take this you bastard! Ventos!" Alden yelled.

He pounded his fists into the ugly beast's eyes as a vicious wind crushed the creature's skull. A geyser of amber blood shot forth as two yellow eyes exploded from Alden's hurricane-like blows. With the right side of its face cracked like an egg the Tadammer's legs buckled trying to retreat. However, unlike before it was too slow as another pair of hands reached up to its face.

"Ventos!" Amara shouted.

Her hands slammed into what was left of the Tadammer's head. Alden's ears popped as her attack's unbelievable strength soared through the creature's bone and brains alike. His blow had cracked its face, but Amara's shattered it. Brutal winds from her hands disintegrated the monster as they entered its mouth and flew out through its innards. Its body exploded into amber ribbons as a once very red room was painted yellow by the Tadammer.

"Amara thank the source you're alive. Are you hurt?" Alden asked. He embraced her as they both were covered in slimy monster guts.

"I'm fine Dad. Good call on the Telendum armor," she said. Amara pointed to the magic which had stopped her being skewered.

"I'm so proud of you, but don't scare me like that. Guess you one upped me," Alden refused to let her go as they were both coated in goo and laughing.

"Dad?"

"Yes, my little conch head?"

"Thanks for giving me the chance to hit it like that. Don't know if I could've completed my trial without you."

"Oh don't worry you would've found a way without me. Besides they don't take off points if you get covered in monster ooze to do it. Now come on we need to burn these eggs and go wash off. Your Mom won't forgive us if we drag this gunk into the house."

We did it, my little girl's gonna be a knight. Never gonna admit how scared I was, but I'm so proud of her.

Alden found his feet and pulled Amara up to observe their handiwork. Not wanting to linger any longer, the pair of monster mustard covered adventurers burned the room with fire spells and then trekked back through the pipes making sure to eliminate any remaining eggs. Once they were back at the docks the Sloll from earlier asked what had happened.

"Well don't think you'll be able to sell that one. Might be able to make a nice jam out of what's left though," Alden said.

"You killed it! How dare you bleedin' knights. That creature cost me a bag of Kolos to get here and you just smear it on your blades like it's nothing. I demand recompense!" he shouted.

"First you're lucky I don't arrest you for endangering the public with that beast, secondly the eggs it was laying could have caused an epidemic of them, and third if you ever speak to me that

180

way again I'll toss your ass into the Tekau so you can swim back to Arigar!" Alden shouted.

The pair walked away down the dock to clean themselves off with a shower as the blue Sloll just stood there, mouth pursed shut. With some help from a harbor hose they were now no longer covered in guts and began to dry in the afternoon breeze.

Trial completed, the father-daughter pair found their way to the nearest train station and took it into Krohfast's center. Arriving at Solarsong Tower they made their way back up to headquarters after about a half hour. Holding his sword up to the door, Alden heard the familiar creaking noise as the massive glass gateway parted to open up. After all the walking they'd dried off considerably and saw Tyreen manning the desk as usual.

"Hello you two, guess the monster hunt was a success, huh? I know that smile anywhere," Tyreen said.

"Yep, turns out I've got a knight for a daughter. She's just passed her trial and covered us both in monster mustard," he said grinning to match Amara.

"Oh that's wonderful, congratulations Amara! Welcome to the Order or rather Berik will do all the formalities I imagine. Either way I'll let you get to him, but I must hear the details you two. Promise me that."

"Course, I doubt I'll be able to stop talking about it," Alden said.

Waving goodbye to Tyreen as she answered another call they kept walking towards Berik's office. The old soldier was by the balcony staring off into the distance as he turned around to face them as they came in.

"Do we have a new knight, Alden?" he asked.

"Yep, she puts my magic to shame and proved to be quite resourceful. I recommend she becomes inducted," Alden said.

"Very well. With the knight's approval, Amara please place your blade on the table. You won't be needing it anymore. Then come over here and kneel before me," Berik said drawing his sword.

Amara did as she was bid and got down on one knee before the old soldier. Sword raised, Berik placed it on her right shoulder and began the pledge.

"Do you Amara Brickborn swear to pledge your own life for the betterment of Heanerath and all her people?" he asked.

"I do," she said.

Bringing his sword over to her left shoulder he recited the second line "Do you swear to uphold the honor of this order and protect the innocent of this world?"

"I do."

"Then stand Lady Amara Brickborn, Knight of the Eternal Abyss, and protector of Heanerath."

The old soldier walked over to a table where a sword much the same as Alden's sat next to its holster. It's only difference was no name was inscribed on the hilt. Picking up the sword Berik returned to Amara and handed the blade to her.

"Inscripa Amara Brickborn," Berik said. The moment he spoke the words a blue light appeared carving her name into the hilt. "Congratulations Amara. Welcome to the Order," the old soldier said.

"Thank you Berik. I hope I can only live up to my father's legacy," she said.

"Don't, exceed it young lady. Make us proud."

Amara grabbed the holster from the table and sheathed her knight sword for the very first time. Looking back to Alden she saw only the face of a proud father and her eyes began to water. His little girl walked over to him and buried herself in his arms.

I'm sorry for all the years I wasn't there Amara, but it seems like you did just fine without me. I will always be here for you my little conch-head. I'm more proud of you than I can ever hope to explain. Sorry I can't help the tears.

Chapter 19: Steel and Spells

Sunlight filtered onto Alden's face as the night's cold embrace was replaced by the humidity of an overcast morning. He planted a kiss on Leonara's cheek before getting dressed and going into the kitchen. *Still can't believe Amara's not a little girl anymore. My little conch-head's killing monsters, but she's not ready for Dreven. A Tadammer is a far cry from that madman. I should head over to headquarters and see if I can find anything out about him. Wonder if Turtan might be able to help?*

Alden walked over to Amara's door and knocked. "Conch-head you awake?" he asked.

"Yep Dad, what's up?" Amara asked.

"I'm heading over to the tower. Wanna see if I can learn anything more about all of this. I wish we had answers, but it just seems like we'll have to make it up as we go for now."

"That's the problem with doing something that's never been done before Dad. Still, I wouldn't mind knowing a bit more about what's happening to us. I feel like so much has changed. What if we never get to be normal again?"

"It's scary, but at least to me it feels like things may have changed for the better. I'm back, you're already a knight, and whatever the future brings you'll be prepared. Besides we never were a very normal family. I explore ruins for a living, before you could light anything on fire you had an ambassador for an aunt, and your mother invents spells. It's ok to be different and maybe this will just be our new normal. You know what may help? You should go spend the day with Batara, explore the city, and you two can trade secrets about your dads."

"Maybe you're right she did seem so excited to see everything. Alright, I'll give her a call and we can talk later tonight. Thanks for understanding Dad."

"Me and your Mom will always be here for you Amara. You don't have to go through this alone. Anyway, I'm sure you'll both have a great time, love you conch-head."

Amara closed her door so Alden went to the kitchen to make himself breakfast. Eating a bit of toast along with an apple was plenty to start the day. He stepped out the front door towards the elevator. Alden pressed the button on the console awaiting the gust of wind from below announcing its arrival.

Normal? What even is normal anymore? If there is such a thing I doubt there's a universal definition. Either way I need to buy her enough time to find it.

Looking up Alden saw the sky was darkening as only clouds remained. Thunder echoed off in the distance, but he wasn't worried as every building was designed to withstand any lightning. Still the sound was jarring and jogged him from his pleasant morning. Alden opened up his vocalamitter and pressed the symbol assigned to Turtan's device. The stone inscriptions lit up as he could see the connection had been accepted.

"Hey Turtan how are you?" Alden asked.

"Fine, still hard to believe this suite Cassara gave us is real. I didn't know people could live in such luxury and I thought we had it good in Henaten," Turtan said.

"You should see her normal place. From what Cassara told Leonara the one she gave you was too plain for her if you can believe it."

"Too plain? If I was still a pirate and stole everything off these walls, I'd be set for one maybe even three lifetimes."

"Yeah well if there's anything I've learned with Cassara is that there's always something nicer. Anyway, I know you're enjoying the apartment, but would you be interested in taking a daytrip. I wanted to head over to headquarters and see what they have on Dreven. Odds are neither one of us is done with him."

"Hate to say it, but I think you're right. No way is he just going to let us walk away. Also Batara said that her and Amara are going to have a girl's day out."

"I suggested it to Amara, thought those two would get along well and it would give Batara a chance to see Krohfast."

"She won't stop telling me how excited she is about it. Wanna meet there at the front desk of headquarters?" he asked.

"Sounds like a plan, see you there," Alden said.

The soulenket's light faded as the call ended. Only a few moments later the elevator arrived bringing a light gust up with it. Alden walked onto the deserted platform, punched in the floor for the train, and began his descent. Wind rushing up through a vent in the floor kept Alden cool as the elevator's humming sound was deafened by approaching thunder. Arriving at the floor he stepped, towards the station and quickly found his way onto the carriage off into Krohfast's center. After a short half hour ride, Alden was staring at the Arcanum tower's lobby where Turtan was standing next to the line for the checkpoint.

Queue the joke about how he couldn't get in. Everyone groans at our humor, but at least us dads can see each other coming from further away than that thunder.

"Glad you could make it Alden. I would've gone on ahead, but somehow I didn't think our friendship would be enough to convince the guard," Turtan said.

"Wouldn't do much good if he let you up anyway. You need the sword just to open the upstairs door unless you felt like taking classes. I could get you a monocle and you'd be right at home," Alden said.

"Not the worst thing I've ever been suggested to wear. Someone once said I should wear an eyepatch."

Alden couldn't help smirking as he presented his sword to the guard. The man barely glanced at the blade before they were allowed to pass and take the elevator up to the entrance hall. Stepping off the platform Alden raised his blade as the doors yielded to them. As always Tyreen sat at her desk fielding paperwork and calls.

"Good morning Alden, I see you brought a friend," she said.

"This is Turtan, he helped me escape the pirate raid after they betrayed him," Alden said.

"Nice to meet you," Turtan said.

"The pleasure's mine. Not often I meet an ex-pirate with so much knowledge of the underworld. I'd be hard pressed to count the number of merchants you've saved with your tip-offs. We owe you quite a thank you even if your help was indirect," Tyreen said.

"Glad to hear I'm actually of some use. I just keep these long ears of mine open and sometimes they hear interesting things. Feels nice to help out honest folks instead of how I got my start."

"Tyreen, I was actually hoping to go over the archive. We're looking for any information the Order has on a man named Dreven Sunsullen," Alden said.

As soon as the words left his mouth her face began to curdle. *Guess I'm not the only one who's got a bone to pick with him. I've never seen Tyreen get sour over anyone. Could there really be something worse than what we already know?*

"I know you've been gone a long time, but Alden you need to understand that's no ordinary name. Come on," Tyreen said.

The wiry Ascendant lady left her desk and started marching down the hallway on the right. Both of them followed trying to keep up with her brisk pace. No one said anything until they'd arrived at the archive at the end of the hall. Surrounding them was the sixteen story library inside the tower which contained the accumulated knowledge of every knight who'd ever served Heanerath. Each shelf was ten feet tall and filled with well-maintained tomes of every shape, size, and color. A menagerie of knowledge, secrets, and stories lived in this room.

The library was a gigantic circle shaped chamber with an elevator in its center. It led to the fifteen separate floors of knowledge above them weaved together by a web of walkways. An enormous Telendum window made up the side of the tower which bathed the books in lightning light every few seconds.

There are no words for it, but I suppose breathtaking will have to do. Centuries of knowledge are in here and our blood has built every piece of it. A wonder worthy of the whole world, no doubt about it.

Tyreen beckoned them to the elevator. "Dreven Sunsullen is perhaps the single most dangerous person in Nisuroth. Your ambassador friend, Cassara, is the person who stole his lordship away after she'd uncovered his atrocities. I remember that book you found was instrumental in sealing his banishment," she said.

"Glad to hear it, but I know you're not one to exaggerate. What's happened since I've been gone?" Alden asked.

"He got wind of what was about to happen and ran. Ever since then he has never stopped his work."

The elevator arrived at the fourth floor where she walked over to a bookcase. Tyreen scanned past several books containing investigation files before she found what she was looking for.

"Here's the bastard. People like him make me feel ashamed to be an Ascendant," she said.

"I saw that book, if a high lord tried to replicate those experiments then I can understand how it would make you feel," he said.

"It's not just that Alden. Back when my people were first created the ritual wasn't the same as it is now. People had to be sacrificed for the ritual to be powered. We discovered quite early that it wasn't necessary, but the new ritual wasn't as strong. So people like him decided to keep killing just to improve their own abilities. He committed atrocities just to explore new magic."

"Dreven seemed to believe everything that happened was an unfortunate necessity. It was strange. I've met people who've done terrible things, but none were so sure they were right. He asked me what loyalty, friendship, and dedication matters in the face of oblivion. If everyone dies if you fail can that really justify any action?"

"His thing between spaces has taken centuries and still hasn't killed any of us. The only people who die are the ones unfortunate enough to run into his madness. Dreven is just another traitor like his father to what it means to be Ascendant. He's a chapter of our history most of us would rather forget and I'm happy to give you the chance to put a period on his life's story. Good luck you two," Tyreen said. With that she set off back to the elevator.

Ancient history doesn't mean much if the pain is real. I had no idea this was so personal to her. Four hundred years ago is ancient to us, but to Tyreen that was just another day in her life. One book started all of this maybe another will help us end it.

"I've got a bad feeling about this," Turtan said.

"Yeah, I know what you mean," Alden said.

With that, the pair found separate places in the library to read over the information and hopefully find something of use. He tucked himself into a nice desk on the bottom level while Turtan situated himself on a bench staring out over Krohfast.

It's been two hours and I'm beginning to feel like Turtan can see the future. Dreven has experimented on hundreds of people and no one's survived except for me. Guess the pirate raid really was something special. He took most people by drugging them in passing on the street. A simple scratch as they walked by from a poisoned needle and your life was over. His resources must be vast for him to keep experimenting after escaping Veferoth and being on the run for so many years.

I was a failure, because I was just another Ascendant. If that's true, then Amara must be the success he's been killing all these people to find. Oh why did I think this was a good idea? Dammit do it for her. If I don't figure out his plan, then we won't be able to stop him. If Amara isn't the goal, then there must be something only she can use to stop the thing between spaces.

All of this only brings up a deeper question. How can Dreven have learned all of this? Archaeologists have studied those ruins for centuries and somehow he was able to not only discover this doom, but also create the ritual which can save all life from it? There's no way he could discover this all on his own. There's no Gray's left to ask about any of this. The Graybuilt won't say and they're the only ones who were even around back then. Could he really have squeezed answers from those talking piles of rock?

Scanning further into the file, Alden found an interesting section speculating on Dreven's true motives. *The Last Well? Is this what Dreven's really after? Of course there's no description of it, but it must be a place only Amara can enter. Question is how could a well stop an unstoppable cosmic monstrosity?*

Brrt. Brrt. Brrt.

Looking down at the table, Alden's vocalamitter began to buzz as someone was trying to reach him. *Batara's symbol? Why is she calling me? Shouldn't her and Amara be out exploring Krohfast. I didn't expect to hear from them until later tonight.* Alden answered the call.

"Hello Batara, how's your girl's day out going?" he asked.

"Hey Uncle Alden, not so great. Amara's not feeling too well. Some hooded jerk carrying crates scratched her arm. Ripped right through her dress sleeve and didn't even stop to apologize," Batara said.

Alden's stomach fell into a bottomless pit as he recalled the passage he'd just read. *A simple scratch was all it took. It can't be a mistake, what do I do?* Alden's eyes grew wide as the terrifying truth dawned on him.

"Batara where are you now?" he asked.

"Going up the elevator to your apartment. Amara said it'd be best if we just went back to her place so she could lie down," she said.

"Okay Batara listen carefully. Me and your Dad are coming straight there. When you get inside I want you to bar the door with anything you can find. The couches, boxes, whatever you can get against that door. Do you understand me?"

"Wait why, you don't think that was Dreven do you?"

"I don't know, but I've got a bad feeling that he's coming after you. Can't explain everything right now, but barricade yourself to buy time, alright?"

"I'll keep Amara safe Uncle Alden. Please hurry."

Batara ended the call as Alden shouted up towards his friend "Turtan get down here; the girls are in trouble!" Running to the elevator, Alden practically punched the console to make it head for the top floor.

"What happened?" Turtan asked.

"Dreven poisoned Amara, I read his tactics in the file there's no mistaking it. The bastard waited for us to separate. She's the key to everything he's planning somehow, I'll explain on the way."

With Turtan onboard the elevator they descended to the entrance. Their feet slapped against the floor as the both of them ran towards the headquarters' entrance. *We can't waste any time. If I use the emergency codes on the carriage, we'll be there in ten minutes. Oh conch-head please be ok, Dad's coming for you.*

189

Alden squeezed through the door's gap and onto the elevator as Turtan followed behind shortly. In less than a minute they touched down in the lobby, but every second felt like an age. *We'll run through the plaza and down the embassy elevator. Should be the fastest route.*

"Knight business clear the way!" Alden shouted as they passed through the checkpoint bypassing security. There was no time to debate, only the dwindling seconds to save their daughters. Buckets of rain crashed upon their heads as the only sound Alden seemed to hear was his heartbeat.

Thump. Thump. Thump.

The plaza was nearly empty as everyone was trying to avoid the rain. They sprinted across it through the downpour until finally piling into an open elevator. Alden inputted his override code and with a few extra passengers staring at them with bewilderment they began to fly towards the ground.

"Apologies everyone, but this is an emergency. We'll be stopping just before the bottom," he said.

Leaving behind the shocked stares, they stopped at the station's level and emerged onto the carriage platform. A train had just arrived and its passengers were disembarking. *A lucky break, finally. We need every second and that just saved us minutes. Hang in there a little longer Batara we'll be there soon.*

"Move! Official Knights of the Abyss business, clear the platform!" Turtan shouted.

I'd say that's my line, but I think he might get them moving a bit quicker.

Responding to the seven and a half foot tall Wekken's command, everyone practically fled from the carriage. Alden punched in a sequence similar to the one for the elevator which would rocket them straight to the apartment. *He looks worried. I bet we both do. Let's just hope we're not too late Turtan.*

The magical doors sealed shut and with the extra sequence entered by Alden the carriage began rocketing forward at a blistering pace. A terrible howling wind began to shriek from outside the carriage as they picked up speed. *I know they say these things are able to take this, but that noise never does get any more reassuring.*

"Is this safe Alden? I want to get there same as you, but we won't be much help if the carriage ends up as a crater on the ground," Turtan said.

"I know it may not feel like it, but they're designed to operate at these kinds of speeds. Most people never see them as their too violent for passengers. It's rough, but I'm not going to give Dreven a second more than I can," Alden said.

"Just make sure I see that birthday with a two in front of the number Alden." Turtan placed his hand on his shoulder.

"Thanks and I know, our stop is coming up. Get ready."

With that final warning, the carriage decelerated into the train station throwing both of them to the floor. Turtan helped pick Alden up as they both sprinted to the elevator. *Alright I'll punch in the code and we're there.* A few moments later the elevator arrived, but there was still one passenger on board. A live Lumenator grenade was placed in the center with a fuse that was nearly spent.

"Look away Turtan!" Alden shouted.

They both fell to the ground to hide their eyes as a deafening explosion rocked the hallway. Luckily they'd both avoided being blinded and jumped onto the elevator up. *Dammit we didn't get here first. I know Batara's strong, but she won't be able to hold out against Dreven. Still if they left the grenade they're probably still here. Maybe we aren't too late.*

"That was a cheap move, but I can't really blame them. They know what we're about to do to them," Turtan said.

"They went after our daughters. That's all the reason I need," Alden said.

Both their heads peaked up over the floor as the platform arrived. Four masked men stared back through the torrent of rain from the storm. Behind them was the apartment door that had been blown to splinters and the door frame was covered in charred ash. Three humans and a Wekken even bigger than Turtan on the right side stood in front of it.

All of them had similar masks, but their weapons couldn't have been more different. Two had crossbows, the Wekken held a monstrous war hammer, and one just left of center had both palms raised for spells. Alden knew just how to take them apart and together with Turtan their combined attack started. The two with bows fired at them first just as the window dissipated.

"Telendum!" Alden shouted.

Opening his palm, an invisible kinetic wall of magic shielded them as the pair of arrows embedded themselves into the barrier. Alden released the spell and the projectiles dropped harmlessly onto the floor. Turtan charged towards the archers, saber raised while Alden decided to take on the war hammer wielding Wekken.

Sure, let me take the big guy Turtan. You get disarmed archers and I get to fight this bookcase. Well no point complaining now. A few good hits and a dodge should do the trick. Just need to watch for spells at this range.

The man swung the warhammer horizontally hoping to crack his ribs. Instead Alden slid under it and stabbed his sword between the separation of plates at the hip. Shouting from the pain the cyclops was still able to hold the hammer and managed to pound his clawed fist into Alden's face. The blow was crushingly powerful as it knocked him onto his back. A giant boot was planted on Alden's chest as the Wekken swung his warhammer toward his head. Instincts honed by a decade of fighting, Alden brought his own two fingers up to meet him.

Sorry big guy, but I hit a lot harder than I look.

"Lumicendor!" Alden shouted.

Lightning erupted from his hand as the two foes were about to collide. Flesh vaporized as the Wekken's hand swung into Alden's spell. Holding his now cauterized stump, the man began to scream as the mage saw his opening.

Dammit, that's not good.

"Flammorta!" the mage yelled. His closed fist pointed toward Alden's head. Unable to move out from under the Wekken's boot, he instead pointed his left hand out along the floor.

Sorry to disappoint you two, but I have a daughter to save.

"Ventos!" Alden shouted.

A gust of wind sprang from his hand, flinging him out from under the heavy boot. The fireball meant for Alden was now hurtling towards the Wekken who'd fallen to the floor. Striking his upper torso, the man burst into flames as his body became a pile of cinders. Alden found his feet and began to run towards the mage. He saw the terror freezing the man in place as he raised his left hand and rushed for the enemy's shoulder.

"Telendum," the man said.

A magical shield enveloped his left shoulder which would stop the spell, but not Alden's sword coming from below. Steel entered just below the ribs as the man's blood painted the stone floor. Grunting with pain, the mage fell to the ground dead as Alden removed his blade.

Immediately upon hitting the ground he burst into flames. *What the? An immolation spell? These are definitely Dreven's men. Wait what tattoo is that?* Alden looked over to see Turtan had just disemboweled his last archer. All that remained of them was a pile of ashes at their feet.

Any investigating would have to wait as they both sprinted over the blackened fragments of the door. A dozen more thugs lay inside with one intimidating man standing distinct from them all, Dreven. His armored black cloak and mask were contrasted by his striking scarlet eyes staring right back at them.

The whole apartment had been torn to shreds as most of the furniture and cabinets were lying broken on the floor. In the corner next to the window was a wounded Batara still guarding an unconscious Amara. Shield and axe in hand she was clearly on her last legs, but in doing so she had protected the pair of them up to this point.

She did it! You held out Batara, thank you. Let us take it from here.

"Batara, we're here shrimp! You're not alone!" Turtan yelled.

"Ah, Alden and Turtan. I was hoping this would be somewhat cleaner, but I guess it can't be avoided. For what it's worth as a father I know how this must feel you two. You have my sympathies, Turtan," he said.

Dreven slammed his fist into Batara's stomach yelling "Nere Vendum!"

Her eye turned white as it rolled back into her head. Nervous system disabled, Batara collapsed onto the floor with a terrible thud. Dreven kicked away her axe and turned to the remaining thugs.

"Take the human girl. Make for the elevator and I'll deal with these two. They're beyond your skill so stay back," Dreven said.

"You'll pay for that you bastard, how dare you harm my little girl!" Turtan shouted.

"I just saved her life Turtan. You really should be proud of your daughter's delaying skills, but she was nothing more than simply in the way."

They both realized their opponent's goal and decided to defend the door rather than take his bait. *Can't let Amara through the door. If they leave I may never see her again. He stole a decade from my family I won't let him take a moment more.*

One of the thugs picked up Amara from the floor and tossed her over his shoulder. The rest formed a semi-circle around the pair as Dreven advanced forward. Drawing an elegant blade from its sheath, he walked calmly towards them. An undeniable cold emitted from him as if there was no passion in his actions, only a certainty of they're result.

"There is no other way Alden. I will not let this world die and if some innocent may suffer for its survival, then so be it," Dreven said.

"A sacrifice everyone, but yourself bears. You're just a deluded villain who hears voices in his head that aren't there," Alden said.

"No, I'm the hero this world needs. My only recognition for my deeds will be scorn, but in the end I will have saved every life that exists and those that haven't even been born. I don't expect you to see any of that though. All you see is a masked man stealing your daughter."

"Words are wasted on someone like you. The only thing left to say is with our steel and spells."

"Indeed. I am sorry it must be this way."

Dreven sprinted towards them as they lowered their swords to meet him. Turtan swung his sword down towards the madman's head and Alden went for the ribs on the right side. Seamlessly the hooded swordsman swung his blade to match the knight's blow while yelling "Telendum!" to create a blocking field on his left hand for the ex-pirate.

Two on one and I'm getting the feeling that may not be enough for this guy. His magic is better than mine and he might not be Bojjer, but that swordsmanship is better than either of ours. I have to find an opening before we end up as just more broken things on the floor.

Everyone released as a dance of blades began. On his own Dreven could outmatch either one of them, but combined they were fast enough to keep him on the defensive. A series of strikes flew between them as they pushed him towards the kitchen counter.

"Ventos!" Dreven shouted.

Erupting from his open palm was a massive gust tossing Turtan into some cabinets. *Gonna have to put up a shield. I won't have time to use counter-spells while blocking him.* Alden yelled "Telendum!" coating his own left hand with a magical shield.

Hoped I wouldn't need this, but he may be one of the strongest mages I've ever seen. My conductivity is far better than when I was human, but Dreven seems to be as good as a master.

Alden gave ground which the madman used to shout "Flammorta!"

The open palm unleashed an enormous raging fire towards him. Directing all his magic into the left hand, Alden's shield grew to endure the flames assault. *Can't see anything through the fire. Where is he?* Dreven rushed forward with his shoulder and decked Alden. The hit stole his breath away as the villain kicked the side of his right knee buckling the leg. Alden looked up as he saw the masked man bringing his terrible blade down toward him. Lunging forward through the pain, he tackled Dreven by the torso knocking him to the ground.

That was close. You're not unbeatable you monster.

Both Ascendant regained their feet as Alden saw Turtan had stumbled out of the cracked pile of cabinets. *Back to two on one. If we strike together maybe that'll create the opening we need.* Alden lunged forward as Turtan followed him, but something was off. Dreven backed up dodging both of their sword blows. The villain raised his palms together just as both of them were lined up in front of each other.

He set a trap and we fell right into it. Brace!

"Ventos!" Dreven shouted.

Skeletal red Ascendant hands burrowed into Turtan's coat before blasting him. Alden felt his skull begin to warp from the pressure wave. *Dammit this hurts.* Both of them were thrown into a wall as the stone they hit cracked like an egg shell.

"Now! You won't get another chance!" Dreven shouted.

The thugs who had been holding back bolted for the door with the masked Ascendant leading them. Alden's ears, eyes, and body felt like they were on fire. Through fading faculties, he watched as Amara was carried through the doorway. *Get up, they're taking her.* He staggered to his feet and stumbled forward. Turning the corner, Alden saw Dreven's masked face staring back at him. They were on the elevator and the magic fields began to appear.

He reached out with his right hand trying to reach Amara. Sight fading to black, Alden collapsed onto the wet stone floor. The elevator descended and with it so did his daughter, they'd failed.

Chapter 20: His Heroic Heart

The darkness began to ebb as Alden came to. Cold seeped into his face as his blood dripped onto the stone floor. Raindrops danced around Alden's legs as they slowly pushed him to stand. Air gushed into his lungs with every choking breath.

"Turtan? Batara? Are either of you there?" Alden asked.

"Uncle Alden, is that you?" Batara asked.

"Yes it's me. Are you alright?"

Alden walked back inside and saw Batara was slowly getting to her feet. Rushing over he put his shoulder under her as a massive paw hugged his chest. Together they kept rising until Batara could hunch over on her own. *Damn Dreven, she's covered in cuts. It's amazing the poor girl's still conscious let alone able to stand on her own. I hope Turtan's in better shape, but where is the old pirate anyway?*

Lying in a cracked crater on the floor, Turtan was still passed out. Dreven's blow had left a raw red crater in his torso where the spell had impacted. *Magic save me what a wound. Bastard must have missed by a few inches. If the spell had actually directly hit Turtan I fear I'd be staring at two halves of him.* Running over to his friend Alden shook the old Wekken awake.

"Dreven really knocked me on my ass with that blast. Ugh, Alden where's Amara?" Turtan asked.

"They got her, she's gone," Alden said.

Grunting through the pain Turtan got himself up. "Only for the moment my friend. We can't just give in. Maybe there's a way to track them down? Did you notice anything on them that was distinct? Mine just burnt up when they died and ashes are next to useless."

"I do remember the mage had a tattoo on his right forearm. Looked like some kind of symbol."

"What did it look like? Might be something we can use."

"A winged axe. Just one and it was all black. Seemed odd looking, but I've never seen the design before."

"Waxxers! I should've known."

"Guessing this isn't the first time you've had a run in with them?"

"I try not to be too familiar with those swill unless I have too, they're a criminal group here in Krohfast. A lot of merchants like to use them to increase their profits. Either by avoiding taxes or helping relieve the competition of their inventory. They're motto is swift as an axe and just as deadly."

"A little on the nose, but I can see why Dreven would use them. Do you know how we could track them down?"

"Actually yes, I told you I do consulting for merchants. I have a contact in their group so I can warn my clients before they're attacked. I'll have him arrange a meeting at their headquarters. This kind of thing is out of their wheelhouse; wonder if these guys were double dealing their boss? Anyway let's get everyone here so we can get a plan together."

"Agreed. I'll make the call and in the meantime there's a medicine cabinet in the laboratory for you two. Get patched up, neither of us is losing our daughter today."

"Come on shrimp you got pretty beat up there. Really proud of you for holding them off," Turtan told Batara.

"That guy just cheated with nerve magic. They managed to get a few cuts in, but you're the one with a crater in your chest," she said. Wrapping her arm around him they started walking to the laboratory.

"Nonsense, look at you. You're the spitting image of a cutting board."

"Least I don't have a hole in my gut."

"You can smirk now, but this is gonna be a really cool scar after this. You're just gonna have a big bruise that fades away. Agh that hurts!" Turtan winced from the pain.

"Don't faint or I'll have to carry you like Alden and you aren't quite so light Dad."

What would I do without those two. They're on the verge of fainting from pain and the only thing escaping their lips are jokes.

Alden pulled out his vocalamitter and stared at the stone. Sighing, he dialed Leonara and explained the situation. Her voice began to falter for a moment before asking if they had any idea how to find Amara. He said that Turtan had a contact who should be able to lead them to wherever she was being held. In an instant, hope returned to her voice and she said they would find their daughter. Alden told her to come over to the apartment so that they could get ready.

After getting off the call he let Cassara know what happened as well. Without even asking, the ambassador told him that she'd come over immediately and would bring a medic. Alden ended the conversation and sat down on the couch to wait.

I can't even think right now, it took me a decade to find her and just like that she's slipped away again. After all this I don't care if the damn Republic wants us to leave for a mission. I'm taking her back to the beach and we'll do nothing for a while. I don't think I can handle any more than that. A half hour passed before Leonara, Cassara, and the medic arrived. Alden got up and hugged his wife as they both consoled each other.

"Sorry I wasn't here honey. That bastard took our daughter and thinks he can keep her. Please tell me we'll find our little girl," Leonara said.

"We will, Turtan knows who helped Dreven take her. They're going to meet in a half hour and hopefully we'll know which door we're ramming down together," Alden said.

"Not likely, I'm blowing the damn thing down. No spell's going to save these thugs from me. If they're lucky I won't peel each of them like an onion."

"We'll find them darling and then we'll save Amara together. Cassara I don't suppose you can help us hit back us against these guys?"

"Of course, I've already scrambled my guard and the Heanerathi military. They're already on alert, we just need somewhere to send them. My medic will patch up those two until then," Cassara said.

"Good I'll head to the meeting with my contact soon and then we can hit them with everything we've got," Turtan said.

"Everyone get ready. I don't care how many swords, spells, and schemes Dreven has. We're bringing Amara home today," Alden said.

Everyone nodded and began preparing for the inevitable fight ahead of them. *All these people are here just to help Amara. Maybe Dreven didn't just separate my family, but instead made us better than we'd ever been.*

Everyone broke off into separate groups around the apartment as they set about preparing for the plan. Turtan called his contact and set up a talk within a half hour. Cassara's guards arrived and prepared to escort him to the meeting. Alden, Leonara, and Batara would stay behind until Turtan gave the word on where to go.

"Thanks for protecting Amara as long as you did. How are you feeling Batara? "Alden asked.

"Better than I probably look. Veferothi medicine is something else. Just wish I could have done more. Can't help feeling like if I wouldn't have let him get the jump on me then maybe Amara would still be here," Batara said.

"Don't beat yourself up you did everything you could. Nothing's gonna stop us from getting her back. She'll come back and I promise to make her finish giving you that tour."

"Thanks Uncle Alden. You know when most people look at me they usually are shaking in their shoes before I even open my big mouth. Amara just accepted me in an instant and acted like we were practically sisters."

"She's always been that way. It's one of the better things she got from her Dad. The propensity for scaring her mother with all the danger she seeks out is also from him," Leonara said.

"Can't argue that, but her combat awareness definitely comes from my wife," Alden said. A small smirk painted itself on his face.

"I can't do all those ridiculous hand motions and rolls. I'll always leave the circus act to you darling."

"I honestly can't believe you did so well against them Uncle Alden. Those guys were no joke. Most brutes I can always just throw over my shoulder like a sack of potatoes, but they made me work for every hit. You and my Dad carved through them like they were butter," Batara said patting Alden on his back.

"It's honestly amazing since Leonara's usually the one who makes dinner. I'm curious do you think you and your Dad will stick around after we get her back?" Alden asked.

"I love the inn, but Krohfast just feels more like a home than that town ever did. Touring the city was incredible and it was like we've been friends since we were kids. I know this may surprise you, but we never fit in around Henaten. Here though it's almost like we've found a family in you guys."

"Batara, it's a miracle that you are able to fit into anything." Alden smiled as his vocalamitter rang, it was Turtan. *Finally, whose door are we blowing down?*

"Alden I met with the contact. He gave up their headquarters, but said that Amara wasn't there. It's not as simple as I was hoping, but my man set up a meeting with his boss. Let's not go in swords swinging and see if we can maintain our surprise against Dreven. I'm not convinced the whole group is in on it and I doubt they'll want to deal with this much trouble for just one client," Turtan said.

"I don't care about them. The only thing that matters is getting Amara back home safe. Where's the headquarters?" Alden asked.

"Building twenty-seven, fiftieth floor. I'll meet you there in a half hour."

With the call completed and the meeting planned everyone made for the elevator. Alden and Leonara went through first with Batara only steps behind ducking through their human sized doorway. Taking the platform down everyone seemed to grow deathly serious. The ride over to tower twenty-seven was quick and soon they were standing in the Waxxer's lobby.

Looking around it seemed like any other luxurious Krohfast office. A large central door with some tall ferns garnishing the entrance. Aetturran art hung on the walls depicting oceanic scenes. *For thieves they have good taste in art. I know that's just paint, but it looks just like someone's made that sunset out of fish scales. Question is did they get these made or is some merchant missing pieces in their collection? Odd home for a bunch a glorified pickpockets.*

"Welcome to the Waxxer's headquarters, I guess they don't sell off everything they steal do they," Turtan said.

"Thieves with a sense of refinement, we'll just need to start spilling wine for them to get talking. This shouldn't take much time at all," Alden said.

A Wekken in a fine lavender coat and matching pants emerged from the double wooden doors. "Turtan it seems you've gotten quite the large social circle," he said.

"Scuthus, this meeting is a long time coming. Hope there's no hard feelings. I'm afraid we have a bit of a problem and I think your boys are involved," Turtan said.

"Naturally, if I'd been involved no one would know who to ask for a meeting. Regardless, my man explained the situation and I would very much like to hear what you have to say. Please come in everyone, we can discuss all of this inside where it's comfortable," Scuthus said.

Not what I expected from a leader of thieves. He's staring down at oblivion like it's just another business deal. The strange get stranger.

Scuthus led them into a large room with a huge polished wooden table. Opulent cherry red chairs lined its sides and much like the rest of the headquarters it was far more uptight than one would expect for a bunch of cargo stealing criminals. Everyone sat on one side while the luxuriously dressed Wekken sat across the table.

Alden spoke first. "Scuthus, some of your men kidnapped my daughter earlier this morning. One of the mages had a tattoo on his forearm of an axe with wings, your symbol," he said.

"Sir Knight, you needn't convince me, but I need details. What were they dressed like? Do you know who they were employed by as it obviously wasn't me?" Scuthus asked.

"Black robes, cloth masks on their faces, and they were working with one Dreven Sunsullen."

"Are you certain, about Mr. Sunsullen I mean? My understanding is that he's quite the wanted criminal. I seem to remember the ambassador was instrumental in the discovery of his particular predilection for ritual murder. What has it been, a decade at least since then?"

"There are no doubts and yes I did everything I could to capture him over a decade ago. Adding syllables to your words doesn't make you any more impressive. You're simply a scoundrel in an expensive coat who steals other people's packages," Cassara said.

I've seen that glare before. It could freeze over a river in the middle of summer. Everyone thinks she's just a dress obsessed old lady, but underneath all the smiles and sweets is a terrifying intellect. If there's something you know that she wants, it's practically her's already.

"You wound me ambassador. While I know our reputation has been besmirched with the occasional lie about some less than legal activities, we would never participate in such an endeavor," Scuthus said.

"It must be difficult, being such an upstanding citizen when the world is conspiring to give you such a poor reputation."

"Do you think men in my position often admit to crimes or associating with wanted fugitives?"

"I could care less about your group's activities, but surely your man told you how they poisoned a Knight of the Eternal Abyss' daughter? That would be problematic for you if that young lady was someone I loved like my own wouldn't it?"

Defending Dreven doesn't mean anything if the money you're paid and the body you leave behind are never found. Honestly knowing Cassara I doubt there would be anything left to find anyway.

"No they neglected to mention such compelling details. Your reputation is no mere myth it seems ambassador. It just so happens I can help you find her, but first I need you to promise me something first."

"Yes?"

"Every man at that warehouse has betrayed this organization. Please show them no mercy, I'd rather not have to clean my rugs after they return."

"Happily, the location if you would?" Alden asked.

"I hope you find your daughter unharmed and we can move past this unfortunate incident. They would have taken her to warehouse eighty-seven in the harbor."

Everyone upon hearing the name jumped up to leave as Scuthus sat there in his chair with an expression that said he'd just narrowly dodged his own death. *We have our location and the people to help take her back. You're coming home Amara. I promise.* They walked back onto the elevator before beginning their descent towards the station they first arrived at.

"Cassara send word to your forces to get down there as soon as they can. Batara, Turtan, you're with us. In an hour we hit the building with everything we have and bring Amara home," Alden said.

At the stop Cassara headed for a carriage to the Solarsong tower. Batara along with Turtan went towards the station heading to the harbor. Alden grabbed Leonara's hand holding her back after they stepped off the elevator. He hugged his wife and held her in his arms as tears began to descend from his eyes. The events of this morning had finally shattered his heroic heart.

"I let them take her, what if they've done something to our little girl? I'll never forgive myself 'Nara," Alden said.

"You've done everything you can darling. How many daughters have had their Dad fight an Ascendant High Lord for them? I can hear her gushing about it to Batara now," Leonara said.

Alden desperately tried to hold onto her as he felt his world shattering once again. Both of them tried to hide their tears, but it was a useless effort. Her warm embrace renewed his resolve and Alden knew she was right. *My conch-head's coming home and we're going to stop Dreven today. What would I do without you 'Nara?*

"Guess I couldn't just bring home a normal villain could I? Then again most husbands don't try to save some villagers, turn themselves into an Ascendant, and give their daughter magical Gray powers," Alden said. A small grin broke across his battered face.

"You are definitely the problem parent of us two, I certainly didn't bring any Dreven's home. You're going to have to clean so many dishes to make up for this," Leonara said.

"Not sure I know how, always just had you enchant the brushes. Maybe I'll ask Amara to help. We're gonna bring her home darling. Tonight we'll all be laughing about this crazy morning. Come on let's go save our daughter."

Alden let her go from his embrace. She nodded and the pair of parents made for the carriage platform. Batara and Turtan turned around just as a carriage arrived.

How did I get so lucky? I'm just some nobody from old town. I wonder if other fathers have to deal with this kind of stuff. Then again they probably don't teach their kids how to shoot lightning out of their hands when they're ten. Wouldn't have it any other way though. Dad's coming to the rescue conch-head and I'm bringing everyone with me.

Chapter 21: A Blow Forged by Failure

Salty harbor air filled Alden's nose as the carriage stopped at the platform. Rain deluged onto the street as dark clouds above them flashed with each bolt of lightning. *Water's still on my right, weather's not as nice, and Amara's at the end of this path too. So much has changed and yet some things about life never do.*

Walking along the overlook to the harbor warehouses Alden eventually spotted number eighty-seven. An inconspicuous wooden building with innumerable poles holding it above the waves. The structure was indistinguishable from any other warehouse except for one detail. A dozen men stood outside the doors; each wore a mask just like those at the apartment.

They're not even bothering with subtlety anymore. What am I missing? Shouldn't he be escaping with her instead of just waiting for the sky to fall onto his head? Something's wrong.

Alden found a bench underneath an overhang that was surprisingly dry. Batara and Turtan went further down the docks for their waiting spot while Leonara sat down right next to him.

"Think they have any idea what's going to come down on them?" Leonara asked.

"How could they? They only antagonized a Knight of the Eternal Abyss, the entire Heanerathi military, the Veferothi ambassador, that ambassador's elite guards, an expert ex-pirate, his giant of a daughter, and the most skilled magess in Krohfast," Alden said.

"We do sound like a small army don't we? Who knows maybe Amara won't even need us. Dreven wouldn't go to all this trouble just to get rid of her and if she wakes up I'm sure we'll hear it."

"True, I'm half expecting her to knock the doors down and walk out after beating them all to a pulp."

"Can only hope. On the off chance she doesn't kill them all how are we going to save her?"

"Been thinking about that and I had something rather poetic in mind."

"Not the first word that comes to mind when I think of a battle plan."

"Do you remember how he snuck up on me in Henaten?"

"You were really drunk?"

"Well yes, but there was more to it than that. I only had two drinks anyway."

"Two drinks of what Batara and Turtan consider booze."

"'Nara what I was getting at was the Venendum spell he used on his shoes, gloves, and grappling hook. The vacuum he applied prevented him from making almost any noise at all. I thought it would be wonderfully ironic to use his own trick against him."

"The Venendum spell. That could work and I can apply it to those two since they can't cast magic. I hope your plan doesn't involve us doing all the work."

"Only what's most important. Cassara's elite guards and Berik's reinforcements can fight through the front without any help from us. Meanwhile we sneak up onto the roof, cut a hole into the back, find Amara, and then have a very loud chat with Dreven."

"Simplicity itself and it'll hopefully be safer for her that way. I hate to think Cassara will get all the fun in this fight."

"All that matters is getting Amara out of here unharmed. Dreven can rot at the bottom of the bay for all I care as long as she's safe. 'Nara I never thought to ask, but what did you think happened to me before I came back from my voyage?" Alden asked.

"I didn't know to be honest. Cassara's soulenket said you were still alive, but then why hadn't you come home? Hope against hope I always thought you'd come through that door again. All you left me with was questions and a little girl to raise. I tried to do my best to turn her into an industrious magess like her Mom, but well you can see how well that turned out."

"It's funny how after all that time she still didn't mind exploring like I did. Guess I was gone, but not forgotten huh?"

"You have no idea. She shares your same enthusiasm for muck and monsters. In a way it was like you never left, although she was much better at magic than you ever were."

"I get turned into an Ascendant and I'm still the lowest rung on the family mage ladder. It's a good thing I know how to swing a blade or I'd be out of a job."

"We are a weird family aren't we?"

"The weirdest and I wouldn't have it any other way darling."

Alden hugged her as he planted a kiss. Holding each other for some time they released as they still needed to keep unnoticed. After waiting a while longer, a Heanerathi guard in a blue hooded cloak approached. *Finally, I think our wait is over.*

"Sir Alden and Mrs. Brickborn your reinforcements have arrived. Would you come with me? Ambassador Ookborne is one block back with the rest of our forces," the man said.

They both nodded and followed the cloaked man through the garden path between the nearby buildings. Walking back behind one final tower, Alden saw a very reassuring sight. Cassara stood before them along with thirty Heanerathi soldiers and a dozen Veferothi ambassadorial guards.

The soldiers wore overlapping metal plate armor and a blue cloth uniform underneath. Their metal helmets surrounded their entire heads like globes shining in the afternoon sun as only a thin visor let them see out. Beside them were the Veferothi guards who wore gallant gold armor mixed with leather pads. Ornate and flexible; it was the mark of a truly elite force. Their helmets were a symphony of melded metal and four golden horns diverged from their faces. Two rose from their temple and one on each side sprang back from the cheek.

Beaming in front of them all was Cassara who wore a lavish dress meshed with golden armor to match her guards. A black metal mask covered her face as an intricate metal helm adorned its top. Only her two red eyes glowed out from the front as her hair did the same as it fell onto skeletal shoulders.

Small doesn't seem quite adequate to describe all of this.

"Sorry for the delay, but I had the hardest time finding room for them all in the carriage," Cassara said.

"I'm glad you did. They should come in quite handy for this," Alden said.

"If I may Sir Alden what is the plan then?" the man with the blue cloak asked.

"The goal is simple; we need to rescue my daughter Amara from Dreven Sunsullen. He is holding her somewhere inside warehouse eighty-seven just behind us. There will be a contingent of Waxxer guards with him and we don't believe he'll threaten her life even if we attack. With that in mind we've come up with a two prong strategy. The first group will assault the front entrance to create a distraction. Simultaneously my team will use silencing magic to sneak onto the roof and cut a hole in at the back. We'll infiltrate the warehouse, rescue my daughter, and then flank them from behind."

It sounds so simple, but when it's your daughter held hostage I can't help but sweat over every detail. I've done this dozens of times and yet I can't help feel none of it has made me ready for this. It'll have to be enough. It will be enough. We'll save you conch-head.

"An efficient plan, I'd expect nothing less from a Knight of the Eternal Abyss. I'm Captain Denerik and we are at your service. Sir Berik sends his regards," he said.

"I wish it were under better circumstances captain. Are you ready to move out?" Alden asked.

"Indeed. If you could give the men a few minutes to get into position, we can be ready to begin the assault on your mark."

"Good, get into place and we'll send up a fireball once we're ready to begin the attack, move out."

With that everyone split into groups. The soldiers dispersed into a semi-circle formation around the warehouse while the captain along with Cassara and her guards came back with Alden. Everyone shouldered up against the stone wall overlooking the warehouse on the street below. Leonara went around giving the infiltration group the Venendum spell on their hands and feet so they would be silent. Alden did the same to his grappling hook which he pulled from his bag. Leonara returned having completed the preparations and sat down beside them.

She always did look so determined in those battle robes of hers. Staff in hand and eyes that will beat you into the dirt. Luckily if her gaze doesn't do it the spells will always be happy to assist.

"You two stay safe and if you could, don't kill the bastard too quickly. I want to get a swing in at him," Cassara said. Her red eyes flared under that elegant helm.

Both of them nodded as Alden turned to Leonara. "Let's go get our daughter," Alden said.

Leonara raised her fist into the air and yelled "Flammorta!"

A scarlet fireball rocketed out of her outstretched hand into the sky. The signal had been given and the assault had now begun. Cassara's elites vaulted over the wall and began to skewer the guards with Telendum arrows. Each shouted the spell with two fingers pointing forward as a bolt of pure kinetic magic rocketed toward their targets. The unlucky guards outside were skewered by countless invisible javelins.

After the group posted at the entrance were dead the Heanerathi guards closed in from the sides and joined the ambassadorial elites. A tide of allies rushed towards the doors as the infiltration team ran toward the right side just behind them. Alden threw his grappling hook onto the roof where it anchored into the soft wood. *Not even a thud and the rope is as taught as iron. I hope the climb is just as silent.*

Alden pulled himself onto the wooden roof putting a hand down to help everyone else get up. First Leonara, then Turtan, and finally Batara scaled the walls even though he needed another father's help to pull her up. Finally, Alden retrieved the grapple for the descent back down into the building.

Alden looked back as he saw Heanerathi soldiers, Captain Denerik, the ambassadorial guards, and Cassara preparing to blow open the door. *This is for busting up our apartment you bastards!*

"Ventos!" Cassara's guards shouted.

Their combined magical might detonated the door into countless splinters. Looking up Cassara met Alden's gaze. She nodded to him before the lady a few years past four hundred began tossing spells into the melee. He turned around and led his group across the rotten roof as rain drenched them. *I appreciate the noise this storm is making, but if we slip then all of our efforts will have been for naught.* Each silent step was another closer to rescuing Amara and everyone took care to pick their footing. Upon reaching the back end of the building Alden quickly found a spot to begin making their entrance.

"Ventos," he said quietly.

Alden pressed two fingers into the roof and began carving a hole with the wind. As Batara pulled the wooden roof up a gaping hole was created pouring light into the dark room below. Attaching his grapple to the roof, Alden made sure it was taught before sliding down the rope onto the floor below. *Can't make anything out yet, but no one's started firing spells at us yet. Hope I'm right conch-head.*

The room was devoid of anyone except for a single person. It was Amara strapped to an operating table and covered in a strange robe with metal strips woven into it. In addition, a tube fed some clear liquid into her pale right arm while another was piping blood into a container on a nearby table. *Amara what has he done to you?* As everyone entered from above Alden's eyes adjusted and he began to see the room for what it was. *This isn't a warehouse it's a laboratory!*

Strange containers of many different colored liquids littered the room. *What is all this? The red is Amara's blood, but why does he need so much of it?* Large Gray artifacts were scattered about the room with optical equipment surrounding them as if someone had been studying their every minute detail. In fact, a strange Gray cube lay on a table with what was unmistakably blood smeared on it's top. The device glowed a mysterious red color just like the ruins on Hemmarasp.

"Amara are you alright?" Alden asked.

Unresponsive, she simply lay there as if in a deep sleep. Everyone else crowded around the table as they took in the horror of the room they stood in. *She's still breathing. We're not too late.*

"Darling what have they done to her? My poor little girl we're going to get you out of here and everything will be ok," Leonara said.

"I don't know 'Nara, but Dreven's not getting another drop from her. Help me get these restraints and tubes off her," Alden said.

Creak.

A door on the room's far side opened as a masked Ascendant entered. It was Dreven. "It won't be much help I'm afraid. I've been quite careful in immobilizing her. A necessary precaution when dealing with someone of her magical prowess," he said.

"What have you done to our daughter!" Leonara shouted.

"Stay your rage, Amara is unharmed. I merely injected her with a sedative to keep the poor thing dreaming. Those suppression restraints were to ensure even if she woke up her magic still wouldn't be an issue. Those metal suppression strips woven into the clothes are the final assurance that your daughter will not be a problem. I have spent decades trying to create someone like her and I won't be stopped by a careless mistake," Dreven began to approach them as they all circled around Amara.

"Why? I saw your soulenket in Henaten. How could you do this to another man's family?" Alden asked.

What could drive a father to do this? He has a family and is still able to inflict these horrors on others? I don't think anything we say will sway him. This is a man who won't cease for any cause. I have to stop him conch-head. If I don't you may never truly be safe.

"For everyone else's families Alden. If I fail, then the horror my father foresaw will befall this world and there will no longer be anyone to care. Look at the cube on the table. That is a Gray artifact. By your daughter's power it is no longer a lump of rock, but instead it's extraordinary magical properties have been revealed. She is the catalyst that will spur this world to salvation. Her body can activate the secrets locked away in the Gray's ruins and with her help I will save this world from what is coming."

"So that's all that matters then. All the families you've broken, villages you've reduced to ashes, and daughters you've stolen are meaningless in the grand scheme of things? What if you're wrong and all this evil you've committed is for naught? What then?"

"You're still assuming I can be wrong, I'm not. I told you once I do not seek to be loved, respected, or admired. This cruelty tears at my heart as a parent, but all my suffering is for the only purpose that life has left me. The only one that matters. I am the necessary evil that will allow all of the good and wonderful things of this world to survive."

"You speak of suffering, but you've given nothing! All you've done is take from others for this insane crusade."

"I've given everything a father can. There is nothing left for me in this world except the knowledge that no one else will ever endure what I have. I see now that letting you live was a mistake. A fellow father's mercy, it was a foolish thing to give. I suppose there only could've been one result."

"Batara and Turtan free Amara. We'll buy you time, now get working!" Alden faced his foe as they both withdrew their blades. *I don't have to win this, only delay long enough for them to free Amara. It sounds so simple, even though it's anything but.*

Dreven leapt forward at Alden as the pair crossed swords, each shaking from trying to press their advantage. His eyes watched every movement the High Lord made as he tried to anticipate the next strike. Every sword swing was another second closer to rescuing Amara. As the third stroke came soaring toward his face Leonara yelled "Telendum!" with her staff aimed squarely at Dreven's head.

Well done 'Nara. Let's buy our little girl some time together.

Dreven rolled away as Alden chased him down determined not to give him an opening to use his magic. Back and forth they swung at each other until Alden heard Leonara wind up another spell.

"Flammorta!" she shouted.

A fireball flew towards Dreven's head at blistering speed from her staff. However, as he moved out of its way Alden shouted "Flammorta!" firing the spell too close to Dreven to dodge. Flames engulfed the High Lord's face as he began to claw at his hood.

We're not just holding him off, but actually holding our own. With everybody's help we've really got a chance against this prick. You messed with the wrong daughter Dreven, ours!

The masked man raged as his robes were consumed like a pyre. Blinded by the fire he desperately cast "Drentos" onto his face. Alden swung for his ribs as Dreven flailed about trying to block. Blinded by the blaze his block missed and the steel sailed deep into his torso. Clear water drained down Dreven's face as blood poured from his side.

That was no flesh wound.

Grunting through the pain, the High Lord yelled "Umbros!" as a dark fog emanated from his left palm enveloping the area around him. *What is he trying to pull?*

Looking back, Alden saw that Turtan and Batara had undone the restraints, but Amara hadn't woken up yet. As he heard Dreven desperately ripping at his hood the sound of battle echoed from the front of the warehouse. *It's gotten a lot quieter out front. Cassara should nearly be done and then this fight will truly be over.*

"Flammorta!" Dreven shouted. A bright flash pierced the fog as Alden saw a flaming red hand appear. A searing noise echoed off the wooden walls as the flames disappeared into the darkness. *He's cauterized his own wound! Not even a whimper from all that pain?*

A blade shot forth from the dark clouds right towards Alden's face. Dodging it he felt a hand as hot as a forge clamp down on his left arm. With his inhumane speed Dreven had branded his forearm with the same spell he'd used to cauterize the wound.

Dammit, he announced it first to catch me off guard and I fell for it like some ignorant lunk. This is bad.

A newly scarred Dreven head-butted Alden knocking him to the floor. Sparks kissed his face as he only just blocked Dreven's sword blow. Life stealing steel clashed only inches from his eyes.

In desperation Leonara raised her staff like a spear and stabbed towards Dreven's guts. Grabbing the staff with his left hand the villain spun around backhanding her face. Dreven seized the advantage and raised his sword to strike Leonara. Alden ripped himself from the floor before swinging at the villain once more. Standing between the pair of them, Alden had blocked the blow as he'd pushed Leonara away.

"Ventos!" he shouted.

Dreven was tossed back as the gust hammered him. *No one hits my 'Nara like that you bastard.*

Picking himself off the floor Dreven flung himself forward. As Alden swung towards him, the High Lord placed an open palm on his chest. "Ventos!" he yelled. *Agh!* Alden was flung into an unfortunately hard relic on the other side of the room. *Dammit where was he keeping that much strength?*

Dreven walked towards the center table with his eyes focused unwaveringly on the still unconscious Amara. Batara and Turtan both swung their weapons down towards his head as he neared the table. With a parry he blocked them both just before tossing them aside with another Ventos spell.

All of us. He just walked through each of us. Wake up Amara! Please get up conch-head! Run!

Standing over Amara, Dreven looked calm as if the center of the room was the eye of a hurricane. The fight around him seemed to have been forgotten if even only for a moment. Looking down he picked up the collected vial of Amara's blood and the cube on the table next to her.

I'm not dead yet and Amara isn't safe. Get up and save her! My limbs feel like they're made of stone, but I can't stop. I won't let you take my daughter again!

Running towards Amara Alden saw Dreven lift his gaze and ready his sword. *We've burned him, stabbed his guts, and none of it's stopped him. I need something even he won't expect. That's it! A blow forged by failure!*

Alden swung his sword towards Dreven's head. The High Lord blocked it easily and locked their blades together. With the two swords stuck against each other he shot his left hand straight for Dreven's guts.

"Lumicendor!" he yelled. Lightning danced across his outstretched hand as it flew forward.

"Telendum!" Dreven shouted.

Magical armor coated the right side of the villain's body. Dreven smiled as he thought he'd outwitted his opponent, but before Alden's hand could strike the magic shield he twisted it up towards their swords.

"You fell for my trap you daughter stealing madman!" Alden shouted.

Grabbing onto his own blade, he channeled all the lightning he could muster into the steel which was still connected to Dreven's. Bolts of blue magic crackled and emanated from their two bodies as electricity coursed through them. Dreven's red eyes grew wide as each man fell to his knees from the unbelievable pain.

"Now Turtan and Batara!" Alden shouted.

An axe and a saber flew into Dreven's back hammering him into the wooden floor. Alden staggered to his feet as the Gray cube rolled away from the table. *I've got you conch-head. Mom's gonna finish this one.* He dragged Amara away from the room's center as Leonara ran towards Dreven for the final blow.

"Stay away from our daughter. Ventos!" Leonara shouted.

She pressed her palm into his bloodied back. A crushing gust drilled into Dreven's body as the floor began to disintegrate around him. Everyone backed away as the wood began to crack and creak. In only a few moments the boards buckled into the sea taking Dreven with them. Alden watched as the monster who'd changed everyone's lives crashed into the waves below their feet.

We won. I can't believe it, but he's lost. Everyone stood silent as the battle in the warehouse had grown quiet leaving only the harbor's waves to hear. Alden looked into the water and suddenly it began to bubble like a boiling cauldron. *No! It can't be, no one could have survived that blow.* A pair of lights erupted from a dark object below the surface which began to move.

A geyser exploded up through the hole splashing the room with sea water. The vessel vanished into the ocean and just like that Dreven was gone. *Amara's safe and he can't take that from us. That madman can run, but it won't change the fact that we won. If only for now, it's over.* Amara had begun to wake up as Alden clutched her in his arms.

"Dad why is your armor smoking? Where are we?" she asked.

"I electrocuted the bad guy by grabbing my own sword and you're right where you should be," Alden said.

He helped Amara onto her feet. "Dad is it bad that doesn't seem outlandish? Now if you told me Mom did that maybe I'd be skeptical, but that definitely sounds like something you'd do."

"Hey it worked didn't it?"

"I guess, but where is he anyway?"

"Your Mom didn't feel like tossing him off the dock so she kind of punched him through it. Unfortunately, it looks like he had a submersible."

"He can go get drenched for all I care. Are all of you ok?"

"Just a few new bruises, nothing to write home about. Honestly your Dad got the worst of it and he did that to himself," Turtan said.

"To stop Dreven from taking my daughter," Alden said.

"It was surprising if nothing else darling. Though you do smell a bit grilled if I'm honest. Where'd you get the idea that hitting yourself with lightning was a good idea?" Leonara asked.

"That was the move that let Bojjer beat me. Figured it'd be perfect for beating his boss with a small change I made. Kinda wish it hurt less though."

The doors to the back room burst open. It was Cassara and Captain Denerik leading the rest of the soldiers. They'd beaten Dreven's mercenaries in the warehouse. *They're looking a little worse for wear.*

"Where is Dreven?" Cassara asked Alden.

"Gone, took off in a submersible after 'Nara blasted him through the floor. You'll have to get that punch in another day Cassara," Alden said.

"Knowing him, that'll come sooner than you think. Still we ought to celebrate today. Looks like we've won for now."

Everyone breathed a sigh of relief and smiled. *Dreven might not be gone for good, but now we know his tricks. It won't be so easy to steal Amara back. He can count on that.* After cleaning themselves up, everyone began to walk out of the warehouse towards home. The storm had ended and grey clouds began to give way to a beautiful blue sky.

Chapter 22: Conch-Head

The elevator finally arrived at their apartment. Alden expected to see their wrecked home, but Cassara's men had already cleaned up all the damage. No ashes remained on the floor and not even a single splinter of their old door remained. In fact, an entirely new and much larger doorway had been built in its place.

"Cassara guessing you had them do a little more than clean up huh?" Alden asked.

"Naturally, your apartment was far too drab dear and Dreven had done most of the demolition work for me anyway. Now Batara doesn't have to fold herself in two just to enter and I made sure the new door had a few pieces from the old one. I may have made a few more changes as well inside," Cassara said.

"Told you Turtan," Alden said.

He pushed opened the giant Nisuri wood door as its intricate design gave way to a completely different apartment than the burnt and broken one they'd left earlier this morning. Leonara who had been silent up to this point quickly revealed just how she felt about Cassara's changes.

"I barely recognize it! Cassara this is gorgeous, thank you," Leonara said.

A modern brown leather couch had replaced the shredded cloth one. Cracks in the wall from Turtan crashing into it had been smoothed over by an architect's magic and all the kitchen cabinets had been replaced with beautiful stone ones. All of them were polished to a shine which the fading sunset reflected onto the floor with an orange glow. A large magical fire pit stood in the room's center around the couch which illuminated numerous new paintings and carpets.

She actually restrained herself for once. I'm honestly impressed at how nice and subtle everything is.

"I love it Aunt Cassara," Amara said. She gave her unofficial aunt a hug.

"I didn't just change up this room. Go on, give your bedroom a look. This is nearly as fun for me as I hope it is for you," Cassara said.

"Come on Batara. I can't wait to see what it looks like."

Two girls from very different families both nearly sprinted into the redecorated bedroom. Not two seconds had passed before everyone else in the apartment could hear how they felt. Alden sighed and wrapped his arm around Leonara with a big grin on his face. Clasping hands, they sat down on the brown leather couch as Turtan went over to the kitchen to fix drinks.

Squealing is so much better than screaming even if it isn't much softer. I hope she has more days like this rather than ones like this morning. Amara deserves better and if I have to electrocute myself a few times for her to have it then I'm happy to make that deal. Still I might need something tall and strong, fatherhood hurts.

Cassara joined them to sit down as they all collectively unwound from the day. Everyone was clearly exhausted from fighting Dreven and as Turtan brought each of them a glass they all clanged them together. Alden brought the delightful yellow drink to his lips and began to gulp. *I've never tasted anything so wonderful. Does lemonade taste better the more peril you get yourself into?*

"You know honestly I can't believe it all ended up as neat as it did," Turtan said.

"What do you mean?" Leonara asked.

"Well we just fought one of the most dangerous people in the world, saved your daughter, and got your apartment redecorated in one day. Turned out pretty well all things considered."

"True, this is a really nice couch Cassara," Alden said.

"Thank you, I actually picked it out for you a while back. Just had to wait for an opportune moment," Cassara said.

"At least we have a break from Dreven. Think I'm going to have to go talk to the Order in the morning about what we're going to do about him. Still I'm way too tired to carry that out until tomorrow. What are you going to do now Turtan?" Alden asked.

"Honestly I don't know. Henaten was a great home, but the inn was more about me and her running it together. She seems so happy here it's almost a cruel thought to take my little girl back there," Turtan said.

"We could use another inn here in Krohfast. What if I helped set you two up to stay instead? You're already living in one of my apartments anyway," Cassara said.

"That's quite generous of you. I'll have to get you a barrel of Batara's Stiff Breeze to celebrate then. Looks like our daughters are going to have the run of the place eh Alden?"

"Only if I try to keep up drinking with you two. If we ever found a mythical lake made of liquor on one of our adventures you two would reduce it to a puddle," Alden said.

As everyone was chatting around the fire pit both of the girls came back from the bedroom. Sitting down they both took drinks that Turtan had left for them.

"Hey sweetie I've been talking to Cassara and I was wondering if you wanted to stay here in Krohfast?" Turtan asked.

"Could we? That would be great, I love it here. This city just has so much to do and Amara still hasn't shown me even a tenth of it," Batara said.

"Good, Cassara has offered to help us open an inn here and I was thinking of bringing Roger up too. Looks like we're moving for good."

"That's great maybe I can finally show you around town without somebody kidnapping me," Amara said.

Well that's officially the scariest joke I've ever heard. I wonder if Turtan has some Stiff Breeze around. Eh, should probably get tomorrow out of the way first. She needs to know.

"Oh that reminds me that you, your Mom, and I need to go to headquarters tomorrow. Representatives from the Republic have asked us to put a plan together to deal with Dreven," Alden said.

"Wish he'd just sink to the bottom of the sea and stay there," Amara said.

"I hope his submersible springs a leak at a couple thousand feet down, but it doesn't hurt to be prepared. No matter what we want, I doubt this is truly over."

"Well if we need a plan then I think I know a place where we can start." Amara pulled the Gray cube from the warehouse out of her pocket.

"That's the artifact Dreven was activating with your blood. Did you fish it out of the harbor while I wasn't looking?"

"Nothing so dramatic; I just found it lying on the floorboards that Mom hadn't collapsed into the sea. Look at this. If I don't put any magic into it the device does nothing, but if I let the energy flow through my fingers." The cube's carved lines began to glow red. A giant scarlet projection appeared in the air above the artifact.

It all makes sense now. She really is the key to their world.

"I can't believe my eyes, I've never seen anything like it," Leonara said.

"No one has, not for thousands of years anyway," Amara said.

"It's Nisuroth, but it's different. Look at these bright spots all over it. Do you think they're?"

"Exactly what Dreven is after."

"Wait I know some of these. These are Gray ruins. Look there's Hemmarasp Isle right there. I knew there were always sites we hadn't uncovered, but they're everywhere," Cassara said.

"Look at Amothis! The whole island is practically glowing." Turtan said.

"Graybuilt isn't just a name. Those golems wouldn't exist without the Gray. Still I've heard that Amothis was the capital of their civilization, but this confirms it. There are so many sites to search. What could Dreven have hoped this map would show?"

"What if they're like the ritual ruins on Hemmarasp that you and Uncle Alden went to? Maybe Dreven hoped the cube could locate somewhere he could make more Amara's?" Batara asked.

"I don't know, but I'm sure he had a purpose in looking at this artifact first. He only had a few hours and out of all of those artifacts in that room this was the one he tried to turn on. It must be important somehow," Amara said.

That's my little conch-head. Bad guy kidnaps her, steals her blood, and she's already trying to figure out our next steps. Give us some time kiddo. I may not age anymore, but if you keep this up I just might find a way.

Everyone sat around the fire pit debating what the map meant late into the night. Still it was more of a celebration than any real attempt at progress. Eventually Cassara, Turtan, and Batara said their goodbyes as they went home. Amara turned in for the night leaving her two parents alone in their bedroom.

"So did you ever think when we set out for Mullentide this would all happen?" Alden asked.

"How could I? You turned into an Ascendant, our daughter became infused with Gray powers, and we had to change our door because our friends got too tall. No, I can honestly say I didn't see it coming, but in a way I wouldn't change anything about it," Leonara said.

"Still a little less kidnapping would have been a nice touch. Oh and being attacked by a giant worm over some fruit. I would have taken that part right out and you know what-" Alden said as he was interrupted by Leonara's kiss.

"I love you."

"I love you too 'Nara."

Alden kissed Leonara deeply. The lights inside went dark as the ones outside their window flickered in the serenity of the night. Under the covers they embraced each other until shortly collapsing not long after from their long day of daughter saving.

Awaking from the best sleep he could remember, Alden placed one last kiss on Leonara's cheek as he left to get ready. First he had a hot shower in Cassara's remodeled bathroom. *Oh wow that's sore. I'm actually having to put effort into blinking. Is this the punishment for leaving for ten years? Ugh, oh this shower can't possibly last long enough to cure this.* Revitalizing hot water warmed his aching muscles as steam washed over him. After finishing up, Alden got dressed and then made breakfast. Only a few minutes later everyone had managed to find their way over to the food.

Both of them are having adventures like me and shockingly they're starting to eat like me too. Good food is at its best when you've had to crawl your way to the table over a puddle of blood, sweat, and tears. Still we really need to get an automated helper for this. If I keep having to electrocute myself for these two I'm gonna start needing breakfast in bed.

"So what do you think they're going to say at the meeting today Dad?" Amara asked.

"If I had to guess we're gonna start with that map of yours. They'll want to find all those sites and see if you can activate them. With any luck they'll help us figure out what Dreven was up to," Alden said.

"Guess we won't be able to just stay at the apartment much longer. You know what happens when they want you to figure something out," Leonara said.

"Eh it wouldn't have lasted long anyway. Amara's going to need training and we both know the morning's ahead of us won't always be this pleasant."

"So you really think they'll want all of us? Our whole family gallivanting around Nisuroth to stop a madman. Can't this morning last just a bit longer?" Leonara asked.

"I just can't believe that story he was telling about those things. What if there really is some terrible monstrosity coming and we have no idea how to stop it? All of us going out there and saving the world. I know that should terrify me, but it just doesn't. I'm ready. Well I have to get dressed first, but you know what I mean," Amara said before heading off to her room to get showered.

"Suppose it won't do if I show up in my nightgown. I'll follow her example darling," Leonara said.

Before leaving for the bedroom she gave Alden a lovely little kiss. With both of them gone only Alden was left in the kitchen to finish off his eggs. *Why do I bother getting ready first? I know they're going to take the better part of the morning just to get ready. All powerful masters of the arcane and it still takes them twenty minutes to do their hair. Some of reality's rules are just absolute I guess.* About a half hour passed before both of them returned to the kitchen.

"Ready to go?" Alden asked.

"The clock hasn't stopped moving forward even a little so I'm afraid so. Just try not to get kidnapped by pirates on the way over. I hate to think what more the world can do to you," Leonara said.

"No promises 'Nara."

223

Alden grinned as he opened the brand new Batara sized door. The family walked over to the elevator as Amara called it on the console before they set off for headquarters. *It's actually a nice day today. A few white puffy clouds, a lovely breeze, and no thunder to be heard.* It only took another half hour before the Brickborn family was standing before the magnificent glass doors into headquarters.

Wait a minute this'll be the first time. We should open the gate together. Dammit don't cry before we meet the representatives. Just enjoy the moment.

"Let's not keep them waiting any longer, Amara would you like to join me?" Alden asked.

"Together?" Amara asked.

"Together."

She nodded as they raised their swords at the same time. With a creaking groan, the immense doors opened inward. As always Tyreen was behind the desk when she looked up to see them. Her eyes lit up as she walked out to meet them.

"Good to see you three are still in one piece after that mess yesterday. Come with me; the others are waiting just upstairs. You've got quite the committee waiting for you," Tyreen said.

It's funny how all of this feels like old news to me, but I'm sure they're dying to hear all the details. Kidnappings, rituals, and world ending horrors. I suppose that is a bit worse than my usual assignments.

Wasting no time at all Tyreen guided them off towards the left side hall. One door on the right was for an elevator which they all stepped onto. Pressing the blue console's button for the top floor they started flying up the tower. At their stop, the door opened to reveal a garden terrace surrounding them as light filtered through a shimmering magic ceiling.

At one edge of the balcony were four people. *Well at least I still recognize two of the faces. That's Berik and Cassara, but I don't remember these two representatives. Hope they're nice.* One was a lady with gray hair framing a sunken aged face, which still seemed welcoming. The other was a young man with blonde hair and olive eyes that seemed ambitious.

"Ahh glad to see we've all made it. Welcome you three, I'm Representative Canthus," the blonde man said.

"I'm Representative Fenma and we're here to listen to your account of yesterday's incident," the lady said.

"It's a pleasure to meet you both. Still I'm guessing you're wanting to hear more than just a story," Alden said.

"Quite right. Sir Alden the Republic has appointed us two as the direct links to the Order of the Eternal Abyss whenever a mission of great importance is discussed. As I understand it you're already familiar with Ambassador Ookborne. What we decide here will require the efforts of both of our countries," Fenma said.

"Understood representatives, then I would assume Ambassador Ookborne has already filled you in on yesterday's events? She's never been one to wait around."

"Indeed, what we would like to ascertain is what should be done to counter this Dreven Sunsullen. The crimes he's committed have already demonstrated his dangerous nature hasn't waned over the years, but our understanding is that he is no longer simply a reckless tinkerer of decrepit relics," Canthus said.

"No, he is responsible for the ritual that changed not only me, but my daughter Amara. Someone or something is granting him knowledge about the Gray."

"This is what concerns us most. We've worked with Ambassador Cassara for some time. It's been common knowledge that Dreven heard voices in his head, but it seems that whatever they've babbled isn't without insight. Gray artifacts on their own are unthinkably powerful and it is all but assured their greatest secrets still remain to be found," Canthus said.

"That isn't the question though. We all know what Dreven has warned about. The things between spaces. If he's wrong, then a madman could be playing with powers beyond all understanding and if he isn't. Well if something is out there we need to be able to defend ourselves. That's where you three will come in," Cassara said.

"You're talking about the map I found?" You want us to explore those ruins and see if my powers can discover something that can help us don't you?" Amara asked.

"I'm afraid so, but you're no longer just some girl anymore dear. Your powers could change the balance of nations in Nisuroth. Dreven is likely only the first person who will want to use you for their goals, not the last."

"So little is known about the Gray. They're knowledge created the Ascendant, changed your family, and may very well shape this world once again," Berik said.

"We'll do this together Amara and I know you're ready for whatever we face," Alden said.

"Good then it's settled. Find the truth and keep our Republics safe," Representative Fenma said.

"We will," the Brickborns said together.

"Good luck you three. Please excuse me and the representatives as we have some other matters to attend to," Berik said.

With their meeting concluded the old soldier and the politicians left for the elevator, but Cassara stayed beside them.

"You know I remember sending you three off to Mullentide. Nearly cried when you finally left. I'm glad you get to go on this adventure together," Cassara said.

"Our first family adventure together," Alden said.

"Don't think you're getting out of helping Cassara. We're going to drag you into this one way or another," Leonara said.

"Oh I'm counting on it dear. I expect you'll rope your two friends from Henaten into this as well," Cassara said.

"Batara and Turtan are as much a part of this as we are. Besides, I imagine it will be so much more fun with them coming along," Amara said.

"I just can't wait to see what you uncover with those Gray powers dear. Just a glimpse of their knowledge created my race. What will this world look like after you've had your say I wonder?" Cassara said.

"Well we can find out tomorrow. I'd rather not do quite so much with today. Hey Dad I was wondering; would you mind if we went to the beach today?" Amara asked.

"That sounds like a perfect idea. Lead the way conch-head," Alden said.

"Enjoy your break. I have a feeling you're going to need some time off before this next adventure. Goodbye you three," Cassara said.

It took the Brickborns a half hour to make it back to their apartment and another half to get a picnic packed into a basket. Taking the carriage out past the harbor and into the countryside, they stopped at a station next to a strip of beautiful white sand. Only a few other people were sharing the beach so there wasn't any trouble finding a spot to enjoy the warm wind coming off the ocean.

"It really is a wonderful day, isn't it?" Amara asked.

"Gorgeous weather, certainly a sight better than yesterday. I haven't seen so little fog in Krohfast in ages. You can almost see through the whole forest of buildings," Leonara said.

"Actually this reminds me of that one day you and me went down to the shore in Mullentide Amara. Remember, we fell into that tide pool looking for shells," Alden said.

"Those waves seemed so much bigger back then. I guess we've both grown to be quite different from who we were. I still couldn't put my clothes away when I was that little and now I'm being asked to travel the world to chase after a madman," Amara said.

"I'd say it was more of a wouldn't than a couldn't conch-head."

"You may be right. You know what might be fun? What if we have ourselves a rematch. Bet I can throw it further than you now."

"Alright you're on. Try not to crack too many stones. 'Nara do you want to get in on this?"

"No, I'd rather give you two a chance to win," Leonara said.

You might be right, but at least hesitate a little before you answer 'Nara. Well I better start making stones. No way am I letting conch-head finish first. Alden and Amara carved a small stack of round rocks. Unlike their previous contest not a single one of them shattered.

"I'll let you go first Dad. Try to at least get past the reef," Amara said.

"You've still got a lot to learn. Take this for example," Alden said.

He wound himself up, tensing his muscles to unleash as much energy as possible. Alden began to let magic flow into his fingertips as he pulled his arm back. *Sorry Amara, but I didn't teach you everything.* Alden shouted "Ventos," firing the stone like a rocket over the ocean.

Skip. Skip. Skip. Skip. Skip. Skip. Skip. Skip. Skap. Ploosh.

The rock flew across the shallows and well past the reef. Amara's face was stunned as she saw how far her Dad had been able to reach. *Control isn't just about knowing how hard to push. It's about where.*

"That was incredible Dad. How'd you get it to go so far?" Amara asked.

"Why do you need to know? You've got this all on your own right?" Alden asked.

"I think so, but what if it's not enough Dad? Am I really ready for Dreven? For all of this?"

"Amara all you can do is prepare and then just give it everything you've got. Throwing that stone further than me is no different than stopping him. I know you'll be able to do it. All you can do is try conch-head."

"Well then, I guess here I go."

Amara wound up into a stance similar to his own. The stone was clutched tight against her calloused fingers. Alden felt the air begin to change and then his little girl threw her rock. *You'll be ready. I believe in you Amara and I always will my little conch-head.* The stone struck the surface of the water and began to bounce.

Skip. Skip. Skip. Skip. Skip...

Epilogue

The Tekau's turquoise waters flowed around the vessel. It's smooth metallic surface carved through the ocean like a knife. He'd made it out of Krohfast without much trouble. Even though he hadn't been entirely successful there was still plenty of progress to celebrate. His still singed hands steered the vessel upward towards the surface and the night sky.

Erupting from the water like an arrow, the submersible splashed onto the top of the sea. Staring through the glass, Dreven saw his ship that he'd signaled for already anchored in place. Pulling up to the side, his singed arms guided the submersible to dock. Depressing the glowing blue release button, the glass canopy opened. Pushing it up to the fully vertical position, Dreven emerged from the jet black craft and climbed onto the ship over the railing. A female Wekken was already waiting for him.

"You're ahead of schedule, I assume all didn't go as planned then?" she asked.

"No, but we've succeeded all the same. Get the men ready to sail for Pekarta. The next stage is now ready with that girl's help," Dreven said. Putting a hand into his coat, he pulled something from one of the pockets. In his hand was a vial of Amara's blood.

"You've figured out how to extend our efforts beyond that bottle I imagine?"

"The Order now believes that the only way to activate Gray artifacts is through her blood. My tests have yielded the truth of the matter. With this revelation and the recent find on Amothis we have everything needed to open the Last Well."

"Understood, then welcome aboard High Lord Dreven and congratulations."

The drenched Ascendant walked to the bow of the ship and stared off into the horizon. *She really is a remarkable daughter Alden, in a way I'm glad you succeeded. This world doesn't need any more pain than it already has. Thank you for reminding me of that.* Grasping the soulenket around his neck, Dreven held it up in his right hand. Opening the metal case, he stared down at his entire world, a single blue pearl surrounded by two long since shattered.

Made in the USA
Middletown, DE
10 September 2019